BLIND
JUSTICE

BLIND
JUSTICE

JAMES BRIDGWATER

Library of Congress Control Number:		2020914349
ISBN:	Softcover	978-1-6641-1220-9
	eBook	978-1-6641-1219-3

Cover Image by Teresa Leyreloup

Print information available on the last page.

Rev. date: 08/04/2020

To order additional copies of this book, contact:
Xlibris
UK TFN: 0800 0148620 (Toll Free inside the UK)
UK Local: 02036 956328 (+44 20 3695 6328 from outside the UK)
www.Xlibrispublishing.co.uk
Orders@Xlibrispublishing.co.uk
817862

PART 1

CHAPTER 1

My name is Blind Justice and I'm the world's first transvestite vigilante. My work uniform is made up of a glittery fuchsia coloured spandex cat-suit with magenta leather calf boots. I wear a cherry silk blindfold with eye holes of black lace. A high quality full length blond wig is my crowning glory. I have a crew cut hair style underneath. My weapon is an épée type blade which my other personality keeps hidden in a visually impaired person's adapted white cane.

I can tell you that even though I've got a sidekick it really is an incredibly lonely life being a solo guerrilla. But then my companion is a Labrador called Willow so we can't discuss my strategies employed for crime fighting here in Tamarmouth where we live. Another thing which makes things hard for me is that unlike the famous characters of Spiderman, Superman and Batman I don't know my other ego. They chose to have two identities where as I have multiple personality disorder (MPD). This means I sometimes have episodes when I have memory loss and have no idea what I did or where. During these periods my other persona takes over my body and so my life. I get the impression my other half is a man called Mark Wilson. Willow is a part time Guide Dog for him due to his eyes working sporadically. He lives an isolated friendless life scraping by on government sickness benefits due to being very visually impaired due to a rare psychosomatic condition linked with MPD.

Multiple personality disorder is usually caused by traumatic events in childhood. The mind breaks into separate parts leaving some to handle the horrendous memories and creating others to lead an uncontaminated existence. I think my other identity copes by using alcohol to dull the pain of the recollections and I have become a vigilante who tries to take revenge on people similar to those that abused him as a child.

Therefore I have become Blind Justice who takes vengeance on corrupt financiers and perverted celebrities as they were the sort of people who abused him as a child in their deprived drug fueled parties. I work as a transvestite as they also abused many women at those iniquitous get-togethers. It all began when my parents died in a car accident when on holiday in Jersey. I was in the car too but survived and after months in hospital returning to health I was put in a local children's home and Jimmy Savile visited it in the 1970s.

Here in Tamarmouth I'm considered to be menacingly stylish by the Police, the Council and all other traditionalists. I scare the hell out of them being emotionally unstable and emblematic of freedom. The austere view of fashion and sexuality taken by the local bureaucrats clashes with my core credence as I encourage original aesthetics. Even Willow has an outfit of Kevlar coated with latex to wear when we are at work and she is being the Heroic Hound. She dons her bulletproof jacket decorated with go faster stripes which has pockets in so I don't have to wear a utility belt. I then tell her to get into Wonder-dog mode by using our code words; "Willow, we must be vigilant!"

Maybe I'll tell you more about what happened in Jersey later if you seem to be responsible but for now I'll just tell you about what Willow and I did last night. We found ourselves down near the Barbican on the Cattedown side of the harbour. I got the impression we had been heading into town in my alter ego's decrepit camper van as I discovered we were parked on Breakwater Hill. In the back of the van I had muddy M and S trousers, aged walking boots and what I called a table-cloth shirt. It had a boring checked design and was worn thin around the cuffs and collar. Being a camper van with blacked out windows I could change into Blind Justice and prepare Wonder-dog in a short time, unknown to any neighbours. Enter the back door as Mark Wilson (as it said on debit card and other wallet contents) and leave as Blind Justice, the Transvestite Vigilante with a marvelous canine companion. The Barbican being what it is and it being early eventide I decided to go out with a rouge feather boa decorating my shoulders.

Something must have stimulated the transformation and looking down to the marina I could see an unusually large cabin cruiser at the end of a walkway being too big to fit in with most other vessels. I crouched down and stroked Willow's golden head fur and straightened her jacket, then took a collapsible telescope from the pouch under her belly.

"Someone is in town tonight Wills!" I told Willow as being down at ground level I didn't think she could see the craft which I was watching. I eased my point of view along the upper deck and saw a deck hand swabbing the stern and looking as if that was the last area to do. Upon the upper deck I could make out a figure which made me cringe. Spread out on the leather settee was a human slug with a right hand flying over a laptop keyboard. The left was alternatively picking up a cigar and a tumbler which appeared to contain a Tequila Sunrise. I recognised one of the wealthiest merchant bankers from Steinbecks Investments Corporation. I didn't know his name because I wouldn't want to pollute my mind with it or dirty my mouth speaking it.

"I believe it's time for us to relieve humanity of an element of contamination again, my furry friend." I folded away the viewing tool and returned it to its home. I then took my adapted white cane from the doorway of my van and locked the vehicle.

We meandered down the sloped hill slowly as my heels were not designed for sloped cobbles and I was planning a strategy of attack, working out the details as we progressed. Willow's lead in one hand and the concealed weapon in the other we soon reached the waterfront and had to find access to the marina. I had skeleton keys in my sequined Gucci handbag and used them to gain entry to the boating complex. The night was getting dark and the Evening Star started to glint in the sky. A crescent moon could be seen over the Citadel skyline as no more than a wisp of cloud adorned the firmament. A stale fishy smell made me feel peaky but it was nothing compared to how I felt about the corruption indulged in by the owner of the boat *Christabelle* and his cohort of parasites. Fortunately no boaters were about so I approached the target knowing there was nobody else on board now. For safety Willow now started to play a Guide dog role and I edged forward using my white cane for awareness of the walkway's edge.

At the gangplank I had Willow go on board and hide while I ensured I could be heard. In this costume with make-up and due to the fading light I would have appeared to be a sexy older lady if not a hot She-man. Being the fat blob my target was he'd not turn away any female attention thinking I was sent by a crew member in return for their shore leave. After all this is Tamarmouth and Union Street isn't just for Navy boys, regardless of country of origin.

He looked over the hand rail and thinking he saw a maiden in distress with impaired vision he asked if I wanted assistance. Like wasps being drawn to cream teas this was a very effective technique for gaining attention.

"Yes please Mister. I seem to have got lost. Can you..?" My friend, a New York drag-queen had taught me a lot about manipulation.

"I'll come down and bring you on board Miss. Be there in a sec." He replied in an ensnared tone.

To be sure I succeeded I ascended the plank to the deck while he came down and once I was on board I was sure I'd not fail.

He seemed surprised to meet me face to face on the upper accommodation deck but not half as surprised when he found he was confronted by a snarling, drooling hell hound in an attractive doggy jacket.

"You are about to receive judgment from Blind Justice! Get down the steps to your stateroom. Try anything funny and I can assure you my hound will be happy to tear your throat out." I spoke watching him wriggling like a hooked worm. He eased himself down the stairs facing them and me. He held the handrails as being so overweight he wanted all the support available. Once on the lower deck he was joined by Willow who jumped down covering the flight of steps in an all in one bound. I came down with my drawn épée a number of inches from the face of my victim. He was sweating enough to moisten his shirt armpits and seemed to be breathing rapidly. One previous victim almost escaped execution by having a heart attack and that was not permitted. I had to get on with my job.

"You and the way you do business are loathsome, you're a blatherskite. Lie on the bed face up with your eyes shut." I gave him instructions as we entered the luxurious bed chamber. I felt uncomfortable, like I was being watched and I saw a tabby cat curled up on the silk pillowcases. It was yawning and staring at us in a surprisingly relaxed manner considering a large Golden Retriever was entering the room. The cat slipped off the far side of the bed and crept underneath. I took some pieces of cord out of my handbag and used them to tie the man's limbs to the corners of the bed frame.

"People like you make me sick. Just seeing you gives me the same horrible feeling I get when I'm walking in the dark and I accidentally stand on a snail. I see you come here where we have Stonehouse and Barne Barton which are areas of great depravity and all you do is waltz around like you rule the world. I wouldn't mind so much if I felt you had earned the money in an honest way but we all know you bankers are as corrupt as the day is long." I explained to this disgusting example of humanity why he was receiving judgment from Blind Justice.

"Still, it's not too late to make a slight difference to the situation. You are going to die, that much is for sure. However, depending on what you choose to do with your wealth now will determine whether or not you suffer a painful death or not. You can tell me you passwords and PINs and I can take money from your account and transfer it to a worthwhile charity. That will get you a painless death, or you can keep your filthy lucre and suffer an agonising death."

As I expected the man was a coward with no moral principles and so we spent the next few minutes taking money from his accounts and transferring it to local charities such as Devonport Regeneration Partnership and the food banks in the area which needed support. Being an honourable person of my word I then gave him an injection of tranquiliser. Once he was unconscious I took my blade and plunged it into his corrupt heart. I was glad to see him gone but I knew there was still so much more to do in my modern version of the Robin Hood story. Also as my list of victims grew I knew I would have my equivalent to the Sheriff of Nottingham on my case soon. I had to let them know this was a Blind Justice case and so I removed his eyeballs and feed them to Willow while I also cut my name in to his chest with a pocket knife I kept in Willow's coat.

"Come on Willow, we need to get home now and wash our clothes. I think we will do best by going back up to the van and changing there. We don't need to worry about forensics as we've left nothing but my shoe prints and your paw prints. Even if you have left a bit of fur I don't think we need to worry about it." I spoke reassuringly to my one companion as I was sure the Devon and Cornwall Police were about to have to implement some more cut backs due to the austerity policies being enforced by the present government. I had heard on the Devon Radio show they had to save millions of pounds and so it was the backroom staff in the offices and laboratories that were going to feel the axe this time.

We decide to reap a harvest from our latest victim and so went to the galley and raided the store cupboards. I took a drawstring bag from Willow's coat and loaded it with some expensive quality wines and spirits. Once we had selected a few things I put the bag over my shoulder. What I hadn't realised was that the vessel's owner was so paranoid about being robbed by his crew he had a hidden camera focussed on the doorway to the wine rack and so I had been filmed selecting the best malt whiskeys. I was only partially in the shot but so was Willow and this was something which would help the person who later become my nemesis. Detective Inspector Tracy Hansard would be to me what Sherlock Holmes was to Professor Moriarty.

CHAPTER 2

Detective Inspector Tracy Hansard slowed her Mondeo as she began driving over the cobbles in front of Dolphin Court. The marina always seemed eerie in the dark and the hint of mist made it worse. Halyards and steel cables knocking against the metal masts produced a very recognisable sound unlike any other. When she reached the two uniformed officers standing at the marina security gate she stopped. One was breathing out clouds of water vapour which seemed as white as little fluffy clouds in the bright artificial light. It reminded her of the light in hospital operating rooms. The smell was a cocktail of fuel, stale water and a hint of fish blowing over from the landing dock the other side of the harbour. She stood by the car and pulled on her XL Sea-spray sailing jacket over her Cornwall rugby top. She put the car keys into her jeans pocket and walked towards the nervous looking Constables.

"Morning Watkins. I hope you have deprived me of my essential beauty sleep for a good reason." She addressed the PC she had dealt with before.

"Yes Ma'am. It looks to be another Blind Justice case. See the biggest luxury yacht in the marina? It belongs to the merchant banker Howard Murtlebury and following a call by someone claiming to be Blind Justice we found he has been murdered and left in the stateroom." Watkins replied pointing to the enormous floating gin palace at the end of the walkway.

"Come with me sunshine and have your friend call the security company and the Scene of Crime boys." Detective Tracy offered round a packet of Extra Strong mints and walked down to the gangplank.

The Empress yacht *Christabelle* was just about big enough to be a floating hotel. It had comfortable accommodation for a Captain, a First Officer, a Chef, a Bosun, and one deck hand with a ship's cat. Then in the top league was the stateroom for the owner, two couples luxurious cabins and quality rooms for either 4 more individuals or another 2 couples. That night the crew were all enjoying a session on *terra firma* having been at sea for weeks. Despite having all the spaces available Mr Murtlebury rarely used his spare cabins. As she boarded the unreal vessel Tracy was reminded of the *Mary Celeste.* She didn't know what the conclusion was in that case but she was sure this was another Blind Justice case. Her problem wasn't proving that, but managing to identify who Blind Justice was.

She half wanted to call her partner but knew this early on a Sunday morning he would have only just gone to bed after a heavy session of binge drinking. Detective Sargent Peter Anderson had numerous personal and family difficulties of which alcohol was a primary one. She knew he'd be a real help but not till he'd had a few hours sleep followed by a shower and a cup of high quality coffee. Probably a bite to eat too. If he'd made it back to his flat a local cafe would get business but sometimes he ended up back at his mum's. She'd do him breakfast as she was also catering for her twenty two year old hairdresser daughter Kathy, who still lived at home. This was due to finance and being caught between two very different boyfriends, Gary and Phil.

Gary was Mum's favourite as he had a good job, didn't mind working hard or putting money away and he didn't smoke. However Phil was funny, unemployed, more interesting and entertaining. He wasn't a local lad and his history was unclear to say the least. No relatives in the area if any alive at all but that was not a real fault as such. Just a bit thin on references.

Tracy decided to leave Peter a message for when he woke up to get down and join her as fast as he could but get set up for a good day's work first so she sent a text. This looked to be the third murder by Blind Justice and one thing which Tracy was having a problem with was personal motivation. Looking at the victims they were all what she'd call 'unpleasant people'. The legalised thieves was the collective name for bankers, money-lenders and brokers round the Police station and she felt so particularly. She'd been too ambitious regarding a mortgage after being promoted to Inspector and her house had been repossessed. She now shared a half decorated upstairs flat with the homeless cats of Mutley Plain in what was known as Studentville. She had a rusty fire escape to her back door providing access for the felines. Her choice companion was Arthur named after the creator of Sherlock Holmes who caught the rodents of the area as the detective did criminals. He was a ginger with strong instinct for hunting and killing rodents as did she with regard to local felons.

Blind Justice had left little forensic evidence previously and she doubted there would be much in the yacht. Certainly no fingerprints but each crime scene so far did have paw prints which she was looking to use in one way or another. Possible curious shoe prints from what seemed to be a large pair of womans boots that confused things. She'd looked around the bridge but soon headed down to the body in the stateroom. She was met by the ship's cat sitting on the sideboard by the porthole.

"I wish I could talk with you pusscat," she stroked him and wondered what he'd seen.

As she expected the corpse had a number of narrow stab wounds including one over the heart. As before 'Blind Justice' had been cut into the torso of the body, after death she thought due to the minimal amount of bleeding.

She stood in a dream like state wondering what had happened and what the life of a super rich man was like. She moved up the bed towards the headboard and could see that as before the eyes had suffered serious damage. The concepts of blindness and justice seemed to be significant to the killer, but she pondered how. A person surely couldn't be a blind murderer so what was it? The justice seemed to be against the wealthy but the first two had reputations for misbehaving with youths and occasionally women so she needed to closely examine the histories of the three victims and see if they were connected. It was a possible lead.

"Here come the forensic scene of crime crew Ma'am and we have got a couple of the crew members. They went to a number of B and B's or hotels glad to be ashore for a night," Watkins called down to her.

"Thanks Constable. It's a start I suppose." She wasn't very optimistic feeling like an albatross lost Mid Pacific looking for an island with regard to finding her devious executioner at present.

She climbed the gangway and passed the officers getting into the disposable overalls used when collecting evidence. She was so despondent she didn't even speak to any of them. Despite one being a friend she drank with from time to time and who was an appreciated Crime Scene Manager (CSM) called John Baldwin.

"We have the Captain and the chef here. They spent the night at the Holiday Inn and were coming back to do breakfast and see what the plan was for today. They wanted to find out if the rest of the crew were needed or could they have a day off," Watkins explained to Tracy. He also described to her that they were Eastern Europeans with limited English language skills.

"Thank you. The first thing I want to know is who was the last person to leave the ship and what time was it?" Tracy addressed the two foreigners speaking clearly and a bit slower than usual. She was glad she didn't have a Janner accent as that would not help.

The Captain took a step forward to represent the ship's crew and said, "Deck hand Stefan do last shift. Swab deck and threw garbage."

"So we need to get hold of this Stefan character next and see what there is on the marina's CCTV," Tracy spoke while making a note in her little black book.

Tracy then told the Captain about the job of the forensics team and asked him to get Stefan to come and join them saying he might well have to join them back at the Police station. However if he cooperated they would not ask anything about his passport and status as an immigrant. Then PC Watkins partner came back from the security department with a couple of disks.

"Here are last night's footage from the cameras at the gates. They all seem to be working so we should have something on here. Of course that's assuming the attacker came that way rather than getting in much earlier or possibly in on a boat." PC Potter gave his assessment of the situation trying to impress the Detective Inspector.

CHAPTER 3

I (Mark Wilson) woke up this morning wondering just what I got up to with my guide dog Willow last night. We had been at home listening to the radio and then I decided to go for a walk at the Recreation Ground at Cattedown roundabout. I don't remember leaving the park and my next memories are when I woke up this morning. I was feeling exhausted despite having been to sleep and my clothes smelling of the waterfront. My shoes were surprisingly fishy for a walk in the local park and Willow had bits of seaweed caught between her claws.

The local kids call us Wallace and Gromit. We live in the part of town that has old gas works and the air smells when the tide goes out exposing mud flats and the water works are just up the river. Ironically I live in Home Sweet Home Terrace. I'm in the ground floor flat and have been for years. I never have any contact with my upstairs neighbour who I think must be in the Merchant Navy or Fleet Auxiliary. I don't hear anything happen upstairs and occasionally post arrives addressed to Miss B. Justice which I leave in the hall. I think she must have a relative or boyfriend or someone to collect it for them as it disappears about every two weeks or so. Especially quickly when it is parcels from Littlewoods, Dorothy Perkins and other mail order clothing companies.

I found my white walking cane was out in the hall way as were my shoes that had oily stains on which didn't look to have come from the neighbourhood park. I am getting concerned about my blackouts which are becoming more frequent. I could understand them if I'd been drinking, especially a heavy session on hard liquor. I'd do that when a payment came from the social or I had a win on the horses, as then I could play at being a millionaire for a day.

I own a camper van but these days I don't have a license and I haven't got the confidence to drive nowadays any way. It's weird but someone seems to be using it occasionally. When I walk down the back road where it's parked I sometimes find it has moved or its state of cleanliness is different. Unless I do something with it when I'm blacked out I think somebody else must have a set of keys.

As well as my mental blackouts which interfere with my memory I have visual blackouts which is why I'm classified as visually impaired. Some of the time my vision is almost perfect but sometimes it decreases until I can hardly see anything more than dark and light shapes in a very hazy cloud. The trouble with it is that it is psychosomatic and so it can come on at anytime with no warning. It's looking to be related to emotional stress but my psychiatrist and I don't yet know what it is I'm getting stressed about. Something seems to have happened when I went out with Willow last night that caused my mental blackout to kick in as I can't recall it at all. But sometimes I'm out and the eyesight goes yet I can remember what happened.

For example last week I got the bus with Willow and I sat in a seat facing sideways rather than forward as those had all been taken. It was at about five in the afternoon on a working day so the double decker bus was almost full. Loads of people on their way home after a long days work, mums with their young kids after shopping in town after school and the older kids going home to play mind corrupting video games, send each other silly messages on this Facebook thing I don't understand, or watch porn according to the national news.

On the other side of the bus on the folding seats opposite me I saw a single mum with her rug rat trying to wriggle free of its containment straps keeping it in the pushchair. She seemed to be more concerned with whatever was on her mobile phone than with child maintenance as the infant had a face well decorated with chocolate smears and fingerprints. It also had a fair amount of saliva spread over the lower half of its face. My vision then moved to the man sitting next to her but obviously not accompanying her. I can gaze at these people without upsetting them or feeling uncomfortable myself, as I wear the dark glasses used by visually impaired individuals. Why we with limited vision are given very dark shades so we can see even less I don't know but that's another matter. Looking at her neighbour I was surprised to see the wild stare his eyes had. He sat in a very stiff posture with his hands on his knees, twitching his head around looking from one place to another. First I noticed that despite being reasonably well dressed his hands were covered with tattoos, disappearing up his arms under his long sleeves. Something about him shouted "Psycho" to me. As I watched him looking around the entire bus my vision started to cloud over and became more tunneled. I could understand why I was feeling stressed in that situation as I don't like packed buses at the best of times, least of all when I think the guy near me might be about to add Tamarmouth to the list of places in which there had been violent gun crimes committed against innocent members of the public. They usually ended in suicide or the criminal being shot by the local constabulary. The bus stopped and we waited for all the kids to come flooding down the stairs carrying their folders, decorated bags and mobile phones. They are such a wild rabble nowadays compared to the previous generation. I'm particularly aware of this as I used to be a bus driver and often did the school run as back then the children didn't shout swear words all the time with the young girls wearing such short skirts they are hardly even belts these days.

Anyway I stayed on the bus for a couple more stops and by the time I had to get off I really was pretty much blind. I asked Willow to take me to the local corner shop as I needed to get some baccy, filters and papers. We took a slow stroll down the road as I was using Willow to provide my navigation. I'd know it by memory from the door of the local shop and I'd be feeling better once I'd restored my nicotine levels. The shopkeeper knew us as I was a regular customer so he already had a little bundle of what I wanted waiting for me behind the counter. That way I never had to put up with running out of the simple things which bring me a bit of relief and pleasure. I'm the sort of shopper who will buy stuff and keep it in stock rather than run out and then have to get more supplies in. I have to do it that way regarding electricity and Willow's food so everything else as well.

CHAPTER 4

Tracy Hansard's partner Detective Sergeant Peter Anderson woke up, and not for the first time found he didn't recognise his surroundings. Peter couldn't remember how he had got to the bedroom he was in or where it was. Still at least he didn't have any U.F.O.s with him like he occasionally did. This was what he called Unidentified Female Others that he sometimes found with him when he woke up in an unfamiliar location. These drink induced blackouts really were becoming a problem. He looked around the room and focusing on the details of the beverages he managed to induce he was in a Travel Lodge. As he had been drinking in the city centre it was almost certain to be the Derry's Cross one.

He staggered out of bed and almost collapsed into the shower, which would be Step 1 in recovery, to prepare himself for another day's work. After a blast of cold water to wake up the still dormant parts of his brain he had a quick wash. He then put back on his clothes and was glad to see they didn't have any incriminating stains on. However the shirt collar was grubby and he wanted to put on a clean one before turning up to work. He suspected Tracy was beginning to have doubts about his performance. Being a good detective she was an expert at seeing little signs and hints things weren't quite right.

He looked at his trusty companion; his Samsung mobile phone. God knows what would happen if he ever lost or broke it. It had so much crucial information in it. He saw he had received a text from Tracy at about three in the morning. It told him to get ready for a hard day's work so he went and invested in a decent breakfast with a coffee that helped raise his morale. He then felt as ready as he was able to for facing work without going back to his own flat or his mum's place. He was now charged up by caffeine and wanted to give his phone the same thing with electricity. However he still had enough left to see he also had a text saying Tracy was at the Sutton Marina investigating what was probably a third Blind Justice case.

A little fresh air and exercise would do him good he thought. So he decide to walk down there as it would only take 15 minutes at the most. It also allowed him to smoke one of the few cigarettes he intended to have that day. Being a Silk Cut it didn't do much for him regarding nicotine but it was just such a habit and he couldn't deny he thought it made him look cool. As he walked past the Brass Monkey drinking establishment he was pretty sure he had been there for a couple last night, but it was a bit hazy after that. He now felt prepared for work and so switched his Police radio on.

"Morning Boss. It's Peter here. I'm heading down to the Marina as I'm in the area. Where are you?" he spoke clearly to make sure she got the message.

"I'm back at the incident room setting up a new board for our latest victim. Howard Murtlebury is Blind Justice's newest object of attention. Executed in his luxury yacht last night. Have a look over the crime scene and see if you can find out whether he was expected in the marina or not." She had a despondent sound to her voice so Peter guessed things didn't look too good yet. However he felt there was something about this case that really got to Tracy. He didn't know if it was linked to who the victims were or how they were killed, but something didn't seem comfortable about it.

He reflected on who the other victims were and what seemed to have happened to them. First had been Spencer Collingwood, murdered in his private garage looking after his Bentley. It looked like he had been out for a spin, probably been to the Staddiscombe golf club for a round with his buddies. Then driven back and either Blind Justice was waiting for him or had followed him. This case showed the initial example of this style of execution. The victim was killed by stab wounds and had **Blind Justice** carved in their chest and had their eyes removed. These events had been done after death. The body was then discovered the next morning when Mr Collingwood's cleaner came in with her own key at about nine. She was Mrs Turner, a local lady doing a couple of jobs to earn enough to pay for her children going through Eggbuckland Community College. An average Tamarmouth single mum.

Second case, found a week later was Anthony Westbrook. Another wealthy, successful businessman but more involved in politics, especially the local stuff. This time he was murdered in his home, a luxurious villa in Mannamead about 48 hours before being discovered. This time he seemed to have put up a fight. There were signs of a struggle, broken glasses and furniture lying on the floor. As what was presumed to be punishment for resistance the desecration was the same but had been given to a living victim. Consciousness could not be confirmed but obviously, hopefully it had been lost. This time it seemed he had answered his front door to the killer and invited them in. The biggest mystery from the postmortem was the dog bites. Mr Westbrook didn't own a dog yet he had fresh marks from canine teeth in his limbs. It was beginning to look as though the killer was taking a dog with him on his murderous outings. He wasn't sure yet, but Peter was thinking that dog saliva from the bite marks may be able to give them a

DNA source. Link it to the dog and then connect the dog with its owner for the killer's ID.

He made a note regarding it in his black note book after chucking his fag-end in the harbour as he came past Dolphin Court. He could see the Police activity on the walkway and the unfortunate man's boat. These victims all seemed to have been living the life of Riley. None however seemed to have inherited their funds. He wanted to see if their was a link between the three men and their earnings in the past. CSM John Baldwin greeted Detective Anderson enthusiastically.

"Morning Pete! I think we've got something here that links this with the previous Blind Justice murder. I've sent a team up to the first crime scene for a more specific search. Dog hairs. I think with a bit of analysis we can determine the breed. Also with it and the saliva we can confirm its individual ID. I don't know of a case where it has happened before; using an animal's DNA."

"Good stuff John. This is looking to be an unique case in a couple of ways. Who should I talk to about whether Mr Murtlebury was expected or did he arrive unanticipated?" Peter found John worked well and was a good source of all relevant information so followed up the boss's query.

"You may want the Harbour-master for that. He has an office over in Stonehouse. Maybe the Manager of Sutton Harbour Marina can help as he works from just over there on The North Quay." John pointed towards to the far edge of the dockside. DS Anderson gratefully acknowledged the information, made notes in his book and began strolling the causeway over the harbour water.

CHAPTER 5

I don't know if this is a good idea but I think I need to explain just how Blind Justice evolved. People need to understand what happened to a little kid to turn him into a killer transvestite.

I was only seven years old when my parents died together in a car crash. I only just survived and I had to spend months in hospital recovering the use of my limbs and restoring my sight. I don't know but having seen the way people behave these days I expect whichever of them was driving was at least mildly intoxicated if not totally drunk.

I don't have any clear memories of being with my family. My first definite recollections are of the time I spent in the children's home I was placed in after leaving the hospital. The Channel Islands are a peculiar place as they are definitely English, but it's like they are in the past somehow. When I was there it was like there was an almost Victorian attitude towards morality and behaviour. Regarding bringing up children they believed, "Don't speak unless your spoken to." Corporal punishment was very much the order of the day. As I had no family I was very lonely. A person can feel incredibly friendless yet still be in a room full of people. I was often in a dormitory with about 20 other young boys yet I felt totally companionless and isolated. I think the staff saw how I was doing with all the other people and some took advantage of the situation. It all began one night when I was lulled into a false sense of security by a devious Deputy House master.

I went to the bathroom from the dorm shortly after 'lights out' and then when I walked back I found Mr Blackhurst was in the corridor. He was walking towards his little apartment at the end of the North wing. Seeing me he approached tentatively, then he crouched down and put his arm around my shoulders.

"How are you feeling Mark? Lonely? … Scared?" He spoke in a soft voice which seemed to sound sympathetic.

I doubt if I even spoke in answer to his questions. I expect I just nodded my head.

"Would you like to come back to my rooms and have a hot cup of cocoa?" His invitation was very appealing as I hadn't had any chocolate for months. Also I was freezing cold as the winter was in full swing and the heating system had broken down again.

I must have agreed as he took my hand and led me down the passage and up to the door of his residency. I felt apprehensive due to some conversations I'd overheard the older boys having. They used to call him Mr Blackheart, but I didn't know why. He opened the door and I felt a blast of heat come through the doorway. Inside he had an open fire burning pieces of coal the size of cricket balls. The room was probably the most alluring I had seen for ages. The shelves were lined with appealing books and children's toys and games. Also the walls were covered with attractive red paper and round the fireplace were a couple of comfy looking armchairs. For months I'd only sat on wooden boards. No sign of padding anywhere for us.

"Sit yourself down and I'll get the cocoa on." He pushed me gently towards the gorgeous heat of the fireplace. I went and sat on the pile of cushions on the chair nearest the fire. He went through a doorway to his kitchenette. I then saw him come back and pick up a bottle of clear, colourless liquid from a collection of other bottles. They nearly all seemed to be clear but some had a range of colours to them; many looked like tea without milk in. I soon found myself drinking from a hot mug. The chocolate had a strange after taste to it but I wasn't going to complain.

As it was so warm in his place he told me to take off my dressing gown as otherwise I wouldn't feel the benefit of putting it on again when I left. He took off his jacket and undid the buttons on his shirt. He also took out his cuff links and rolled up his sleeves. By now I was feeling a bit queasy and it was hard to keep my eyes open. Then he crouched down next to me and I remember he stroked my hair. I can vaguely recall him rubbing my upper arms and my thighs saying he wanted to make sure the heat got right into me. The next thing I'm sure about was I woke up in his bedroom and I was in his bed without my pyjamas on. What I did have on was a blindfold so I couldn't see. After that I woke up back in the dormitory and I had a stinking headache. I can't explain it very well but I felt incredibly dirty and guilty. Later that morning I saw Mr Blackhurst and he reminded me I had promised him I'd not mention that episode to anyone else as obviously he couldn't give cocoa to all the boys in the home, only one or two who were his special friends. He said he had picked out a couple of us for particular care and attention as we were the most sensitive boys there. We couldn't tell the other boys as obviously they would become jealous.

I never found out who the others were. But about once a month or so either I would bump into Mr Blackhurst in the corridor or occasionally he would come and get me saying he wanted a word with me and then he would turn out the lights in the dorm and take me back to his hideous chamber of horrors. I hated him but there was nobody I could turn to for help amongst the staff. The only friend I had in the children's home was a boy who had no memories about how he had got there. He was called Michael Evans and he was the one who went on to be Michelle, the Rocket Queen. He already showed signs of being gay and I think that is what put Mr Blackhurst off him. It's weird as he liked to mess about with little boys yet a gay one put him off. Maybe he just didn't find him attractive, I don't know.

Maybe later I'll tell you about the terrible parties Mr Blackhurst used to organise in the summer holidays, as that was when the rich and famous people used to come and visit Jersey. Not now though as I've thought about it enough for now.

CHAPTER 6

The other night after dealing with that scumbag in his yacht I was feeling elated and I wanted to boast about my work as the Transvestite Vigilante to someone. I don't have any local companions to talk to but I do have my lifelong friend from when I was in a children's home on Jersey. To me he is Michelle, the Rocket Queen. When I left the Channel Islands to go to the UK he hung around for a while. Once he had raised some money and had come out to his friends about being gay he decided to go to New York and work as a drag queen.

He was a real hit in places like The Stonewall Inn in Greenwich Village. They used to love his English accent when he was performing. We stayed in touch with each other by regularly writing to each other. Being the more successful of us regarding finances he would come and visit me or offer to pay my air fare to go out and visit New York. We also phoned and talked to each when we had some serious news to pass on. This would be things like getting a promotion, a new boyfriend or a good one night stand. These days we regularly use Skype so I can see his latest costumes and he is the only person that has seen me as Blind Justice while knowing my other identity. It was early in the morning by the time I had got back to my upstairs flat in Home Sweet Home Terrace after parking the camper van in a back alley. I had also given Willow a shampoo and blow dry as a reward for being such a loyal companion. I then got changed into a nightie, some leg warmers and put on my silk kimono which I had got shipped over from Japan. I hadn't shown it to Michelle yet and I was excited about what he would think of it. It had got to just after five so I knew it was just gone midnight in New York. Being a weekday Michelle would probably be in by then so I called on Skype.

"How are you darling? Been having a good time with your new show?" I greeted Michelle while lying on my chaise-longue drinking a G and T.

"Great. Yeah, I've just got in as I went out with Joey for a meal at Lorenzo's. We are really getting on like a house on fire. We both make each other raging hot." Michelle spoke to me while sitting at his dressing table and taking off his make up. I could see his lipstick had been smudged so he and Joey had obviously had at least a decent goodnight kiss, but I expected it was more than that by now.

"Yes, he sounds a real sweetie. Nice that he's moved in to the Village to be closer to you." Knowing how promiscuous 'Shell was I had my doubts about how good an idea that would turn out to be for him. However that was not my problem. I lit up a pink Sobranie Cocktail cigarette. It occurred to me that he threw male friends away like I did cigarette ends.

"I like your kimono. It suits you, as do most silk garments. That shiny look works for you. How are you doing in your glossy cat-suit?" Michelle moved around his bedroom changing into some pajamas and brushing his hair.

He had provided it for me by going to a costume shop in the Village with my measurements and having it handmade. Nobody else knew of it. Most other Blind Justice accessories I had bought via on-line stores.

"Well that's why I've called tonight. I took out another of those bastards tonight. There are countless fuckers out there, but I feel so exhilarated each time I get one. It reminds me of that film Highlander with Sean Connery in. It's like I take a burst of energy from them when they lose their life force I receive it." I drew again on my Sobranie.

"Is BJ in the news yet? I expect you will be now you have done three. But I suppose it's hard for them to cover the story unless they have a picture of you. Still escaping CCTV? It's a shame as it's a lovely outfit you've got there." Michelle put some Revitalift Night Cream on his fingertips and began working it in to his cheeks and forehead.

"I'm still only known to the Police and, not the public as no sign of any photos yet. I may have been caught on film last night though as the place was surrounded by security kit. It was a posh yacht marina." I lent forward and stroked Willow as she came over and nuzzled up against my thigh.

"Wills is looking good. I'm thinking about getting a Pekingese puppy. It could be helpful in my drag act as I've got some ideas about saying how it's a dog's life." Michelle yawned, popped a few vitamin tablets and stretched his arms up in the air showing how well he had shaved his armpits.

"Yeah. I agree with what Edgar Allen Poe said regarding them as company. He said something about their dedication, and how they can be relied on unlike people." I could see the Rocket Queen was looking burnt out and I was pretty exhausted so I decided to end the conversation there and then.

We finished by blowing kisses and wishing the best to each other. I felt my other personality rising and so chose to leave my den of iniquity and get into a Mark Wilson outfit downstairs to return to my other life.

Willow and I left all signs of Blind Justice and the Heroic Hound in my secret lair. I had been washing the cat-suit while talking with Michelle and so I hung it up to dry. I was clever enough to at least try and remove any forensic evidence. There was a small toilet just off the landing in the top flat and that was where I transformed from a Vigilante to a Mister Normal.

We got down to the hall and locked the door to the upstairs flat behind us. I went into Mark Wilson's place which was so different from the place above it. His place was the most dull, uninteresting home you could imagine. So dark and dingy it was almost like being inside a cave. The windows were so dirty the curtains didn't need to be drawn to keep out the light. The grime did the job. Yet upstairs was a festival of colour, especially pinks and purples. It was like comparing a blackbird to a peacock. It really is incredible, the variety between two personalities who share the same physicality. A real case of Jekyll and Hyde. Now I had to sit back and wait and see what if anything I'd left for the cops. I felt sure they would get something from the crime scene this time as it had been a spontaneous attack, rather than planned and organised like the others. I was getting confident in my ability to be a killer. In fact I had become so cocksure I was thinking about either writing to the Police or maybe the local press.

CHAPTER 7

Detective Inspector Hansard was pleased to see her partner looking good when he arrived at the incident room in Charles Cross Police station. She could see he probably hadn't been home last night from his five o'clock shadow. He only ever shaved with his cut throat razor. One of his idiosyncrasies that she found appealing. She couldn't complain as he put up with her superstitions such as saying 'Good Morning' to the magpies.

"How was your weekend Pete?" She greeted him and waved to him across the room.

"Basically OK, but due to seeing my father on Saturday I was a bit disconcerted so had a few drinks on Sunday evening." He had a confused look which was often the case regarding his relatives. Tracy didn't need soap operas, she just kept up to date with the people in her squad room. That was quite enough nervous tension for her.

She knew what the situation was regarding his dysfunctional family. His parents had divorced due to his father Jack being an alcoholic. He had been in the Navy and suffered from sleepless nights, anxiety and mood swings following the Falklands conflict. It was probably Post Traumatic Stress Disorder but he couldn't admit to his fellow sailors he, a Chief Petty Officer had a mental health problem.

Jack had moved out when Peter and his sister Kathy were still at school and spent a few years pretty much out of contact with his kids. Peter's mother Sue felt he was a bad influence and was happy if they didn't see him. She thought they were out of touch but in fact Peter did see Jack occasionally as they bumped into each other at various bars.

"What do you make of our latest crime?" Tracy inquired of her partner.

"It's in a more public place so I think BJ is getting more confident. Also nobody seems to have been expecting Mr Murtlebury so I don't think this one was planned, like I reckon the others were. It seems to have been spontaneous, sort of opportunistic." Peter spoke while noting things down on the briefing board.

"Yes, I agree. I think we have a few lines of inquiry to follow for the moment. Firstly, we'll see if there is anything on the CCTV from last night. Second line is the forensics. We need to search the first site for dog hairs and possible paw prints as it's looking like Blind Justice always has his pet dog with him when at work. Possible paw prints as well, as it seems he is wearing gloves each time." Tracy went through things in the same methodical way she always did just about everything.

"Ma'am, I was wondering what you were thinking about the motive as things don't seem to be missing and the guys all have their wallets still undisturbed in their pockets each time so far. So it's not robbery." DS Anderson raised the point which was a real mystery to DI Hansard.

"Yeah, I've wondering about that. I think we need to see if these men have any link with each other in the past. Did they ever work together, live in the same area or maybe they shared a holiday or something. I'm sure they have a connection somewhere in the past. Do they have any history?" Tracy was sure they had something in common. So far it was just that they were wealthy but what else was it, did they know each other?

"We'll start looking at schools and universities and then check out where they made their money; what companies they are involved with." The detective sitting at the computer keyboard answered Tracy as he typed in the next piece of information.

"How come they have all been in Tamarmouth? Are they from here or did they move here? We have quite a few different lines to follow up guys so let me know when you have anything nd for now I'm going to the mortuary with DS Anderson." Tracy allotted each couple of cops different lines to follow up before going off to do one of the parts of her job she really found disgusting. How someone could work as a pathologist was beyond her. She didn't like dealing with any dead animals and so was freaked out when she came back to her flat in the evening and found that one of the cats she cared for had killed a mouse or a bird.

Tracy drove as usual and Peter sat in the passenger seat as they went out towards the hospital at Derriford. It was a good chance for them to talk in a fairly relaxed environment. It was where they often talked about more things such as relationships or lack of them anyway. She had gone into the Police force after studying criminology as University. Peter had been in the Navy for a few years, as had members of his family for numerous generations. It wasn't quite right for him so he had left and become a Police officer. Fortunately he had avoided any really threatening situations unlike his father. There were no real life threatening posts since the Falklands for the sailors. Not to the extent there were for the Marines and the soldiers anyway.

"How was your dad on Saturday Pete?" Tracy wondered what had happened between the two of them that had made Pete go out and get drunk on Sunday night.

"He was alright. We just met by chance at the Brass Monkey, though we both know we may well bump into each other there. The issue is that Mum doesn't want to deal with him and she thinks Kathy and I are out of touch with him. A bad influence on us Mum says. Well, I want to know my dad but I think Kathy suspects we've made contact and she feels caught between the two. It's tricky as I think she knows I'm talking to Dad again now. I think she wants to, but she's still living at Mum's place so she feels obliged to her." Pete gave Tracy the latest episode of the reality drama Cops Lives.

"How come Kathy isn't living on her own or with a boyfriend? As I recall she has plenty of assets, both physical and incorporeal. Good looking girl working as a hairdresser if I remember rightly." Tracy went through her mental index cards and picked out the latest one for Pete's sister Kathy Anderson.

"She's stuck between two guys at the minute. If she could choose which one she really loved and make a commitment to him she could start making progress but decisions have never been her strong point." Peter explained the problem. Then he said about how he had arranged to meet one of the potential brothers in law on Sunday evening. Phil had come along and been very generous with the drinks; Pete got the impression Phil was trying to buy his favour. However it was known by the family that Phil was out of work. He however was the Prince Charming in relation to Gary who was more reliable but not such a laugh. A difficult decision to make. It was clear however to Kathy that Sue, her mum preferred Gary. Peter was reminded that he had said to his sister he would check on the Police National Computer to see if Phil was on there as a few bits of his past seemed slightly unclear.

They pulled in to a parking space for official visitors to the mortuary. The weather matched the way Tracy was feeling about her next task. It was grey and somber but it was inevitable it would pass.

"Right, let's see what Dr Morton can tell us." Tracy spoke, bracing herself to see a particularly unpleasant sight. Not just a dead body, but one that had been spitefully desecrated. She was worried about this case. It had the potential to have a serious effect on her future. Positive or negative; depending on how long it took to solve and to what extent the disturbed killer got inside her head.

CHAPTER 8

I, Mark Wilson, don't usually pay much attention to the news as it doesn't affect me and it's all about people I don't know. I reckon the closer to home things are the more I think about them. I read a weird thing in the Herald the other day. I don't usually buy the local rag and I only had a copy then because someone had left it on the bus. The headline caught my attention. **Blind Justice Killing Spree.** I read that there was a serial killer going round Tamarmouth killing rich people who had ill gotten gains. He had written to the paper as he had killed three so far and so was getting smug in his confidence regarding out witting the local Police.

Blind Justice
Who knows where?
11/10/18

Tracy Hansard
Detective Inspector
Devon and Cornwall Police
Charles Cross Police Station
Plymouth PL4 8HG

Dear Tracy Hansard,

Thank you for being such a useless detective. I really appreciate your pathetic attempts to catch me. I and my companion the Heroic Hound are working to clean up the twenty first century's society here in Tamarmouth. There are so many abusers, paedophiles, low life criminals and other rapscallions in the world today I think you need help removing them. I'm specialising in the perverts but any large scale cheats are within my range. Until you catch us we are going to carry on finding them and administering justice to them. We will give them all the death penalty but it is more than what they deserve. They have corrupted, damaged and defiled so many people over the years it is what they have earned. I was abused as a child by authority figures and occasionally a celebrity. I'm taking my revenge now as I have nothing else to live for.

Yours contently

Blind Justice

The strange thing about it was I could understand what he was saying. I felt that the world we were living in these days had a lot more drug dealers, prostitutes, pimps and other undesirables in than it used to. Also I felt that the justice system had gone to pot. Everyone was let off with weak sentences these days. So many got probation, suspended sentences and community service. They had to be a criminal for years before they ever got sent to prison. Even when they did they were sent to places like corporate hotels. These days prison cells have curtains and full beverage making facilities. I knew of people who had been homeless and had got themselves sent to prison to get a roof over their head and be provided with three meals a day. This particularly applied around Christmas time. I didn't know but I expected they got crackers to pull these days. Jail was supposed to be a place people were frightened of and would do anything to avoid, not a place they chose to go to by any stretch of the imagination.

I was so inspired by this article I decided to do something rather radical. I'd go out to my local drinking establishment and socialise a bit. Willow and I got off the bus at Embankment Road. I smoked a rollie as we walked carefully to Commercial Road where we entered The Eagle pub. It had been my local for years and suited me just fine. It is the kind of place you wont go into unless you have a good reason to. It's not very appealing to look at from the outside, and not much better on the inside to be honest. It's typical of back street boozers in deprived areas. Half of its population were in the Armed Forces and are drinking to subdue their Post Traumatic Stress Disorder while the other half are unemployed, probably on the long term sick. Like me they are slowly wasting away their lives smoking, boozing, gambling and using the neighbourhood whores about once a year. It was one of the few places I could go where I was known.

"Good evening George! How are things going?" I greeted the barman with a surprisingly energetic voice as I followed Willow up to the bar.

"Well as you can see I'm not rushed off my feet, but then it's a winter weekday evening so I wouldn't expect to be. The usual?" George strolled down to my end of the bar after putting change in to the hand of one of the few other customers in the room. He pulled me a pint of Tribute and placed it in front of me.

"Do you want some water for Willow? How about a packet of pork scratchings for you two to share?" He anticipated my next activity as I had a definite pattern of behaviour when coming out for an hour or two.

"Just the pork scratchings. Thanks. Who's a lucky dog, hey Wills?" I bent over Willow and stroked her on the head and played with her floppy ears. George placed the plastic packet on the bar and went to the till. Fiddled about with it for a moment or two then turned and said, "Four pounds please."

I gave him a five pound note after putting the newspaper which I had carried tucked under my arm on the bar.

"Have you seen this mate?" I asked George as I pointed to the headline.

"Yeah. It's weird but it makes sense I suppose. Last couple of times there was a killer on the streets the local working girls got scared. This time they feel the nutter is on their side and it's the pimps who have got frightened." George described the situation as he gave me my change.

"Right. He seems to be after the 'fat cats' rather than the nobodies. Quite a few people think he is doing a good job. The coppers don't do it these days." I opened my packet of pork scratchings and took out a rather burnt one. I turned and saw Willow was watching me like a cat about to pounce on a bird.

"OK Sunshine." I threw it up in the air and she caught it a couple of feet from the ground. Crunch.

"The news is on TV in a minute or two. Shall I put it on to see what's happening? We can see the sport results too." George picked up the battered old remote and pointed it at the TV. Nothing happened; George banged the handset gently on the bar and tried again successfully this time. The set flickered into life.

Looking at the program they showed the original copy of the letter which had been sent to the detective woman. It had not been done on a computer printer but by cutting words and letters out from copies of local newspapers. I was interested to see the word 'rapscallion' as I didn't think I knew anyone who used it except myself. I called Willow a rapscallion if she was being especially mischievous. They then mentioned some CCTV footage they had from the marina but for some reason it was not being shown to the public yet. I wondered if this was just them lying to try and disconcert the killer. I'd worked my way through my pint and my bag of pork rind by the time the news show was over and so I decided to get out while the going was still good. It was approaching the time when men might come in after work so I gently pulled Willow's lead. "Home."

"Good night George. See ya again sometime." I called to the barman over my shoulder as I reached the front door.

I reached my hallway and found a card from the Royal Mail saying they had been round with a parcel for Miss Justice but had to take it back to their depot as it needed to be signed for and didn't fit through the letterbox anyway. I had a feeling she might be in Tamarmouth but staying with a boyfriend or something as recently there seemed to be some footprints in the hallway and the post had been dealt with the other day. I just put the card on the shelf to wait and see what happened next and when.

CHAPTER 9

I got done up in my best pulling outfit and decided to seduce and then kidnap my victim this time. I had consulted The Rocket Queen for techniques and got hold of some Liquid Ecstasy. That had been bought for me in New York and shipped over. I had a whole evening in which to find a target, get him back to my place and entice him in to my chamber of ill-repute to have my wicked way with him.

I was taking a big risk as I chose to leave Willow behind. It meant if I got stressed it was possible I'd lose my vision, maybe even blackout totally. Still I was confident now and my psychosomatic condition would take time to come on. It would not just go from full vision to blindness in a second or two but it faded away over a few minutes. Therefore I'd have time to get to the toilets and deal with the situation from there. I'd probably go to the ladies lavatory despite not actually being one myself. I certainly appeared as one.

The Voodoo Lounge was a place I liked so I thought I'd start there. I'd just have a drink there to get in the right mind and build up my Dutch courage. I had to get the right victim as if not I'd wouldn't be cleaning up the pollution from the streets as I'd said in my letter to the world. I'd get to know him by chatting with him and once I was sure he was what I was looking for I could give him a dose of Special K. The

Theatre Royal bar seemed to have a better clientele due to its ridiculously high prices. This meant it was used by the 'culture vultures' who had some money rather than the students, matlows and other scum. I'd see if I could get a single fat cat there.

I took a taxi from Cattedown roundabout so as not to reveal my address to anyone. I was dressed up in my pink cat-suit and was carrying a Thela mini handbag. It was done by the Japanese designer Shoko. I particularly like it as it has a monster on it, although it is a dinosaur. I had my wig under a silk scarf from Aspinal which I adored. This meant I had my hands free to manipulate someone with my feather boa. I might be able to tie them up a bit before getting them secured with a pair of handcuffs I had.

I'd booked my taxi with the company that send a text to say what the vehicle would be and gave you the driver's name with the car's registration number. Then there was a second text to say when it arrived. A silver Vectra being driven by Robbie pulled up beside the pavement and it had the company's advert on the side. I opened the back door and stepped in from the curb.

"Evening sweetie, taxi to drive Miss Justice to the Voodoo Lounge?" I asked in my Little Black Dress voice. It was sexy but it was not too blatant.

"Yes, evening darling … You're looking hot tonight! Meeting your fella in town later or are you out on the pull? If so I reckon you'll have a good night." The driver quizzed me about my intentions with stereotypical conversation.

"That's it. I'm looking for some fresh meat tonight. I'm in a real Man-eater mood tonight I tell ya. I keep thinking of that Rollin' Stones song '*I can't get no satisfaction.*' That had better not be the case tonight or someone will feel my fury." I explained things to Robbie.

"I'm reminded of that song '*Killer Queen*' done by Freddie Mercury and his mates. 'Twas on the radio earlier today. *Killer*

Queen reminds me of your namesake Blind Justice. That crazy person in the news this week. Seems to be getting rid of the bad people but not doing it the right way." Robbie talked to me while eying me up in the mirror.

I was glad to find out I was at the centre of attention and I guessed I was being talked about over coffees during fag breaks.

"Yeah, I know what you mean darling. Can I ask you a question about nightclubs?" I said this in my alluring posh dress voice as I wanted a good answer to it.

"Fire away pet!" Robbie smiled looking at my reflection in the mirror.

"If a well heeled businessman was in town and asked to be taken to a deluxe venue for a night out where would you drive him to? If he wants a place with quality customers and decent escort girls, but still in the city centre not out of town." He could see from the look in my eyes what kind of thing I was looking for so he thought for a moment rather just blurting out the first thing he thought of.

"A couple of places come to mind but if you want the city centre I'd probably go for Tigermilk, the cocktail bar in the cellar of the Duke of Cornwall. I've not used it myself but I've heard good reviews and as it's new the staff there are still pretty fresh and on the ball. You know what I mean?" This was his considered answer and he obviously meant it.

"Oh yeah. That could be good. Cheers." I got out my compact and touched up my make up, putting some fresh lip gloss on.

The cab pulled up at the University end of Mayflower Street which was fine. Just a couple of steps to the benches at the back of Voodoo Lounge where the smokers would be wetting their whistles.

"Keep the change Rob." I gave my chauffeur a five pound note.

"Knock 'em dead!" Rob's exclamation seemed a bit ironic to me and put a real smile on my face.

I teetered forward on my heels but moved forward much better once I'd got my balance. After a few G and Ts I may even be up for a spot of dancing. It was during the half term holiday of Christmas term on a night no band was playing so the place wasn't crammed full of students fortunately. Therefore I didn't have to queue to get to the bar.

I caught the attention of the two lads behind the bar. One whispered in the ear of the other and the older looking of the two approached.

"What do you fancy sweetheart?" He asked and it was immediately clear he wasn't a local.

"Any cocktails on offer?" I answered in a flirtatious style, blinking my eyelashes at the mirror behind him.

"I expect you'd like Sex on the Beach but it's hardly the weather for it so for two quid I'll give you a Slippery Nipple." He spoke leaning forward far enough to put his elbows on the bar and then support his head in his hands, gazing towards my falsies bosom.

"I'll save that for later I think. Just give me a double G and T for now. With Plymouth Gin if you have it." I reached in my handbag and pulled out my fluorescent pink purse.

He quickly got the drink and I saw from the optic they did have the local brand in stock.

"Three pounds, luv." I gave him the required coins and then turned to scan tonights party animals.

Basically there were two classes of revelers in the joint. The freshers who were all under twenty five and the mature ones in their thirties or early forties. People older than that didn't use this place in the evenings. Fine for just a drink and a chat then move on and get down to business.

The Theatre Royal bar was on the way to the Duke of Cornwall and the show had started for tonight. That meant anyone in the bar was not looking for a night watching a show. Here we had some potential focuses of my attention. These guys certainly had the money. I just needed to get under their skin and bring down their defences. It should be easy enough. I took the lift up to the second floor bar to leave the street trash behind me though they didn't frequent this place. I popped into the ladies to guild the lily and ensure my phone was set as required.

Over to the bar where a group of mature gentlemen were relaxing at a table round a couple of bottles of white wine. One empty, one half gone. I saw they were watching me and at least one nodded at me then at the empty chair next to him. Could be perfect.

"Good evening boys. You seem to be lacking company." I meandered around the table going behind each in turn. I had my long sleeve gloves on and I stroked them across the back of the neck or the shoulders as I chose a seat. I saw who had wedding rings and who didn't. There were two without bands. I sat between them. The other said he'd get me a glass from the bar while picking up the next bottle.

"Thanks. A real gentleman." I smiled at him as he ambled away to the mens room.

"We are not locals and our partners have already crossed the channel to Roscoff." The man on my left with a relaxed face spoke. I noticed he said partners, not wives and he was not wearing any rings. He did have a solid gold bracelet and something about him said entrepreneur. The other, on my right had a couple of sovereign rings and he seemed less interested. He appeared more of an executive. If these two worked together I felt Mr Bracelet was the risk taker and Mr Rings was the financier. Tricky. Bracelet would be easier to attract but Rings was more likely to have a dirty secret.

"Our friend is a dedicated husband; just enjoying a night out free from his wife." Mr Bracelet made things clear regarding him.

"Does anyone fancy a Christmas cocktail just round the corner in a much more appealing site? Mistletoe provided." I knew most of the tables there were only really comfortable taking two drinkers.

"Yes, I need a bit of seasonal cheer and merriment," said Rings as though he had been evaluating the situation and had given it a positive assessment now.

It became clear over the time of just under an hour that Rings was the brains of these guys looking to set up a restaurant in the Royal William Yard. Bracelet would be the manager and the gentleman was a retired chef auditioning potential senior kitchen staff to take his place once they were up and running. They knew each other from University in London but there were family connections to Tamarmouth.

I carefully entertained them all while attending to Simon (Mr Rings) under the table. First with feet and then hands including an arm round his waist occasionally. I felt he was on the edge of going for me; hook, line and sinker. Time for the romantic candle lit wine bar. Lose the other two, or at least get them at a greater distance from us.

"Okay chaps. I'll just get freshened up. Then we can try the liqueurs and Christmas spirits." I acted drunker than I was. Leaning on Simon when I stood up.

"Fine BJ. We'll see you down by the main entrance as we will be having a cigar or something." Simon talked to me and I had told him my initials but not my name.

I flounced to the ladies through a pretty empty bar. The show had finished and the bar emptied fairly quickly. In the room I was alone and I revitalised my make up. Put on a fresh spray of Yves Saint Laurent Opium. Checked I had the little dropper bottle of knockout drops in a small side pocket with a flap over the top but not done up for easy access.

I just needed to be certain Simon had a dark past and I didn't think it would be difficult. In fact one concern was he'd admit to something he hadn't done just because he thought

I wanted him to. I was worried he thought I wanted a night out with somebody who admitted to a skeleton or two in the cupboard to be more exciting. Still I could work on certifying facts once he was kidnapped and in my grasp. Tonight was just about seduction.

"There you are. It's just a short walk round a few corners to our next venue." I slid down the stairs looking like a cross between Cruella de Vil and Jessica Rabbit, the attractive wife of Roger Rabbit. The gentleman put his overcoat round my shoulders and the three lambs followed me to a dark basement below a listed building over one hundred years old. Survived the blitz and so had character and style.

"Welcome to Tamarmouth's speakeasy gents. This is an exquisite piece of living history for you to enjoy." I buzzed the locked door to get us let in as that was part of the format here. We were duly let in by the doorman tending the entrance at the bottom of the old granite stairway. The Victorian Gothic architectural masterpiece loomed above us.

"Simon, can you get that table over there while I fetch you a cocktail? I've a surprise in mind for you. Let the others stand by the bar or find a table for themselves. I think they know we're together now for the evening." I whispered to Simon by resting my hands on his near shoulder and reaching up towards his ear while we stood inside as the door was closed behind us.

"Sure angel. I see the dark corner you have in mind. The table has a bottle holding a burning red candle." He made his way under the carved rock arch enjoying the atmosphere.

I went to the bar and picked the fanciest item on the specials of the day blackboard. I had my back to Simon and took the opportunity to splash a few drops of liquid cosh in to his glass. Fine. This was a one way road now. To hell and torment for him. It would give me total power and control over him.

CHAPTER 10

Following the post-mortem report by Dr Morton, Peter Anderson had a chat with Tracy about what to do next. She decided it was time to give a press release following the letter the Herald had published. It needed answering so she would write something, clear it with the Superintendent and then send it to the office. Meanwhile, the DS was to go and have a conversation with a forensic psychologist who worked as a profiler for the Police. He was a quirky man who taught at the local University when he wasn't doing research at either the prison or the mental health department of the hospital. DS Anderson had his mobile number still after a previous case so he'd arrange a meeting over lunch.

"Morning Professor Larsson. It's DS Anderson here. Can we meet up and talk about a case we'd like you to have a look at? I think you'll find it interesting."

"Sure Sargent. You can meet me at the refectory about one o'clock. Bring all the case notes you can; crime scene photos, victim details, you know the sort of things." The teacher spoke with a weak Scottish accent.

"Thanks. See you there for lunch." Peter finished the conversation and then went back to the station and picked up the files to make another copy.

Peter produced a copy of the files for Professor Larsson and found he had a spare hour before he needed to head down to the Uni to meet him. Time to check out his sister's potential partner Phil, on the Police National Computer (PNC). He had been cautioned for cannabis possession over a year ago. Thinking about the history of his sister's relationships he remembered that Gary had gone to school with Kathy but had been in the year below. Phil however she had met in a pub just under a year ago. Peter was happy to accept this in the 21st century, especially as it was decriminalised in some States of America. He guessed she may well already know about this as it didn't need to be kept a secret. He knew Kathy had certainly been aware of cannabis use in the past and she may well have at least tried it in the past. It wasn't as if he had a record of violence towards women.

He put on his tatty black leather jacket and went out to the courtyard where the cars were kept. Just enough time to drive to the salon where Kathy worked and have a little chat with her. It was about time they got together for a proper talk about the family, the future and where their lives were going. He pulled up outside the salon and walked in, not knowing how she would react to seeing him. She sometimes seemed pleased but not always.

"Hi Pete! How's things with you? You and your boss were mention in the paper the other day. I take it you're working on this Blind Justice case." She was in one of her lively, bubbly moods he was pleased to see.

"Yeah, that's right sis. I was in the area so I thought I'd pop in to try and arrange a proper meeting later in the week when we can talk, but it can't be at home as we need to discuss Mum and Dad as well as your mates." He spoke in his sensible organised voice. She guessed from that he had some news or information for her. "By the way, your hair is looking good. Orange as flames. I like the variety of different tones."

"Thanks. I'm trying out some new products before we sell them to the customers. It's a new colour and conditioner combination. Do you know which evenings you'll be free? Well, how about Thursday as that's also late night shopping so we should be able to manage something then in the Drake Circus mall as it's just over the road from your office and I can keep myself occupied there for ages." She answered Peter while cutting the hair of a pensioner who was using the reduced rates in the morning scheme.

"Yeah. Okay, I'll give you the details then but having looked up Phil on the PNC I don't think you need to worry about his past." Peter was pleased to be able to help his little sister and he gave her a hug before returning to his car and heading towards the Uni.

He parked in a little side street as he knew all the local roads and alleys like the back of his hand. He could understand why most serial killers at least started in areas they were familiar with. It made you feel a lot more comfortable being somewhere you knew, for sure.

He had a short walk to the refectory and resisted the urge to have a cigarette. He walked through the herds of students thinking how they were inheriting a world in which cyber crime had so many potentials. He was glad he didn't have any children to worry about in the twenty-first century and he knew Tracy felt the same. Global warming, Islamic terrorists and the short sighted politicians. The future didn't look very bright.

As he approached the double entrance doors he saw Professor Larsson coming towards him from the other end of the corridor. He had an Apple Mac under his arm and was dressed in a colourful waistcoat over a dark plain shirt as usual.

"Professor!" The DS called to the forensic psychology scientist waving at him.

"Mr Anderson. I would say it's good to see you but we only meet at times of personal tragedy for others. Still, I hope I can help you with this as I did before." The researcher headed towards the counter and just grabbed a packet of sandwiches without really looking to see what they were. He then picked up a tray and by the time they had reached the till between them they had a wide range of foods and two coffees.

"I'll cover this," said the Sargent knowing he was only being seen as a favour and he believed that teachers didn't get the respect they were due these days.

The two men sat in a quiet corner of the sizable hall, away from the entrance and exit doors where most of the noise was being made as they knew it was important work they were about to do. Peter described the situation to Professor Stefan Larsson, showing him all the documentation and explaining when ever he had a question. What he liked about the way the scientist worked was he could set him up with the information and top it up as more things were discovered. Then leave him to work alone and in less than 48 hours he'd receive a profile. It wouldn't be an exact description of who the killer was but it would say things about his demographic groupings, his position in society and why he used the *modus operandi* (M.O.) he did.

So if they could have this information about Blind Justice they should be able to start getting inside his head and looking at the world as he did. Maybe start predicting which group he was targeting specifically. Soon begin to looking for previous appearances in the system; maybe prior offences or run ins with the psychiatric hospitals or such like. Peter was pretty sure he had some sort of history somewhere. He just had to find out what and where.

CHAPTER 11

"Detective Inspector Tracy Hansard will now talk to you and update you on the Blind Justice case." Chief Inspector Harris spoke to the crowd of media reporters gathered in a conference room in the Charles Cross Police Station. There were also members of the public in the audience. It had become a national event and the Channel 4 and ITV news crews had sent down their back-up teams. The local BBC Spotlight crew was known to the staff of the Police station.

Tracy sat behind a table in her uniform next to the CI Harris. They both had microphones and unlike him she planned to just read off from the script she had been working on all morning. It was one of the reasons she didn't see herself as a senior officer. She needed time to prepare. Spontaneous, off the cuff didn't suit her. Usually at these sort of things there were relatives of the murder victims either sat behind the table and asking for the members of the public to support them. If not that they would be in the audience looking to ask the difficult questions nobody else wanted to say. But this was different.

"Ladies and gentlemen I will read this statement and then you can ask questions. The first victim was Mr Spencer Collingwood. He used to be a city banker and was found murdered in his car garage at Staddiscombe. It was on the property of his mansion where he lived alone. Second to that was Anthony Westbrook, found a week later. He was as some of you will know and remember a Plymouth City Counsellor in the 2000s and was found dead in his Mannamead villa. A couple of days ago Mr Howard Murtlebury came in to the Sutton Marina on his yacht *Christabelle*. His crew left the vessel to spend a night on shore and when they returned they found he was dead. Murdered in the same way, using exactly the same M.O. as the others, but that seemed to have been spontaneous. Not planned like the other two." Tracy read off the sheet in a slow monotone voice. She didn't want to express any emotion. Certainly no sign of weakness as it was possible the killer was in the room at the time. Pretty certain he would see the broadcast of the press release anyway. After being insulted in the anonymous letter she couldn't look phased in the least.

"Each man has had his eyes removed and has had the words *Blind Justice* cut into his torso. The cause of death is a stab wound to the heart but not with the blade used to cut the name. This will be a very distinctive piece of weaponry and will be very recognisable. Assuming the letter published by the Herald was from the killer and not a troublemaker he has a dog he takes with him. We have footage taken from the marina which will be very helpful in identifying our suspect once he has been apprehended." Tracy finished the crib sheet and sighed. She could feel she was sweating and she was aware the worst bit of the process began now as she would be unsympathetically quizzed. She felt like a sacrificial lamb.

"Any questions?" Tracy tried not to show fear in her voice.

A group of the reporters talked to each other and a few near the front raised their hands and their voices.

"Miss Hansard. I'm from The Times. Do you have any DNA from crime scenes or from the letter?" A smartly dressed well educated man asked her, while looking at her with cold hard eyes.

"We do, which means identification will be easy once we catch our prime suspect." In fact the only certain DNA they had was from dog saliva but the killer didn't need to know that.

"I presume from the wording of the letter that you are expecting another victim in a day or two as Blind Justice says he is looking to clean up the whole of Tamarmouth. How are you dealing with the pressure that puts on you and your fellow officers?" A man Tracy recognised from the Herald asked a question knowing that she was partner to a DS with a drink problem and knowing that the Police had suffered financial cuts at the cruel hands of the government.

"Well, we support each other and we know we have the support of the Tamarmouth public and obviously the media too." Tracy answered the man she knew but was watching someone she wasn't familiar with. Something about this rough looking lady made her think she had a tricky question she was about to send to her. Like a bowler setting up a googly.

"Miss Hansard. I'm from the University. I represent the LGBT crowd. We saw the letter and that Blind Justice is looking for revenge following child abuse. Is that a link between these three men? Were they all three paedophiles? Coz if you can't catch them at least Blind Justice can and does. How do you feel about a mad member of the public doing your job for you?" It was about the difficult moral side of the case. Tracy believed Blind Justice had been abused and so sympathised to a degree. But she couldn't be seen to relate to a serial killer in any shape or form.

"A number of things link these men in the past and the present." She could imagine what the LGBT crowd would say about her and the operation on Facebook if she wasn't very careful. She didn't want the social media supporting a serial vigilante, but following the Jimmy Savile uproar the celebrity/

well off abusers were very unpopular at the moment. Murder was far more acceptable and understandable than child abuse.

"Okay. That will do now. As you can accept we have a lot of work to go and do." The CI interrupted and saved Tracy before she made a mistake.

The reporters milled around the conference room and started to phone editors, contacts and even private detectives they planned to use for more information.

After the room was cleared the cleaners came in to get rid of the empty cardboard cups and biscuit wrappers. Tracy remembered her start to the day and suddenly felt tired and drained; emotionally and physically. She needed to go home and relax. A good nights sleep would help her a lot. She knew what Peter had been doing and that he was looking to connect the men to each other next day and so see if there were signs of others would be in the same group.

She doubted Professor Larsson but was willing to try anything this time. Still now all she wanted to do was get back to her flat. Have a hot bath, a drink, a decent meal to eat and then forget everything linked with right and wrong. Her cats helped her do this as obviously feline ethics and human ones were very different. She wondered about the motivation of Blind Justice and his conscience. He didn't seem to feel guilty which implied he had at least psychopathic personality traits.

CHAPTER 12

Once Simon and I sat together in a booth round a candle lit table his two friends soon realised they were making a crowd and I discovered later he sent them both a text saying they should go back to their hotel rooms and see him again in the morning. Being across the table from him worked well especially in the poor lighting conditions. He was close enough to see me looking attractive with my quality make up and well attached wig. However he couldn't manhandle me and feel that my breasts were silicone implants attached to the inside of my cat-suit.

"How have you made your wealth my darling and what do you spend it on privately to enjoy yourself? Tell me your dark personal secrets." I murmured towards Simon as I stroked his hand on the table, enjoying flirting with him.

"I'm just a successful businessman. As we explained earlier we are in the restaurant trade. I started off with my friends doing stalls and wagons at events and festivals. That worked well so we moved up to permanent establishments doing quick easy meals at good prices." He spoke while looking at me over the rim of his cocktail glass. His speech seemed to be slowing down and becoming slightly slurred.

The Liquid Ecstasy seemed to be working with the alcohol. It also had a bit of a truth serum effect too. Time to press home my advantage.

"Nobody does that well with a clean record these days. You must have cheated, lied or manipulated people in the past somewhere." I just wanted an admission of guilt to satisfy my conscience.

"We employed immigrant workers paying them minimal salary to work in the kitchens and do cleaning. Occasionally we used their friends who worked the streets to put on wild parties especially if we had gigs with celebrities. That publicity guy Max Clifford was one we dealt with when in London." Simon smiled as he talked clearly remembering good times.

This was just what I wanted as he had been found guilty of indecent assault. Time for Blind Justice to take a hostage and really take revenge.

"How about we pick up a taxi and go back to my boudoir darling? I think I can give you a few unique experiences and a time you wont forget in a hurry." I took out my mobile phone from my handbag with one hand as I stroked Simon's hair with my other.

"Splendid. Yeah. Go for it sweetie." Simon replied taking my hand to be led out like a lamb going to the slaughter.

I phoned the taxi company I had used before and we were soon in the back seats of a Vauxhall driving towards Cattedown. To try and conceal my lair I got us dropped round the corner from my abode. Also I felt a little cold air might help me clear my mind. I tied my feather boa round Simon's wrists and used my silk scarf as a blindfold. I then led him along, like a slave in captivity. In to the hallway and past the door to Mr Wilson's flat. Up the stairs to my residence and into the bedroom.

"This smells divine and beautifully feminine!" Simon mumbled as I pushed him onto my four poster bed. As I had planned the event I had plastic chains round the corners of the bed with straps on the end so I could secure him in a St Andrew crucifixion position. I did that after removing his suit jacket. He was just conscious when I finished off by placing a strip of duct tape over his mouth. I took his wallet from his trousers pocket and also took his mobile.

I then went into my living room and was greeted by a hungry Willow. I knelt down and hugged her as she licked my face affectionately.

"Okay sunshine." I led her into the kitchen and dispensed a bowl of Butcher's for my furry friend. I got myself a Silk Cut and relaxed on my piece of French furniture. I lit a rose scented candle and used my mobile phone to email Michelle. I wished I had someone to accompany me locally.

I then used the BBC iPlayer to watch the news and see what DI Hansard had said about me and my activities. I decided to send her a credit card from Simon Richards and a photo as well. Just showing Mr Richards in his position of restraint. I didn't think my bedchamber could be recognised by anyone except perhaps Michelle in New York. I used my phone to take the photo and then printed it off via my Epson wireless connection. On the back I wrote, "Blind Justice is looking at this scumbag now. He will soon start to suffer as retribution for my past." I put the two objects in an envelope which I addressed to DS Hansard in the same flowery handwriting as I had used before on an envelope.

I was interested in the attention paid to the LGBT reporter from the University and so decided to at least look that group up on Facebook. Knowing what younger people were like when it came to activism I wondered if there was a group who were anti-abusers who might at least support my actions. I found the LGBT group met once a month to talk about things happening and share each others company. They had a Christmas party scheduled for a couple of weeks time which I thought I might attend.

I thought if I went along in a good outfit and had a few drinks I was sure I could ask people how they felt about Blind Justice and see if I had any sympathisers. Also I might be able to find out if there was a support group for people who had suffered abuse as children as the students were often good at setting up a wide range of groups to help each other. I knew they had things like that in London and I guessed that Tamarmouth being such a high population university might well do so too.

I felt sleepy and as the bed in my flat was being used by my hostage Simon I'd have to use the downstairs one. I changed my clothes and went downstairs leaving the letter for DI Hansard in the hallway. I put it on the wooden box which had the flats electricity key meters in. I turned back into Mr Wilson and went into the downstairs flat with Willow.

CHAPTER 13

"Willow, can you take me to the laundry?" I asked my best friend in an easy voice. It was time to go and do a weekly wash. Then probably get something to eat like a pasty as I didn't like to sit in the laundry doing nothing. Also I had found a letter which needed posting left in the hallway so I'd do that too. Maybe go to the local Coop and buy some food and drink as it was pay day.

I loaded up my rucksack with all of the last week's dirty clothes. God knows when I had last washed some sheets. I either bought new ones in somewhere like Wilko's or from a charity shop. I could get a fitted sheet once a month or so with matching duvet covers and pillow cases for a price that made the hassle of washing and drying such things seem foolish. I threw away my dirty ones as they often had a cigarette burn or two and if not I'd just put them in a big green bin thing on a street corner which the Salvation Army used to collect clothes and other donations.

I saw the letter to post was addressed to the Police station which I thought was strange; still not my business. I always try and go to the laundry on a weekday during school hours as I find it is quietest then. There is some cliche about not airing your dirty laundry in public but it just makes sense to me to keep it to myself. There is something very equating about a laundromat and having to show your most personal items of clothing to all and sundry. Still, I didn't have airs and graces so I didn't mind.

I put my rucksack on my back and went out into Home Sweet Home Terrace with my white stick in one hand and my harness to Willow in the other. A brief walk up to Embankment Road and we were soon putting the money in the slot and wondering what to do next. Along to the Post Office to get my money out and then shopping. As I was recognised in the pub so it was in those places.

"Morning Mr Wilson! How are you and Willow today? Not too cold?" I was greeted by Pam who had been working at the Post Office counter ever since she and her husband took it on with the local newsagent store. In the time I had lived where I did I had seen them have a couple of kids, watched the kids go to school, primary and secondary and leave home. I felt sorry for her as her daughter had been hit by a drunk driver years ago. She had gone from a free spirited nymphet to a wheelchair bound victim of modern society. The driver had been a drunk property developer visiting Tamarmouth looking for areas to demolish and replace with student flats.

"I'm okay and Wills is always fine if she has a good walk and a bone to chew in the evenings. Christmas bonus of my extra pension money from my old bus driving job any day now. How about you?" I didn't feel talkative but what I get in return for at least being polite made it worthwhile.

"Well, do you believe in poetic justice? Sort of like what those Asians call karma I suppose. I need to check the details but I think that one of those clowns taken out by that nutter Blind Justice is related to the bastard who ran over my daughter Julie." Pam seemed to be uplifted by this sort of revenge event. Blind Justice was certainly doing well regarding quantity of media attention I thought.

"It's weird isn't it. Killing paedophiles is pretty much seen as okay. They really are seen as the lowest of the low. I reckon the cops will have trouble catching Blind Justice as he'll be supported by the public. I was thinking about it the other day. Some of the police who don't have perfect character and morality maybe inclined to let things slip or look the other way now and then." I talked to Pam as she counted out my money and took out the TV license charge. I took the letter out of my pocket and slipped it across the counter, with no concerns as it already had a stamp on.

"I'd be inclined to help against those scumbags," she admitted.

"Bye." I put the cash in my wallet and left the dingy shop to find a bite to eat. Despite the greyness of the sky I was feeling surprising content with things and so decided to splash out on a proper lunch rather than just a 'meal deal' at the supermarket. It was the local takeaway but it had seating too. Reasonably quiet at this time of day. I went in to browse the price list but already knew what I'd probably have.

"Hi ... I'll have Spam fritters, medium chips and mushy peas please. And a pickled egg, thanks.That's to eat in." I followed Willow to the table farthest from the door and slumped in the chair. I stroked her head and rubbed under her chin telling her what a lucky dog she was to get pickled eggs. She sat in an alert posture enjoying the smells in the chippy.

After a few minutes my meal was brought over and I enjoyed the battered Spam soaked in oil, dripping with cholesterol; not that I cared about that. I did nothing to try and live a healthy life as I saw no future either for myself or for the modern world. I was glad I didn't have any kids as the world seemed to be killing itself to me so I may as well do the same thing. I took the pickled egg and watched Willow focus her attention on my right hand. I threw it up in the air and Willow snatched it in her jaws, gobbled it up and then licked her chops then her paws.

We returned to the laundry after popping in to pick up a few microwavable meals from the Coop. I also bought a bottle of scotch as it was on offer for Christmas and it helped dull the pain. I agreed with people who called this time of year "the silly season" and I could understand why it had such bad statistics regarding suicide rates. Most people said they loved Christmas but I hated it as I remembered it in Jersey years ago.

CHAPTER 14

D S Peter Anderson sat looking at the I.D. photos of the three victims. The trouble with criminals these days was they didn't look like criminals. They either hid behind the internet or used one of the many beauty therapists to get a posh haircut and make over. There were so many tanning shops, gyms and spas these days it meant everyone could at least look good on the outside, even if they weren't good inside. Peter was sure these three men had a link in their past. They hadn't gone to the same school or University, but they were all pretty well educated. Collingwood had divorced after marrying a fellow student at the London School of Economics. He was from London originally. Moved to Tamarmouth to leave the City, his cheating wife and his business partner behind. Still worked but pretty much freelance as he didn't need the income. He had a bunch of friends at the local golf club but didn't socialise much in Tamarmouth City Centre. Different to Mr Westbrook who was a Tamarmouth lad, done well. He went to a good private local school and made it to Oxbridge. He had studied law and politics and came back home to work in the Courts. Became a local counsellor and had done a lot for the profile of the city. He was almost a local celebrity often being in the press due to attending events and raising money for charities in the area.

Then there was Mr Murtlebury, the one who didn't live in the locality but sometimes visited on his floating home. He had still been married but was very separate from his wife. She lived in the United States now with the kids. He had been in the Navy for a few years but wasn't from a naval family or from Tamarmouth. Been a bit lost for a few years and so had been a mature student when educated. Then went and worked at Canary Wharf with all the dodgy bankers and got rich just before it all fell apart. Maybe his wife was a local girl? That needed to be checked. All the mens siblings needed to be checked out too. After all the majority of murders were committed by family or close friends. That obviously wasn't the case with a serial killer.

Peter was about to go and get a coffee but then he remembered hearing caffeine didn't just have an immediate effect but messed up your sleep patterns for ages after so he left it. He looked at a photocopy of the letter sent to the Herald. So they knew BJ had been abused as a kid. The question was where and by whom.

He then thought about the press release Tracy had made earlier. What really bugged him was the idea that the question from the Uni girl had something to it. If Blind Justice had been after men that were paedophiles how did he know who they were? Were they all part of a network and had they all abused him sometime in the past. He decided to draw up time-lines for the three victims and see if they crossed anywhere. Assuming they did he could then investigate that point and see what he came up with.

He also needed to check the first person to find the body in each case. The cleaner for Mr Collingwood. Mrs Turner had arrived and seen one of the garage doors open which was unusual. She went over to see if Mr Collingwood was there and found a dead body on the floor beside the Bentley laid out naked from above the waist. She saw it was a gory mess and phoned the Police immediately. They had arrived in minutes and turned it into a crime scene. They set up base in the garage from which they could move out to search the house once the garage had been forensically examined.

The second body had laid in place for longer as Mr Westbrook missed a meeting with his P.A. and failed to answer e-mails or calls for a day. This aroused suspicion and so his P.A. called round to his house after a day in the office. A smashed glass panel in the front door aroused suspicion. Feeling brave but suspicious due to the darkness and the silence she walked around the back garden. She knew the house layout having been there twice before. A birthday barbecue that summer and also to collect some things for Mr Westbrook. He had been busy before flying over to America so she collected his luggage for him. She had been new to his employ then and explored the house in an estate agent type visit to size up her new taskmaster. She couldn't resist it. Any chance after that TV series "Through the keyhole." It was before all the current reality shows but maybe helped to start the trend. She looked in the kitchen window and saw a designer place with the only culinary island she knew. The mess and smashed glasses meant that what was expected to be perfection was a scene of tainted chaos. She decided to call the local police and report a missing person. Being part of the establishment he was soon under investigation and she was talking to an officer face to face in under 12 hours. They came round and broke in using the already damaged front door. A struggle was soon apparent and the master bedroom revealed a bloody body in St.Andrew's crucifixion position. Eyes removed again and **Blind Justice** cut in the chest again. In a way this one was more disturbing than the first as it showed for sure a psychotic killer not just a one off individual event.

Peter looked and saw Julie Mason was the P.A. he needed to talk to and he knew that dog hairs were found at that crime scene too. Two non-keepers of dogs but both murder scenes were laden with them. He decided to call the forensic lab and see what he could find out about these dog hairs. He was presuming they were the same dog in both places and he also must confirm with the forensics lab that they matched those found at *Christabelle.*

"Hello, Dr Pai at the forensic lab? This is Detective Sergeant Anderson at the murder investigation team. I just wondered if you have anything regarding the dog hairs at crime scenes. Can ya match them up and give me a breed?" Peter was clearly eager.

"Yes. Detective we can confirm it is the same dog at all three crime scenes. Having compared them with others we know we dealing with a Labrador. We could match it to a particular dog so find the dog and so find the killer." The voice was recognisable as a man of studious behaviour. "We have a few paw prints which might help in I. I don't know how submittable they would be in court. Better check that with Crown Prosecution Service as it would definitely be able to confirm the dog's ID."

"Thanks, that's all useful," Peter was pleased to have something to tell Tracy which put him in a better frame of mind as he was going to see her after work for a drink. He thought about the tip off regarding the crime on the boat. It had only made a couple of hours difference as the returning crew would have found the body at about six in the morning. Instead all the investigating officers had to turn up on the docks at about three in the morning. It was like Blind Justice was particularly trying to annoy them personally. Also Peter thought it probably had been Blind Justice calling from a phone box as he seemed to be gaining in self-belief.

PART 2

CHAPTER 15

"Arthur, I hope you are having a better day than I am." Tracy greeted her cat as she came in to find her hungry friend waiting at the top of the stairs. She took off her waterproof jacket and hung it on the overloaded coat stand in the porch. "I'll just have a shower as Peter is coming over for a drink and to give me an update regarding the forensics."

In the kitchen, with its parquet floor, tongue-and-groove ceiling and wooden doors on all the cupboards, she felt she was in the farmhouse where she had grown up. Shame she didn't have an AGA stove to top it off but they weren't practical on the first floor. She still dreamt about having a wood burner, either there or if she moved again, at the new place. Great way to get rid of documents, evidence and any dead birds given to her by Arthur. She pulled a cold beer from the fridge and looked at her watch. Not enough time for a shower as she wanted to wash her hair. She always felt like doing that after visiting the mortuary.

"We'll deal with Peter first and then I can choose between a shower and a bath. You don't know how jealous I am of you and your ability to have catnaps at any time of the day." She took the last pouch of turkey and beef out of the box and put it in the empty dish without rinsing it. She placed it on the mat by the water bowl and topped it up with water left in the kettle.

She sat in the chair which gave her a view over Tamarmouth towards the ferry port. She took a good pull from the can of lager and thought about all those people out there, each with their own dreams and nightmares. She loved the fact that she was high enough to see nearly all of the municipal districts; she felt like a ruler looking out over their empire. She just hoped Blind Justice wasn't feeling too powerful and emancipated. She was getting the impression he was psychotic and so the norms of civilised society didn't really concern him. These were the worst ones, as they weren't worried about being subtle or tactful. Yet neither were they concerned about hiding evidence, as a rule, which helped.

The doorbell rang as she was wondering what she really felt about someone killing paedophiles. She hated what they did but what was the essence of justice and the law? Obviously different people saw it in different ways. When is a terrorist a freedom fighter?

She answered the door and was greeted by a cheerful looking Peter, carrying a plastic bag containing a four-pack of beers. She knew from that there was some good news. If not, he wouldn't splash out on a drink to share. Their quality and quantity reflected the situation regarding the case. The one occasion he had called on her to say they had caught the offender, he had been standing on her doorstep smoking a cigar with a bottle of champagne wrapped in tissue paper.

"Okay, Peter. Come on up and tell me what you have found out." She was enthusiastic and had finished her first beer just before he arrived. He went up the stairs and straight into the kitchen. He knew she had a well-decorated and comfortably-furnished lounge but, like the parlour of the Victorian era, it was only for significant, official visitors when making a good impression was important. She took his cans and placed them in the fridge, using them to replace the two she extracted.

"Thanks, Boss. The forensics have come through. The same Labrador at each crime scene. It looks like we can use DNA from its fur to identify it. Then with that, we can link it to its owner." He gave her the updated information in a burst, knowing it was helpful. It would be an aid to convicting Blind Justice but not much help in catching the sod, which was Tracy's principal concern for the time being. She felt she was on an emotional roller coaster as she was lifted seeing Peter but then plummeted down again knowing she still had the real job left to do, apprehending the killer.

Peter saw the disappointment in her face and told her that Professor Larsson had a profile for them tomorrow. She tried to look inspired by that but couldn't help going to the cabinet where she kept her supply of spirits. She felt like a train driver at the top of a steep descent. She still had the brakes on for the moment. If she took just one glass of the lethal lubricant she was pretty sure she'd lose grip on the brakes. Then the momentum would gather and she would go crashing down towards the Slough of Despond. Certainly, if Peter was on the train with her, the two of them would make an entropic dive, which it would be very difficult to recover from. She knew Peter would find it almost impossible and she couldn't betray him like that. That would be treachery.

"Okay, Peter. I'll see you in the incident room tomorrow morning; bright and early. We'll give the others an update with the profile and the forensic report." She spoke as she turned away from the drinks cabinet, which she didn't open as it would be akin to opening the Gates of Hell. Letting Blind Justice get the better of her before they had even had a fight. Submission was not a characteristic of her personality.

"Sure, Ma'am. I reckon we'll crack this one with sheer slog, basic police detective work. You know: blood, tears and sweat." He said this as he walked down the stairs to the flat door, which led to the communal hallway. She didn't need to show him out. He knew when to take responsibility for himself. A short walk to the bus stop, then back home to his mum's for a good night's sleep and breakfast in the morning.

Whereas she needed a steaming hot Radox-esque bath to lift her inner energy levels and make her feel both human and humane again, to restore self-belief and faith in her own ethics and morals. Arthur was permitted to kill because it was his instinct, in his nature. He couldn't help himself. Blind Justice was not the same. He chose his victims but Arthur attacked things due to being stimulated. Which was why he jumped on feathers, pens, lipsticks and unlucky birds.

A dose of purple bath salts, a good splash of bubble bath and a tub loaded with belting-hot water, together with a relaxing CD of ambient music. A couple of scented candles on the shelf, where she kept her perfumes and, in the morning, she'd be ready to be Tamarmouth's No. 1 Crime-Fighting Lady again.

CHAPTER 16

I crept into what would be my torture chamber as quiet and dangerous as a flea carrying bubonic plague. Blind Justice was about to equate to The Black Death as far as Mr Richards was concerned. I didn't know what he thought about things such as souls, eternal life and fate but he was going to find out about karma. In Paradise Lost, if I remembered right, there were nine levels to Hell and so pain, suffering, misery and torment could go a very long way if I so chose. In a way, I intended to take years of emotional, psychological anguish and convert it into a period of unbearable, endless and relentless physical agony. How long it lasted would depend on his strength, will power and determination; yet also on my skill at maintaining his life in the darkest, harshest place tolerable without falling into the abyss of oblivion. How long can a life be held on to at the pain equivalent to the event horizon of a black hole without tumbling inescapably to the singularity of death at its core?

I had composed a manual over the years as I invented or discovered more regarding the infliction of pain and studied it as a science. I should be a Professor of Pain Application and could have written texts such as Dummies' Guide to Torture and Suffering. Really it could be in two volumes as physical and mental hurt were both very different and were caused by very different techniques. Combined methods were effective too. For example: take the blindfolded victim and allow them to hear electric current sparking between contacts. I would take some hair and fur left in brushes and electrocute that as the smell of its burning really is disgusting. I'd never been in a situation where any dead bodies were burnt but I imagined that at least contributed to the unforgettable, soul destroying odour. This would induce such fear enhanced by the victim's imagination conceiving such hellish pictures as Hieronymus Bosch would be proud of.

"Don't worry, Mr Richards, I'm not planning to keep you for a while… I'll keep you forever." I impressed myself with just how psychotic and criminally insane I sounded. Even Willow seemed to hardly recognise the voice.

Mr Richards tossed and turned his head from left to right. He had not clearly, consciously moved till then since I entered the room but, as I'd hoped, he was awake. A hangover, hunger, thirst and now demonic plaguing to torment him.

"Time to see if you are foolish or sensible. If I undo the gag, permitting you to speak and consume some sustenance, it will obviously be to your advantage. However, if you are stupid enough to cry out for aid, I can remove your tongue. You are being detained in a remote warehouse and it will be easy and pleasurable for me to extract your tasting organ and vocal chords. My dog will eat most offal and tongue is a rarity nowadays so he'll be grateful to try human. Not that I see you as much of a human but a distorted, corrupted and contemptible specimen." The threatening words dripped from my mouth as blood does from a sacrificial, slaughtered pig. Thick, dark and heavy.

He froze as I spoke; then slowly nodded in agreement with my demands. I reached over to his face, untied the cloth and pulled out the wadding stuffed in his mouth when out cold. I left the blindfold over his eyes as he couldn't know he was in my flat, not a warehouse as I'd said.

"W–Water, please... If you can." He uttered in a surprisingly soft, child-like voice. Intentional or not, this failed to evoke sympathy in my cold heart, which may as well have been pumping liquid oxygen through my veins for all the warmth I felt towards this beast.

I took a straw from an already prepared water bottle as I had expected this. I touched it to his mouth and he eagerly sipped like a camel at an oasis.

"Time for some questioning. I'll ask you questions; some I know the answers to and some I don't, but you won't know which are which, so I advise you to give true, correct answers to them all. If you give me an answer which I know is wrong, you will pay for it." I laid out the interrogation sequence.

"Which of these people have you dealt with in the past; Spencer Collingwood, Anthony Westbrook and Howard Murtlebury?" I started with a good, simple query.

Mr Richards was sweating profusely despite being almost naked in an average temperature room. I saw him give a deep gulp and his Adam's apple bobbed up and down in his throat. He clearly knew at least one of those names.

"I once went to a sort of party weekend organised by Anthony Westbrook. It was attended by Howard Murtlebury. It was on Jersey and he turned up on a flash boat. That was quite a while ago now and he had only just got it then. I think it cheered him up as he had just split with his wife. To console himself while missing his kids he came to Jersey, took coke and fucked about with the kids at the local children's home. That was the same one Jimmy Savile went to, but I never saw him." Simon talked, giving me the impression the more talking he did and info he gave, the more likely he thought I was to let him go.

I knew from when I'd captured Westbrook that he'd known Richards, but now Murtlebury was linked in with Savile as well, which helped me see who had done what.

"Thanks for that." I needed to get my bathroom ready for a serious butchery job once I'd killed this worthless paedophile and so, to help me get in the right frame of mind, I retired to my lounge and set up a Skype link with the Rocket Queen. We had a bottle of vodka each as we both had memories to block out, which we were reminded of. Also things were about to happen for both of us which we knew were going to be unpleasant, and so it would be better faced through a haze of drunkenness. I had to kill Mr Richards in my bedroom, cut him into pieces and feed him to Willow and the local feral hounds. Some bits needed to be dumped, probably off Laira Bridge. But I needed to check for CCTV cameras first. I'd take some photos to send to Detective Hansard once I'd got going as that would boost my morale. Maybe to the local media too. Meanwhile the Rocket Queen was about to stop orbiting Joey as a black hole called Franklin was applying a seriously unavoidable attractive force from Manhattan. At least Michelle now had the decency to tell lovers when they had gone from strong attractive force to weak, which was better behaviour than before. Joey was meeting Michelle that night, about to suffer an emotional supernova so a litre of vodka would help fuel the Rocket Queen to reach the required escape velocity. I felt sorry for Joey as he'd been looking forward to a romantic New York Christmas with Michelle, but was about to find himself in a very poor atmosphere, feeling like Major Tom.

CHAPTER 17

"I get the impression you have dreams occasionally, Willow." I talked to my hound as I saw her twitching in her sleep, which she sometimes did before waking up. "I don't enjoy my dreams, usually and that's a good thing about alcohol: I don't remember them if I'm drunk when I go to sleep." We had enjoyed last night as I'd worked my way through most of my bottle of spirits and Willow had a tin of premium dog food. We demolished a few pork scratchings between us too. Watching Willow, I wondered whether she could remember her past, being a puppy and having family. I knew some people who seemed to be more interested in their history than their future. A lot of people, including some celebrities these days, were mad about genealogy. It seemed pointless to me as, whatever one knew about their past or not, it didn't change who you were now. So what was the point in getting so het up about it? I didn't like what had happened in my past and wasn't bothered I could hardly recall it. The future didn't look too good either, but at least I had a chance to influence that. I had a few more years with Willow and then it would be a real hassle to get another guide dog. I'd probably stay at home more then as I expected my eyesight to decline; it'd certainly not get any better.

Perhaps then I'd go into a community or a residential place but I got the impression the current political movers and shakers were cutting budgets for all those places now. 'Better to burn out than fade away.' Can't remember where I'd heard that but I suppose I agreed. The Romans had said 'Carpe diem' – seize the day; it made sense.

"Let's go for walkies. I fancy getting a local paper today. Maybe pop in the bookies too; we'll see." Willow was awake and I could see she was ready for a little exercise.

We just missed a downpour as it had chucked it down earlier. That was good as an umbrella was tricky if I had my white cane in one hand and Willow's harness in the other, not that I needed both at the same time. I felt more secure with both though. I didn't know if it was a seasonal thing but I was having quite a few blind episodes these days. Sooner or later I'd have to talk to my Community Psychiatric Nurse (CPN) about it. Maybe see the psychiatrist again, though I had doubts about him. Like my dentist, he didn't look old enough to have the qualification he purported to hold. Certainly not the real life experience anyway.

We went for a walk down towards the Barbican. I enjoyed looking at the boats bobbing up and down in the marina. I hated the seagulls. I saw them as flying rats; utter vermin. I might see a swan or two as there were a couple in the harbour somewhere. We were happy going down Southside Street today as, in winter it wasn't full of tourists and holiday-makers. The students, even if on holiday, cluttered up the streets in summer but went home or stayed indoors when gray skies prevailed.

"Give us a packet of Gold Leaf and some liquorice papers please; and this Herald as well. Cheers, love." I picked up the smoking gear and stuffed it into my jacket pocket. Took the rag and rolled it up to carry in the same hand as Willow's leash. I caught sight of the picture on the front page and headline too. "Blind Justice takes hostage!" The picture was of the unfortunate victim, Mr Simon Richards strapped to

Blind Justice's four-poster bed. I paid and walked out of the Co-op towards the Hoe. After just a few paces I started feeling dizzy, and my eyesight began fading. I stopped at a bench I was familiar with to take stock of the situation and rolled a smoke, though I did that so often I'd have no trouble doing it with no eyesight.

"This really is becoming a problem, buddy. I'm going to have to go and see Dr Kirkwood again." I talked to my soul-mate as I stroked her head. "I don't think my CPN can actually do anything to help whereas he might have a treatment or some kind of therapy we can try. If I remember he said he thought each time it happens, it is triggered by some external activator. I'll need to try and find out what they are and keep a diary of them. Then, once we know what they are, he can do something to negate their effect on me. I think hypnotism was one way he said they could be cancelled." I got up and threw my fag end in the harbour. I was holding Willow's lead and the cane while in an area I was familiar with, yet I didn't feel comfortable so decided to go home via the quickest, shortest route.

"Let's go over the Sutton Harbour footbridge." I didn't like that way because it meant walking through the flats at Teats Hill Road, which I saw as the local slum and so felt vulnerable if travelling it when I couldn't see. However it was not too bad during daytime, which was why I'd risk it now. It was also better doing it when the kids were still at school, which was why we could manage it if we got on with it now. The lock gates were in the closed position, which meant we could walk straight over the bridge without waiting.

It was a surprisingly short walk from the posh shops and restaurants on the Barbican to the underclass flats at Coxside. Then, out the other side to Cattedown, which was in between the two regarding status. As Willow led me past the National Marine Aquarium I thought about the possible activators. I knew stress triggered a response so what had I just encountered that was something to be freaked out by? Buying baccy in a well-known shop certainly wasn't. I remembered the incident on the bus a while ago, but I could understand that. I'd been stressed by the weird looking guy on the seat opposite me. Everything today seemed ordinary and comfortable. Just getting some smokes and a Herald; I even recognized the store assistant so that wasn't it.

"I don't know what's going on, mate." I spoke to Willow as we walked down Gashouse Lane at the side of Barbican Leisure Park. A dirty, dingy backstreet lined with relics of pleasures past; used condoms, empty bottles and a few syringes. It made me glad I didn't have any kids or family to worry about. Technology may be advancing in leaps and bounds these days but I didn't feel humanity was improving at all.

CHAPTER 18

D S Peter woke up in a room he had known since he was a teenager and had decided to take The Good Way. A lot of his friends at the sixth form college had started driving and drinking, combining those activities and a few other criminal pastimes. Back then car theft was a lot easier, kids didn't have the virtual world to play in and drugs were not as abundant.

Until recently many shops provided 'legal highs' and with the Government encouraging kids to get degrees in chemistry and biology, more youngsters knew how to make crystal meth in their garage or use hydroponics to grow skunk or spice. Back then being a celebrity meant something. He and his sister used to watch 'Jim'll Fix it!' They were both appalled to see him and Rolf Harris get convicted as paedophiles. Peter had lived in Tamarmouth all his life and when his parents were still together they'd all had holidays in Cornwall and the Channel Islands. They had seen the children's home which had shut down under allegations of being a hub for child abuse and other depraved activities.

"Morning, Petey.! Do you fancy a cup of filter coffee? I'm bothering to do it as you and Kathy are both in for breakfast today. We usually make do with Douwe Egberts instant." Peter heard his mum shout up the stairs over the sounds of the home

preparing for another working day. Peter had never got used to
his dad not being there after he moved out to Ernesettle when
he'd split from his mum, Sue.

"Yeah. Go on, Mum. Do as much of a full English as
you can. Today's going to be non-stop after our briefing from
Tracy." Peter called back as he made his way to the bathroom.
He knew Kathy would be out running at this time of day as
that was part of her routine. Like her dad had done in the
Navy, she worked via routines and established practices.
Therefore every morning she rose, exercised, returned for a
shower followed by coffee and cereal. Then she would watch
the news while breakfasting and catch the bus to work at the
salon on Wolseley Road. This wasn't a family bathroom any
more, but a girlie one, occasionally visited by a guy now and
then. Peter found all his shaving kit and wondered whether
either of Kathy's boyfriends had stayed overnight yet. There
were a few possibilities on that front. Phil was the one most
likely to do so but he'd do it secretly, either stay in Kathy's
room and leave early before Mum was up, or maybe even hide
in Peter's room till the house was empty. Gary would let Mum
know if he stayed in her house and would probably stay on
the sofa or in Pete's room. He'd join them for breakfast before
going to work. He seemed the better option if Kathy wanted
an orthodox lifestyle. She was still in touch with friends from
school via Facebook and some of them had successfully gone to
Oz or the States, either with, or, to find partners. International
transmigration was far more common these days following
the refugee crisis in Europe. Pete didn't see himself leaving
Devon but he could imagine Kathy and Phil running a gym/
spa-type place in a hot sunny country where English was the
predominant language. He shaved and washed while thinking
of the family's potential future.

He descended to the open-plan kitchen-diner and found
his mum leaning on the breakfast bar over the newspaper. The
coffee was steaming and she had bacon and eggs ready to fry

now he'd come down. The local radio station was mumbling in the background as it had done for years. He took his phone and plugged it into the charger before going and hugging his mum from behind.

"Sleep well, darlin'?" Mum asked the same question every morning and it was then followed by a comment on the latest story in the paper to catch her attention.

"I guess you're busy with this Blind Justice case? Now that someone's been kidnapped it's all over the national papers. Good luck with it, son." She spoke as she worked over the hob, frying the bacon and eggs.

He noted what she had said, as she generally didn't mention his work, knowing he couldn't talk about it. This time he wouldn't have, even if he could because he was quite disturbed by this case. It was almost like something on TV or a movie. He knew the Armed Response Unit were ready to go charging in if they could just find an address to send them to.

The quality coffee steamed in his own personal mug. It was adorned with a picture of Homer Simpson drinking beer. In a way he wished his life was as simple as Homer's. At times he hated the fact his decisions could have such life-changing effects on the lives of others. Also he worked so hard that, unless things changed, he would soon be a bachelor for life with no children. He remembered when he joined the force and had laughed at those lonely older men and women; the joke was they wed their warrant cards. It'll never happen to me, he had thought but time waited for no man and could not be bought. He'd be particularly lonely if Kathy moved abroad and had kids there. That was one of the things he wanted to talk to her about when they met up later that day at the mall, after his shift. He had to find out how she felt about her father as Peter was in touch with him, but in a sly, covert way which made it seem like a dirty secret. That wasn't right.

"Doing anything today, Mum?" He asked dutifully.

"Depends on Shirley. We might go up to Asda for a big shop and use the café there too. I'm just waiting to hear if she is over the flu she had." This made him think it must be great to have a soul-mate to discuss any and everything with. His mum Sue and Shirley had lived within a couple of miles of each other for almost seventy years. Since primary school they had been spiritual Siamese twins knowing all there was to know about each other. Working together and then sharing holidays. Adopted and adapted parents for each other's children. People just didn't build relationships like that any more; it was all Facebook now rather than face-to-face conversations. He knew his mum would never be big on social media. She liked to see people and be able to touch them. It was the way she'd grown up and wouldn't change now. She'd rather take a walk round to Shirley's place in the rain than talk to her on the phone. He guessed that was what she'd do after washing up the breakfast pots and pans.

CHAPTER 19

Peter felt on top form having had a good night's sleep in his favourite bed and then a good breakfast talking to his mum. He had also confirmed with Kathy they'd meet in the evening for a discussion about family and future. He entered the police station hoping to find Tracy in an optimistic mood as she had seemed reasonably up-beat when he had left her last night.

"Peter, can I have a word with you, then we'll do the briefing? Tell everyone to gather in the incident room and we'll see them there in a couple of minutes." Tracy had a roughness to her voice he didn't recognise and when he turned to face her, he was surprised by what he saw. She wasn't exactly a model but she always had reasonable make-up and could dress up if she wanted to. He was shocked to see her looking scruffy and in the same clothes she'd been wearing last night.

"Ma'am." Peter acknowledged her then shouted over the noise for all the officers involved to wait in the incident room to start the meeting. He then went into her office and shut the door behind him. The blinds were already closed.

"My cat, Arthur was really sick last night. I found him just when I was about to run myself a good bath with all trimmings; you know, bells and smells? First I nursed him for a couple of hours as I'm pretty familiar with cats and their health, especially having grown up on a farm on Dartmoor. He seemed to be getting worse and I thought he had been poisoned. I took him to the Veterinary Hospital at Estover, which is the only place open 24/7. They saved his life, I reckon; he's still there now. I couldn't help thinking it wasn't an accident. Say Blind Justice followed me home to see where I live and I was targeted. It's paranoid, but I couldn't get it out of my head early this morning so I didn't go home. I spent an hour or two at Estover then drove round for a while. Eventually I parked up and slept for an hour or so." She burbled to her junior officer in a very uncharacteristic manner, which was almost tearful. Her eyes were red and puffy and the swiftly applied make-up failed to conceal it and, if anything, made the problem worse.

"Ma'am, we can send uniforms over to your road to have a look around. Even do a little door-to-door if you think it's worth it? Let's just get through this morning's update and I'll tell people what we have from Professor Larsson." Peter was as accommodating as he could be. He imagined it was just an accident with poor quality, meal-in-a-minute cat food. But in this case they were dealing with a very disturbed killer. Nothing was really beyond the reach of such a damaged mind.

"Thanks, Peter. I've already been in touch with the Superintendent about it and he has offered me a safe house tonight if I want." She explained things as she sifted through the paperwork on her desk and checked emails and texts on her mobile. "Obviously we are examining what we've got in the way of forensics and someone is analysing the handwriting, but Blind Justice isn't stupid so I'm not holding my breath."

The two officers went into the incident room and briefed everyone regarding the psychological profile, the letters from Blind Justice to the media and the constabulary, and finished off with orders for plain clothes constables to do door-to-door along Tracy's street. They were to ask about suspicious looking people in the vicinity in the last twenty-four hours but not mention Blind Justice specifically. The psych report didn't really tell anyone anything they hadn't expected. They were dealing with a loner who was fairly clever and didn't have many meaningful relationships with people. Probably from a dysfunctional family, showing psychopathic tendencies and would be a middle-aged, white male of average strength. He would be a local and had a property where he could act as he wanted without worrying about neighbours causing trouble. The dog companion was an interesting point and, from the CCTV footage from *Christabelle,* it looked to be a guide dog. Tracy's next move was to check with the RNIB for records of guide dogs as there could only be a few in the city. She wasn't going to let anyone not working for her know about that valuable footage, as that was certainly an ace she had up her sleeve, and she was going to keep it that way for as long as possible.

Tracy finished the meeting as she always did by reminding her officers they were the Pilgrims of the Law. The officers dispatched, everyone knowing what to do and where to go. Peter decided it was time to check out the victim's next of kin so he started by looking up Spencer Collingwood's ex-wife. They had been divorced for quite a while and she was still living in London. By now she had had enough time to get over it so he'd give her a call and find out about his history.

Tracy got in touch with the RNIB and found out the Guide Dogs for the Blind Association was separate from them, which she hadn't known or expected. She was disappointed but hardly surprised to find the nearest office was Exeter and they covered the whole South West region from Bristol to the end of Cornwall. Despite there being about five thousand Guide Dog users in the UK, she couldn't get any other information as they had a privacy policy, which worked in similar fashion to medical confidentiality. Therefore people would just have to keep their eyes open for guide dogs and Tracy sent a message out to the local PCSOs to keep an eye out for them as they walked the beat. Tracy thought it worth going to the local drop-in centre but was shocked to find Tamarmouth didn't have one, despite it being much bigger than Exeter or Paignton where they had better services. Also the Royal Eye Infirmary had recently shut down and been sold to make executive flats by the railway line, a short distance from the main station.

As Tracy flitted from website to website she couldn't help wondering whether Blind Justice had been watching her, and had followed her to her flat. It did look that way. She asked the Duty Sergeant and it seemed the door-to-door round her place had turned up a weird-looking woman in the back alleys of Greenbank around sunset the day before. Tracy wanted them to get the police artist to make a photofit picture by visiting the eyewitnesses with the best memories. However this wasn't going to work though as the visitor's face had been concealed by a scarf and a woolly hat.

CHAPTER 20

I was sitting at my make-up table looking at the reflection looking back out at me. They say the eyes are the window to the soul and I was feeling pretty soulless at that moment. That was because of what I intended to do next. I was about to go and deal with Simon Richards, or the first part of the job anyway. It was such a big job it would probably take a couple of sessions to do the whole thing, and getting rid of all the parts afterwards would take a number of trips to local refuse sites for getting rid of bones and also a few trips to places where wild dogs are known to hang around. I had been in Tamarmouth long enough to know where these areas were and also the handy places to throw things into the river and lose them for years.

Clothes and things could be taken to the local charity shop if I found they didn't fit me, and that was a good way to disperse any material goods that remained. Thinking about being soulless and getting rid of leftover items, I couldn't help remembering the mountains of shoes and spectacles left over at the German concentration camps. I recalled the one thing about that which I had found so incredibly hard to believe. How easily people had gone from being average, normal members of society to killer guards in such brutal institutions.

To make things easier for myself I decided to poison my victim first. Then, when he was dead, I would cut my name into his chest and take some pictures. I'd forward these to the police and then dispose of the body rather than leaving it to be found by someone. I had no plans for what to do after that but the wantonness of my activities was something which gave me more freedom. Not following any particular pattern or trend made it harder for the police to work out who I was and what I was up to.

"Okay, Willow. It's time to start preparing our guest to pass on to where he doesn't don't want to go. A good dose of ketamine and he'll be no problem to deal with. He'll still be aware of what is going on though, so he'll be suffering psychologically even if not too much physically. We gave him that earlier with all the electricity and insertion of pins to conduct to the shock points. That meant he felt the pain deep in his joints and bones due to where the shock came from and went to." I explained to Willow. As I did so, it suddenly occurred to me that feeding Willow or the feral street dogs meat laced with ketamine could cause them a possible problem. I didn't worry about the wild ones but, obviously, I didn't want to poison Willow. I needed to find out more. It was the sort of thing I could probably find out from Michelle or, at least, indirectly from him as he knew some medical students. Did ketamine stop having an effect due to its breakdown or was it just that the effect only lasted for a period of time after consumption? These were the kinds of things I was worried about.

I was in no particular hurry to deal with the mess in the bedroom so I decided to call the Rocket Queen and find out about Franklin. That would also boost my level of confidence. Being early evening where I was, it was the kind of time when Michelle might be having a siesta, so it seemed reasonable to try a Skype call. I sat down with a few new items of make-up to break the ice and start the conversation moving.

"Willow, come and keep me company." I called my furry friend over and she sat down on the floor. I sat on my chaise-lounge. Pretty much immediately I got through to Michelle and found he was waltzing around his apartment in a disco-style outfit. I remembered he had said Franklin enjoyed dancing but had assumed that was a reference to more ballroom style activity. I would have to ask about it.

"Hi BJ, how's things in the little lemon?" Michelle greeted me with a mention of her nickname for Tamarmouth, it was in contrast to the Big Apple. It also seemed appropriate as I was getting a sour taste in my mouth thinking about what I had to do later.

"Just great. Look, I now need to do the least pleasant part of the job. You know, it's like having a real banquet: the preparation is bearable because one still has the anticipation of the feast to come, the hideous bit is the cleaning up afterwards." I talked as I lit a thin menthol cigarette and lay back, blowing clouds of smoke into the already-scented air.

"Frankie and I are having a few friends over tonight for drinks and a private dance party. We've only invited pairs or, at least, couples so everyone will have a partner to dance with. If my apartment was a little bigger we'd have live musicians too as Franklin knows all sorts of artistes." Michelle was clearly in a good mood.

"That sounds good. One reason I called you was to do with your contacts, actually. I was wondering if you know anyone with a bit of medical knowledge. They don't need to be qualified by any means, just a bit of basic training should be enough." I was sure that someone in his entourage would fit the bill.

"Yes. Thinking about it, I've got connections in the cosmetic surgery and beauty therapy fields. Would that be any good?" The Rocket Queen was looking at the computer screen half the time and at his own reflection the other half of the time.

"Ideal. I need to know what ketamine is like regarding its residue. I can ask them myself if you want to give me their contact details, or you can ask for me. The question is, once something has ketamine in and then that is consumed, will it have an effect on the second consumer? I'm thinking about Willow eating contaminated meat; would it be dangerous?" I stroked Willow as I talked, rubbing under her chin so her muzzle pointed towards the webcam.

Michelle knew the benefits I had from having Willow as a companion. It was immeasurable, both psychologically and socially. Also, the exercise was very advantageous, physically.

"I think it best if I ask someone and then forward the answer to you. I can either put it in an email or just send a link to a website, which will tell you what you want to know." Michelle's answer was clear and confident and helped my morale. I really felt that I could bite the bullet and at least make a start on the job now. Once started it would be alright. I had been procrastinating for too long now and just needed to begin.

"Thanks. I hope you have a good night with Franklin and company later on. I'm thinking of going to a student Christmas party, organised by the LGBT people, as I think some of them may be supportive of my ideas. At least they are very unimpressed by the suspects turned up via Operation Yewtree." When I said that to Michelle I meant it. I also felt he would benefit from a good partner to share his life with, in every sense.

CHAPTER 21

I had an appointment with Dr Kirkwood and it was important we began to make progress regarding my psychosomatic eye condition. I had made a record of all the times the blindness struck me. I also went out of my way to try and note what I had been doing just beforehand. This was because it took a few minutes for it to take effect each time so I had a window of opportunity to gather information.

The most significant episodes were when I was outside as they were the ones that would be most dangerous for me. If I was at home or, at least, indoors I could just sit down till it passed. However now I had the details of the last few months episodes, which I had shown to my CPN, Jane Vickery. She had reviewed them and sent a report to Dr Kirkwood which was the reason for the appointment.

"Mr Wilson, it seems to me, having spoken with your nurse, Mrs Vickery that we do have an idea. If you can go out with her, she can see what is around and maybe notice something you are not aware of. If the two of you take a walk around the areas in which you've had trouble in the past, we'll see if there are any triggers." The doctor spoke in a very monotone voice. It was almost as dreary as his suit and the office decor.

"I suspect there is a connection between the reaction provoked in your vision and some trauma from your past but these things aren't always obvious or direct. If Mrs Vickery can give us another viewpoint of the situation, we may be able to find a treatment via Cognitive Behaviour Therapy."

"Thank you doctor. At least we have something we can do now. I'll make an appointment to see you again in six months and I'll see Mrs Vickery as soon as I can." I talked to Dr Kirkwood wondering about the latest mental health statistics I had heard regarding frequency of effects.

"Good morning, Willow. Today we are going for a walk with Jane. I don't know if she has a route planned or if that is my job. Thinking about NHS cuts, it's probably best if I come up with a potential itinerary. She can pick us up from here as I've had a few episodes here. Then we can walk past the aquarium to the Barbican via the swing bridge. Cross there and wander around the little cobbled back streets that give it such a unique character. Probably stop for a coffee and a fag somewhere. Yes, if I remember rightly, Jane smokes too so that shouldn't be a problem." I carried on talking to Willow as I cleared away the breakfast things and settled down with a run-of-the-mill cup of tea to watch the latest celebrities making fools of themselves. It really disgusted me, the amount of money these people got for the minimal contribution they made to the world. Particularly awful were the football players, pop tarts and show presenters like Chris Evans, Russell Brand and other DJs.

The TV was on in the corner but I wasn't watching it closely. I began thinking about my past and what had happened to cause my personality disorder and psychosomatic blindness. A local news flash came on. I saw the police were doing a manhunt both for Blind Justice, the criminal and his hostage, Simon Richards. Then there was a little piece on whom they thought these two people were and what connected them in the past. There was some speculation that it was a case of a victim taking revenge on an abuser. This reminded me it would be Christmas soon, which I was not pleased to hear. Time to get in a good supply of strong drink and maybe make plans to go somewhere like the local Salvation Army hall for a Christmas meal. I couldn't recall any good Christmases. Still, at least, this time I could do things to stop it being a miserable occasion in contrast to the earliest ones.

I couldn't help memories of my last Christmas on Jersey seeping into my consciousness. There was a very strict regime exercised over Advent and there was no money to waste on decorations, luxuries or anything that would make the place pleasant. The winter just meant we had to do more exercise to try and keep warm. Also we were more likely to behave as punishments such as a run round the field were agonising in the winter chill. I was reminded of a favour Michael Evans, as he was known then had done for me, which I still appreciated now.

Michael and I had been in the gym without any members of staff, which was not allowed but it was the only way we got to play together, as we were in different classes and dormitories. We were kicking a ball around when Mike suddenly jumped on me and pushed me to the floor.

"Get behind the vaulting box! Give us the ball, Mate…" Mike hurried to the other end of the room.

I rolled the ball towards him and crawled behind the apparatus. He started kicking it against the far wall near the main entrance, which led to the changing rooms. There was a small door at my end, which went straight to the courtyard. This was how we had got in: we had left it open the last PE lesson.

The lights came on in the changing room and I heard footsteps echoing in the open space. We could usually tell which teacher it was via their tread and we knew it was

Blackheart. There was no escape, he was an unavoidable nemesis. As he came into the room dressed in his snow-white gym kit, Michael kicked the football so it just missed him and banged into the wall beside his chest.

"What's going on? Evans, what are you doing in here with no staff?" Mr Blackheart exploded with rage like a round of grapeshot fired at the Spanish Armada. He grabbed my friend by the ear and almost lifted him off the ground. "Who else is here, or are you alone, you little yahoo?" Mr Blackheart pushed Michael against the climbing bars on the wall with a hand around his throat.

"J-Just... m-me, S-Sir." Michael spluttered as best as could while being half choked.

"I'm going to teach you a lesson here and now... You dirty little lout." Mr Blackheart turned Michael around and then took off his size 10 plimsoll and held it up in the air in his right hand.

He whacked Michael six times and then dragged him whimpering out through the changing room, locking the door behind him after turning off the lights. Then, as Michael was escorted back to the dormitory block, it gave me a chance to get out and shut the back door behind me, ready for Monday. Michael had saved me from a very painful experience while I was still recovering from a previous one.

I found that having thought about those things for a few minutes, my eyesight was starting to cloud over again. I heard the doorbell ring and got Willow to help me to the front door. As I expected, I was greeted by my CPN, Mrs Vickery.

"Hi, Jane. You'd better come in now as something has just triggered a response in the last few minutes. Let's see if we can work out what it was." I welcomed Jane in, hoping we could make some progress with things here and now. I told her what I had done so far that day and what I'd been thinking about. We talked about my previous episodes and concluded that any stressful event that would effect anybody, caused a response in me. But specifically, I got a response in reaction to the subject of child abuse, particularly that of my past. Jane said she'd talk to Dr Kirkwood about it so they could make an appointment. Then they would do some tests involving giving me certain stimuli and measure the response.

CHAPTER 22

Having killed Simon Richards and begun the most unpleasant part of being a killer of abductees, I decided I needed to go out and raise my spirits before losing a few large bones. Via the lemonrock.com website I could easily find out what gigs were on and who was playing where. I'd spent the afternoon shaving and making other preparations for a good night out. Now I had to make the most important decision of the night: to go in a rougher, shabbier outfit and look like a mature student, or put on a bit of style and stand out a bit. These were the times I could really use a partner. The weather was going to be a factor for sure. At least it hadn't got so bad that it was frosty, but there were wet leaves on the pavement, which were very slippery. I'd have to leave off the heels. Still, I knew the LGBT crowd would be okay with whatever I was wearing. In the end I decided on a good pair of Doc Martens and a pair of dungarees, which had been tie-dyed. A sweatshirt from Primark promoting New York finished things off with a snood in my hair to wear as a scarf round my neck if that needed protecting from the cold or anything else later that night.

I then loaded up my handbag with a wide range of accessories including make-up, purse, mobile, cigarettes, lighter and medicines. I also included a hip flask which I had loaded with brandy as the pub prices were ridiculous. I took my cane and left Willow in the flat to be a guard dog. Mutley Plain was a good place to start. It had a good population of students, being so close to the main campus of the university and there were plenty of drinking establishments around there. There had been loads around the dockyard but now they were situated near the uni as that was where people gathered these days. I was already getting bored of the Christmas adverts and it was still a couple of weeks until The Day actually arrived. Some people called this 'the silly season' and I could understand why. It was a time of the year when families came into focus, especially people's kids and grandkids. Those who were alone were made to feel jealous of those who had offspring to attend to. I wasn't surprised it was the most popular time of year for suicide. The worst affected group was young men and I was glad I wasn't one of those any more, not that I felt much better being who I was.

I arrived at Mutley Plain in a taxi and we pulled up across from the Hyde Park Inn. I paid my driver and then crossed the road to the island which had the pub situated on it. I decided to have a smoke to start the evening off, while the weather was still acceptable. I didn't like the fact we had to smoke outside these days but it was a good way to break the ice. I sparked up a Sobranie Cocktail with my Zippo, decorated with a Scrimshaw chip picture of an old sailing boat and a lighthouse. I saw a few people I guessed were students using the outdoor furniture for rolling smokes and to rest their drinks on.

"Hi, guys! I'm not from around here but I was told to come to this area for a drink. I can see there are numerous places on this road, but are any of them particularly LGBT orientated?" I spoke to the crowd in a nervous, apprehensive tone of voice as I shuffled towards them and joined them under the parasol advertising Tribute beer from St Austell brewery.

"There's a question. Um… I'd say nowhere here, especially but at the far end is The Junction. It's a music venue and I've seen trannies and gays in there. Maybe due to a certain band playing." A handsome gentleman with a crew cut hairstyle talked to me from a nearby bench under an electric heater. He looked to be one of the older members of the little group. He was smoking a real roll-up cigarette while others of his company used e-cigarettes.

"Do you know where The Barbican is? There are a couple of real gay bars there. I think OMG is the biggest, best club like that after Bristol. So I was told anyway." This came from a little girl in a tracksuit who I imagined would need to show ID when buying alcohol. She had lovely, wavy blond hair, which I'd have loved to stroke as it reminded me of Willow's golden fur.

"The other one near there is The Swallow. It's more of a pub that does music than a full-on club like OMG. Friday tonight so I expect they'll have an act. They have Drag Queens, cabaret shows and karaoke. Is that the sort of thing you are looking for?" This came from a chap I imagined was a really socially awkward, geek kind of a guy.

"Well, I think they are probably worth checking out. Thanks." I thought to myself how good a social chameleon I was, as I could blend in with all different types of people depending on whom I was with and whom I wanted to be.

I thanked the students again and decided not to buy a drink yet but started walking towards the Barbican. I could easily stop off and buy a cheap bottle of cola, tip some away and top it up with the brandy I had in my hip flask. Walking in the dark wearing my dungarees and Doc Martens it was hard for people to tell if I was a guy or a girl until they got close. I went in the Spar on North Hill and picked up their own brand of cola to make a strong brandy and coke for my handbag.

Just for the thrill of it I walked from there down past the Charles Cross Police Station. It was exciting thinking that Detective Hansard might be in there sweating over the case and how to catch me. I reckoned I had given her a few clues but not enough yet. Things would get difficult for me if she put a picture of me out on *Crimewatch*, especially if they showed me with Willow as well. There couldn't be many people with Guide Dogs in the city.

I then made my way to The Swallow to get warmed up and then I could go to OMG if I was in the mood for it. I made my way in and saw a band were just setting up on the stage at the far end of the main bar. There was a guy dressed in a sparkling dress with sexy black patent leather ankle boots on testing the sound levels of the microphone while the others milled about and connected up cables.

"Do you have any warm mulled wine as I need something to heat the heart of my cockles after being out there in that big freeze?" I asked the chap behind the bar as I rubbed my arms and hands to try to bring myself back to life.

"Sure darling. Do you want a large one or a small?" I was answered with enthusiasm by the member of staff in his brightly coloured Christmas waistcoat. He obviously felt hot as he was wearing nothing else on top.

"Give us a large one so I can thaw my hands wrapping them round the glass." I talked to him as I looked to see who else was in the bar that night. I saw a number of couples, a few groups and a scattering of individuals.

"Okay, give us a minute as I need to heat it in the microwave." He turned and started measuring shots and red wine in to the glass. He mixed in a sprinkling of spices for flavour and popped it in the cooker. "That's four pound fifty."

"Allow me to get that for you!" A voice came from behind me as the night's entertainment shimmied over to me and sat on the bar stool beside me.

"Sure sweet … Do you know this band?" I replied as I nodded to the preparing musicians. "This is a new place to me so I know nobody and no one here."

"Yes, that makes sense as I think I'd recognise you if I'd seen you before. I'm a fairly regular customer here." The answer came quickly with the confidence imbued in to it which comes from familiarity.

"As this our initial meeting I'll give you my initials. I'm B.J." I was trying not to sound to cocksure, not in any sense.

"Mmm … Interesting, you can call me Paige. So what are you doing in Tamarmouth in this season when you don't know the place?" This was elusive and evasive as Paige is one of those unisex names which could be masculine or feminine. The character was wearing a dress but that didn't mean much in a place like this.

"I'm checking out the action in the place as I'm moving house, but I haven't decided where to yet. I know students are a big thing here. What is this place like in the summer?" This gave Paige something to mull over while I appreciated my warm wine.

"Plenty of holiday romances. It's thick with tourists in the summer and getting more and more international these days. Does that appeal to you?..It does to me as now I have friends I met here but being sun worshipers they live in fairer climes presently. I'm welcome to visit if I choose." Paige smiled while talking and I guessed there were good memories.

The mulled wine was hot and spicy, the way I liked to live life. Also quite dark which suited me as well. "I could do with a trip abroad I think. I've been stuck in England too long I think. I doubt I'd emigrate but I want to travel and get a new perspective on things … It would help me with my work; well it's more of a hobby nowadays."

While I was talking Paige's phone rang a couple of times and was answered. It was impossible to be sure if Paige was male or female via the voice and I was very curious. Maybe even a transgender, I couldn't tell.

Paige's expression changed while on the phone, from a beguiling face ready to seduce to a look of intense concern. I imagined something was wrong.

Paige looked at me in the eyes and I felt a tumult of emotions; good and bad, strong and weak. "I'm sorry B.J. but I've got to go. Would you like to go to a house party next Saturday? It's at my place so I can't not turn up." Paige spoke while delving in to a shoulder bag and passed me a business card with all contact details. Name, address, website, Facebook, Twitter and Email.

"I'm must dash off now but I hope to see you again!" Paige smiled alluringly while getting off the stool and gave me a knowing over the shoulder glance when heading to the door.

CHAPTER 23

D S Anderson had a frustrating day talking to the relatives and friends of Blind Justice's victims about their histories, trying to find elements of their past that they had in common. There was clearly a link between the murder victims and their involvement in clandestine groups connected to child abuse, particularly in establishments such as children's homes. Things went from bad to worse after lunch because the post arrived, and it contained a new delivery from Blind Justice. This time it was photos of Simon Richards with *Blind Justice* cut across his chest. Also, the eyeballs had obviously been extracted, and something had killed the victim. The cause of death was uncertain, however, as the injuries were brutal and would have caused great pain but would not be lethal.

He kept himself in a good frame of mind, knowing that after the shift he was going to meet up with his sister, Kathy. They had always been very close, especially after their parents split up and their father, Jack, moved up to Ernesettle. At the time they thought he was responsible for the divorce, so they sided with their mum. It was only as they grew up and heard about things like PTSD that they began to understand why he had done what he did. Until he went to therapy, he couldn't really help himself.

Pete now knew his father was still struggling with alcohol but was doing better than he had been in the nineties. The two had been speaking in bars over the last six months, and it was clear how Jack felt about his son. He was missing his family, feeling lonely and worried about his health, fearing dementia.

"Okay Pete, I think you may as well wrap up now," DI Hansard called to her partner across the incident room. She was attaching copies of the photos to the board about Simon Richards as the originals had been sent to the forensic lab to be checked for prints. They weren't holding their breath, but it was still a worthwhile exercise.

"Thanks, ma'am. I think Blind Justice has told us more than intended with those pictures, you know." Peter decided to try to boost his boss's morale, thinking she was going back to her flat – it seemed that Blind Justice had gone to her flat and poisoned the cats in the neighbourhood. "Looking closely at the architecture of the house, which I'm sure is the offender's home, it is clearly an old building, so not on a new estate. Built well before the war, I'd say."

"Yes, I was wondering if we could talk to a town planner about where we are likely to find a house with a bedroom with those dimensions. See if we can recognise a likely area. It's obviously not somewhere like Mannamead, which has old houses, but only ones." She discussed with Peter as they walked down the corridor towards the exit.

"See you tomorrow!" Peter turned towards the front door and reception desk to leave, while Tracy moved to the stairs that led to the secure police car park where she had parked her Mondeo.

It wasn't too late, but Peter knew that Kathy was happy to have a bit of retail therapy at Drake Circus shopping centre. She had texted him earlier saying that she was in Primark trying to find herself a new Christmas jumper and looking for potential presents for family and colleagues. He eventually found her in the lingerie department trying to find some sexy undies to go with her fiery red hair.

"Evening, sis. How are things on the boyfriend front? Who are you looking to impress with that new outfit?" He used the boyfriend subject to break the ice and get the conversation flowing before raising the subject of their father. He was sure that living with their mum meant that Kathy had been given loads of negative propaganda about what Jack was like and why he had done what he did. Having thought about it for months and watched documentaries on iPlayer and YouTube, Peter felt that he understood PTSD much better now. These days it was relevant to his job and had obviously affected his father after the Falklands War.

"Hey, Pete. Do you think I should go for black to contrast with my hair or a red/orange outfit that matches it?" she asked, trying to discern what kind of a mood he was in.

"I don't know. I just fancy a bite to eat, and I want to talk to you about the future of our family. How about we go and have some sushi, and I'll tell you what I think after that?" He knew she loved seafood in all shapes and sizes.

"Sure. You obviously have a clear agenda for tonight's meeting. Let's get that out of the way." She put the clothes back on the rack and followed him towards the door to the food stalls.

"When did you last see Dad? Was it a few years ago at the family get-together for Uncle Alan's funeral?" He was pretty certain that was right because he'd have heard if she had seen him in town.

"I think so. Why?" She looked at him a little suspiciously.

"Well, I saw him recently for a chat, and I believe part of the reason he and Mum split up was because he's got PTSD. That's why he used to get so drunk. To block out the memories of the war," he explained in a reconciling tone of voice, knowing she missed her father's presence in her life. He was also aware that she'd want to be given away by her father at a white wedding one day.

"Yes. Mum often slags him off, but occasionally she reminisces about the good old days when they were happy together. It seems she just threw him out because she thought that was the best thing for us." Kathy was telling Peter what he wanted to hear. They both sat down and ordered a selection of sushi dishes.

"Do you think we could get them back together sometime over Christmas? Maybe get Dad to meet your boyfriend and all go for a meal or something. I haven't got a special friend at the moment, but I know a couple of ladies I'd be glad to take for a meal. Proud to introduce my family to them." He put forward the suggestion to start work on restoring his family.

"I reckon if I mention it to Mum one evening when she's feeling lonely, she might well be interested. She's never really had another guy since him, you know." Kathy was clearly keen on the idea. "Have you arranged for him to meet us here?"

"No, but he often drinks around the corner at the King's Head as he's got a buddy in Exeter Street he stays with some nights. I'll buy you a drink, and we'll see if he's around." In fact, Pete was almost certain he'd be there.

They talked about possible plans for Christmas and New Year's and what was on the horizon. Peter was convinced that he should try online dating as a New Year's resolution because he felt he was slipping down the slope towards being a police bachelor, which he didn't find appealing.

They left the shopping centre and headed for a pub a couple hundred yards away that had been there since the mid-seventeenth century. The atmosphere in places like this was one of the things Pete particularly enjoyed about Tamarmouth. They walked in and found a reasonable number of drinkers and saw their dad near the door to the beer garden. Pete bought a whiskey for himself and a glass of white wine for his sister. They then walked over to their father, who was very surprised to see his daughter for the first time in about five years. Pete left them to get things going and popped out for a smoke – his second of the day, and it was about nine o'clock. He was breaking his addiction to nicotine slowly but surely.

Kathy gave her dad a well overdue hug. She then sat down next to a shadow of the man she remembered her father being during her school years.

"Daddy, how are you these days? Pete told me you want to try and at least get back in touch with Mum so you are not lonely over Christmas."

"That's right, my dear. I don't know how she is nowadays, but I can admit that I'm responsible for a lot of the problems we had then. Also, I've only got a couple of real friends these days for a number of reasons." Jack was obviously looking for support over Christmas, as are more and more elderly people these days.

"As you know, I don't have any children of my own yet, but it is definitely a possibility as is moving away from England. I would like them to know their grandparents on my side of the family, even if it's just via email and Skype." As Kathy spoke to him, she remembered what seeing her granddad had been like years ago. It had been a very special day because back then, Navy Days was still an event on the bank holiday weekend, and they all went on board active ships. These days, the Royal Navy, like her father, was a fraction of what it used to be.

Pete came over and joined them sitting around a barrel that had been fashioned as a table, and he could see that Kathy was happy to be there.

"We will talk to Mum about getting together. I'm sure she misses you some of the time as she's never had another serious relationship since you." Kathy explained her ideas about her mum; since she still lived at home, she knew her mother better than anyone else in the family. The three of them could certainly get on like this, and nobody was proposing that Jack and Sue would become a couple again, just good companions and maybe grandparents in the future.

CHAPTER 24

I 'm becoming increasingly worried about my friend Mark in England. For years he's had a personality disorder, but that wasn't a problem when he kept to himself and only interacted with social services staff, medically qualified practitioners and, occasionally, members of the public. As he gets older he seems to live in more of a fantasy world and less in the reality that actually surrounds him. He has multiple personalities, and the uninhibited one, Blind Justice, seems to be growing stronger and controlling most of his life.

I was talking to my previous boyfriend about it a while ago before we split up, and since then, my new lover, Frankie, has said that he is very disturbed by what Mark Wilson's dominant character is up to. He seems to be going on a killing spree. He hasn't gone out on a mad rampage killing schoolchildren or anything, but he has killed enough people to qualify as a serial killer.

We have been friends since we were in a children's home together. We had both lost contact with our families, and so, having sworn a vow of allegiance to each other, we've both trusted each other through thick and thin for many years. I swore my oath to Mark Wilson, but it's Blind Justice, a totally different character and personality, who is becoming the psychopathic murderer now. Allow me to describe a recent episode while I was at mine with Frankie. We were getting to know each other while sharing cocktails and a spliff or two. Frankie wasn't new to my apartment but wasn't familiar with it either.

"Have you ever had 'two kids in a cup' before?" I asked Frankie as he settled himself down in one of my beanbags.

"Oh…no, never. I've had a few of the common things like a screwdriver, tequila sunrise and a few slippery nipples. I'll try anything once, I reckon," Frankie drawled to me and pointed towards my desktop computer to let me know a Skype call was coming in.

I passed Frankie his glass, having poured the drink in to it. I then sat at the desk so that when I received the call, I would be in view of the webcam. Frankie could see the screen, but Blind Justice, the one calling me, couldn't see Frankie.

Understandably, I'm not sure Frankie even believed what I had said previously about my old companion.

"How are things in the Big Apple, Queenie?" Blind Justice talked into his mobile instead of the computer speakers.

"Lovely, thanks. Trying out some new cocktail recipes." It wasn't intentional, but I failed to make it clear that I had company. Thus, Blind Justice didn't feel inhibited, so he walked to his bathroom carrying his phone, allowing me to see the room's condition. Blood stains were on nearly every surface. It was a feminine room; there was a lot of pink and white décor, so someone taking a quick glimpse might not be able to see the red smears and patches.

Frankie saw the room and was clearly shocked. What had previously been rumour and speculation was now confirmed as fact. Knowing that he might be heard by BJ and to avoid the camera lens, he wrote me a note. From behind the screen, he held up a piece of paper. Written on it was 'Really is a fucking psycho!'

I remembered the information about ketamine that I had passed on to Blind Justice, specifically how contaminated meat is alright to feed to a healthy dog. I was having an internal debate regarding morals and ethics. Half of me supported Blind Justice because I had been abused as a child myself. However, the other half couldn't help but think that what was happening was crude justice. Being treated badly is not an excuse for a person to treat someone else badly in return. I then saw movement, and the dog, Willow, trotted over to her master. She had an enormous bone in her mouth, which I guessed was that of a human thigh. It was stripped of flesh but still had fresh red stains. Looking at the dog's facial fur, I was sure that she had recently eaten bloody meat.

"In apartments in the States you nearly always have waste disposal units, don't you? I suppose I've got an organic waste disposal unit here." BJ stroked Willow and scratched behind her ears. "We've done the worst of it and threw the skull and pelvis into the back of the rubbish truck the other day. I've fed the local dogs a free meal, and I've now stocked up my freezer with dog food."

It was like I was watching a horror movie, but in reality I was staring at a person I'd known for years, a person who was no longer the victim but the psychotic killer. I'd never been so glad we were living miles away from each other. I was thinking that, if this were happening locally, I'd probably let the cops know, and I couldn't help thinking I should contact the UK police. I didn't know what to say to this person I'd known and trusted for years but who was now behaving in a totally crazy way that was making me feel increasingly worried about his future.

"Are you feeling alright? You're looking as though you're stressed about something." Blind Justice knew me well enough to see that I wasn't entirely comfortable with the present situation.

I knew I had to persuade him that I was reasonably happy with things because despite being horrified by what I was seeing and appalled by the behaviour he was engaging in, I had to keep in touch with him. I had a nasty feeling that I was the only person in the 'real world' he was regularly socialising with. It worried me that if he broke contact with me, he would disappear and would be difficult to find. It also seemed to me that if I was going to stay in touch with Frankie, he might well want me to separate myself from BJ. It wasn't a ridiculous concept considering what he'd been doing recently. Also, people like this rarely seem to quit; rather, they get worse and worse till they are caught or killed.

"I can't have a talk now as Frankie's sent a text saying he'll join me for cocktails. I'll call you back." I hung up, hoping that Rocket Queen was still a good enough liar to fool Blind Justice.

CHAPTER 25

Tracy contacted the veterinary hospital and arranged for Arthur to stay there another night as he was still suffering from what had now been confirmed as a poisoning. That meant that she could spend the night at the police house rather than returning to her home, the location of which Blind Justice now seemed to know. She managed to keep a good distance from most criminals, so she could put them out of her mind at the end of a shift.

Blind Justice was different, however. This one was getting to her. She was angry about her cat being messed with – that made it personal. Obviously, BJ was a dog person, unlike her. She had felt some sympathy for him when she discovered that he had been abused as a child and was now seeking revenge. But that was no reason to hurt her by putting out contaminated food for one of the few loves of her life.

She drove to one of the constabulary's properties for putting up visitors and providing emergency housing as and when required. She chose to stay at a shared house rather than a flat because she didn't feel like being alone that night. She knew it would probably result in her having to listen to new recruits discussing *EastEnders* and eating a takeaway supper. She left the office and drove to the co-op nearest to the house so she could buy a bottle of red wine to help her relax that evening. She also picked up a local newspaper to see what was in the letters page as she knew this case had certainly received media attention. It was the kind of case that was very divisive. Some people thought the police weren't as good as they used to be, so someone else catching paedophiles was not a bad thing. Of course, most members of the public didn't approve of murder, but if anyone were to be killed, those on the sex offenders list were the top priority.

Tracy drove up the drive and parked in the double garage that had been left open. She unscrewed the lid of the wine bottle and took a generous sip before putting it in the little travel bag she kept in the car with a supply of toiletries, makeup and other overnight essentials. She locked the car and walked up to the front door of the pre-Blitz house. It reminded her of the place she'd have owned a few years ago if things had worked out better financially. One big enough for a family of a couple of kids, each with their own room. She went in to the lit hallway as at least one person was in already.

"Hello...DI Hansard arriving. I'll just put my things in a free bedroom upstairs, and then we can make plans." She spoke loud enough to be heard in the kitchen and living room.

"Fancy a cuppa? The kettle has just boiled." The voice from the kitchen sounded friendly and local.

"No thanks. I could use a wine glass though." Tracy headed upstairs to see what condition the bathroom was in and placed her bag on a single bed in the room looking out over the back lawn. She drew the curtains to keep the darkness out and the warmth in, reorganised a few things in the room and then went back down with her wine bottle.

She was greeted by an elderly officer who had been in the force for years but had never held a rank above sergeant because he wanted to stay on the streets of his hometown. Also, it was difficult not to get involved in politics if one got to be a senior rank.

"Evening, darlin'. I'm just here for a night or two as I move to a smaller house. Here's a wine glass for you." He passed an average wine glass for her to pour the very ordinary wine into. She saw he was already at work preparing a meal. "I can easily give you a helping of my cooking if you don't want to order a delivery."

She was reminded of someone she'd known when she was growing up in the wilds of Dartmoor. In particular, the man's dress sense and style. He was wearing a shirt and tie, and his tweed jacket was hanging over the back of a kitchen chair. This made him look very much like an uncle she hadn't heard from for years. He had his sleeves rolled up over his elbows, like he might have done had he been engaged in serious food preparation. Another thing that caught her attention was the little badge pinned to the lapel of his jacket. It was a small fish symbol, which Tracy recognised as a Christian sign. She didn't go to church very often these days, but if asked, she would have said that she is a Christian. She accepted his offer and asked him if he'd like a glass of wine, which he accepted modestly.

They found a radio and started playing some light classical music in the background. They had time to fill while they waited for the meal to cook, so they sat down at the kitchen table. She was on her laptop while he browsed the local paper to see what was happening as Christmas neared. He explained he was moving to a bungalow now that his wife had passed on, and that the extra finances would help support his children and grandchildren. The conversation drifted but remained related to how people should behave and where they get their ideas from regarding morals and ethics.

"If a thief stole from someone whom they knew were corrupt or who had gotten their money from drug dealing, does that make them better than a person who just takes the money because they know they can get away with it?" The older officer asked Miss Hansard. Her answer was that they were all bad, but the drug dealers were the worst of the lot. She particularly despised dealers of class A drugs rather than cannabis suppliers. Personally, neither of them knew any victims of multiple sclerosis, so they couldn't ask anyone who used cannabis as a form of medication how effective is it. In America, where it is legal in some states and illegal in others, things did seem too difficult and confusing.

"Well, it's time to forget everything to do with work and enjoy a good hearty meal. It's something I don't think you can get in any café, and you wouldn't find it in a restaurant. It's ideal for this sort of evening as many ingredients are kept in cupboards. My specialty...corned beef hash." He opened the oven as he talked and took out a large casserole dish filled to the brim with crispy golden-brown baked mashed potato. Around the edge, Tracy saw a rich gravy bubbling, and there was melted cheese adorning the top, placed on in thin slices rather than grated. It was something Tracy hadn't had for years but had often eaten when growing up in a cold Devon farmhouse.

She was very pleased to have a family favourite and so got on with draining the vegetables while the chef took plates out of the oven where he had put them to warm for a bit. She thought he had probably gotten into that habit when he lived somewhere that had an AGA cooker in the kitchen. People didn't do that kind of thing nowadays. She felt she didn't live in the past but was securely rooted there. Two generous helpings of a rich, quality meal served with local veg killed the conversation for a while. Tracy reflected on what her life would be like if she ever found a suitable partner; he'd definitely have to be a house husband. She couldn't imagine it ever happening, and she didn't feel that motherhood suited her, either.

She looked across the table to her companion and saw that he looked spent, emotionally and physically. When thinking about why he was there, she guessed that he might not have made the dish since he had been with his wife. She poured the last of the wine into her glass and took a hefty swig.

"Thanks for a good meal. I'll do the washing up in the morning as I usually get up at about six with plenty of energy. I'll say goodnight now. You look like you could use a good rest; I suppose moving house is a physical drain given the packing and moving furniture." She'd had a better time than she'd expected in the shared house and hoped her one-night colleague would have a happy time in his new home.

PART 3

CHAPTER 26

I was becoming increasingly concerned about what was happening when my other personality takes over my life because recently I'd woken up in bed unsure about the previous evening's activities. Willow was the problem – she had stains on her fur. I couldn't remember noticing this the night before, but dark patches were now apparent around her muzzle; I was reminded of the nature programs where wolves are stained with blood after eating a moose or some such animal. My next appointment with Dr Kirkwood wasn't for a while, but after my sessions with the CPN, I thought we might actually be making some progress. I just needed to survive this Christmas and New Year's season, and I'd been given some Diazepam to help me relax. However, I'd been told to avoid mixing it with alcohol. This led to another question regarding my alter ego. A few nights previously I had decided to have a drink instead of taking a blue tablet because I had found a brand of whisky with a flavour that I particularly enjoyed. I opened my drinks cabinet and was more than a bit surprised to find an open bottle of Pappy Van Winkle's Family Reserve 23-year-old bourbon. I didn't realise it till the next day when I looked it up on the Internet using the Central library that it was valued at nearly £1,800 per bottle.

"Where on earth did this come from?" I asked Willow as I poured out a glass of the liquid gold and wondered about its history. I couldn't think of anywhere in Tamarmouth that sold anything in that sort of league, not that there was any reason I'd know of it anyway. I remembered there had been something in the local news a week or two previously about some expensive drinks going missing from the gin palace in which a murder had occurred. As Christmas approached, and since it was supposed to be 'the season of goodwill to all men', I decided it was time to socialise a bit with the other members of the underclass of which I am a apart. I remembered an event I'd been told about by my CPN – a Christmas lunch organised by the local church. I was a bit of a traditionalist, so I enjoyed the old Christmas carols too; I'd find out when there was a decent carol service. The meal at least would be the kind of event where I might see some of the local people I used to hang around with before I became more housebound.

I got up on the morning of the lunch and decided to get a bit dressed up. I put on a shirt that was still in decent shape despite the fact that I hadn't worn it since it had been dry cleaned after a funeral and wake for a neighbour and drinking partner I'd known for years. Then I had to choose a tie and I chose my Tamarmouth Bus Company tie as it was one of the few things I still had that I was proud of. It is very recognisable to people of my generation who were also Janners. I'd even gone to the trouble of polishing my smart shoes the night before. I gave Willow a brush down, and we set off on a walk in the park on the way to the church hall. In the passage that led to the upstairs flat, I noticed that the pile of Christmas cards had disappeared, so I guessed my neighbour had been in that night and maybe still was. I was particularly surprised to see that a card for me had replaced the others. I opened it and found this message inside: 'Happy Christmas and have a Good New Year. Love to you and Willow, from BJ'.

I decided to bring my own alcohol to the party because I doubted there would be much, if any, provided. To be clever, I poured the last of the Pappy Van Winkle's into a hip flask, and I planned buy some cans or a bottle of something, depending on what the local supermarket was offering. I picked up a bottle of sherry as I knew a lot of the local ladies would enjoy that and also topped up my smoking supplies and invested in a box of cigars as a Christmas treat. I also bought Willow a bag of pork scratchings to show her how much she was appreciated. We walked on the pathway, looking at the skeletal trees and the chilly glistening sapphires of frost coating everything. I enjoyed this time of year as it reminded me how life could be brutal yet beautiful at the same time. I and my faithful hound exhaled clouds of vapour as we watched the birds being frustrated by the layer of ice covering the pond. Life could certainly be harsh, but generally I believe in karmic justice; if you deserve a comeuppance, you will get it sooner or later.

We turned up at the hall after I had a smoke and walked around it, checking it out. As I expected, it was mainly populated by Old Aged Pensioners, but there was also a table at which sat younger people. They were probably there because they either had mental health issues, were homeless or were drug addicts. I decided to sit at a table where I was with the people of my generation but close enough to hear what the others were talking about. I knew I could use Willow as an icebreaker if I wanted to introduce myself. The staff came around asking us if we wanted the usual Christmas dinner or a vegetarian option. They were also pouring glasses of fruit juice to whoever wanted one. I took a glass but filled it with my sherry and also gave one to a woman named Mary who had come and sat beside me. We recognised each other from the local Co-op but hadn't really talked to each other before.

She was definitely mutton dressed as lamb, but beggars can't be choosers. We soon progressed beyond the introductory pleasantries and got down to a serious conversation. Mary had come out despite the fact that members of her family had tried to persuade her to stay home due to the murders being committed by Blind Justice. Her daughter particularly had said that the streets were not safe these days. However, Mary had seen the *Herald* and read the letter saying that Blind Justice was only after criminals, especially nonces, so she felt secure. I had to admit I could understand what she was saying, but I asked her why she felt she could trust such a deviant, violent person to keep to his word.

She admitted that her husband had been an occasional lawbreaker, and she had learned about 'honour among thieves'. There was a sense of ethics and morality even in the lowest parts of society. She had volunteered with homeless people and drug-users in the past and knew, for example, that stealing from Marks & Spencer was okay, but taking someone's stash of alcohol or their filthy sleeping bag was not the way to behave.

Considering we had only been asked to make a donation rather than purchase a ticket for the event, were being given a surprisingly good spread. We had Pringles and Twiglets with our drinks, followed by a choice of soups. There was homemade beetroot borscht or mass-produced tomato soup for the less adventurous. After that, we had a traditional Christmas dinner of turkey, roast spuds and parsnips, sprouts with chestnuts, pigs in blankets, Yorkshire puddings and of course gravy and cranberry sauce. We were both very impressed by the meal, and Willow enjoyed it too. We had done so well, and at about half past two in the afternoon, there was a break before we were presented with a choice between Christmas pudding and mince pies, both of which were served with ice cream or local clotted cream. To finish what was one of the best meals I'd had in a long time, there was filter coffee or Earl Grey tea. I had really enjoyed the meal, but the company was also a major contribution to the event. I felt I had made a new friend, so Mary and I exchanged details.

Neither of us had mobile phones, but she expected to be given one by her daughter as a present in a week or two.

I was feeling that to finish off a great meal I'd like a cigar, so I admitted my dirty habit to Mary. She said that she had guessed as much by my nicotine-stained fingers. She had work-worn digits but said she occasionally had a rollie if it was made with a liquorice paper, so she carried a packet in her handbag. We laughed at this. We'd finished the bottle of sherry by now and had also given some to our tablemates. We left the table to get some fresh air, and I took Willow too so she could relieve herself. I rolled Mary a smoke with one of her papers and then sparked it and my Hamlet cigar. We both stood quietly, admiring the view of Tamarmouth harbour. We were both very grateful for the charity we had received.

"I was just thinking about a quotation I used to hear my husband say: 'With malice towards none, with charity for all, with firmness in the right as God gives us to see the right.' Comes from an early American president, I think." Mary seemed to be getting a bit emotional, so I thought it was time to end our first encounter.

"Right, yes. It makes sense. Would you like a taxi home, love? I'll pay, of course." I offered her a £10 note.

"Thanks. I'd appreciate that. It's been a long but very enjoyable day. Doubt I'll even eat tomorrow. Let's get Christmas out of the way and then we can meet up for a chat, yeah?" Mary was the sort of woman I wished I'd met years ago when I had a decent life and worked on the buses.

"Sure. Willow and I will now go for a stroll through the park and then watch a classic old film like *Spellbound* or *Notorious*. I do like a good Hitchcock film." I gave Mary a peck on the cheek and headed towards the recreation ground while she made her way to the taxi rank, happy that she didn't need to use a bus since she had consumed more alcohol than she had expected to that day.

CHAPTER 27

I had been looking forward to Saturday with exponentially increasing excitement. It was a chance to see Paige again, and since it would be an intimate house party, I guessed that there would only be a few select guests. I had been thinking and fantasising about this night on and off ever since our brief encounter. I'd had to go to the street and walk past the house to see where Paige lived so that I'd know what to expect. Based on my first impressions I'd expected and imagined a modern, open-plan penthouse flat kind of place. Probably an exclusive block on the Barbican, like Discovery Wharf. However, I could not have been more wrong. It was an old street in Cattedown full of small houses that I'd call cottages. The one at the end of the terrace was Paige's.

The one thing I hated about parties was choosing what time to arrive. I could be early if I knew the host well and was comfortable having a one-on-one conversation with them. Obviously I didn't want to be late because in small houses, there is often very limited seating, and people tend to settle in and, once they're comfortable, are unlikely to move without good reason. I was also assuming that most of the guests had already met one another, and some were likely to be good friends, maybe even partners. I guessed that most of the others would be quite intelligent, even if not necessarily formally educated. After all, I knew I had a good brain without the certificates to prove it.

After hours wondering about it and a few lengthy heated discussions with Rocket Queen, I'd plumped for a fairly simple full-length black velour dress with a few decorative sequins. I wore a pair of black leather ankle boots that matched my handbag. I wanted to look sophisticated rather than showy; there's a definite line between the two that I wasn't planning to cross. I also brought a bottle of white wine as a gift and to show my gratitude to Paige for the invitation because I was still playing the part of a greenhorn regarding Tamarmouth. I couldn't relax, get drunk and let my guard down, which was frustrating as I hadn't been to a good saturnalia for a long time. I'd arrive in a black cab just after the estimated time of arrival. That way, I wouldn't be stressed at home waiting for someone to arrive. It was during that time that I'd get something akin to stage fright, pacing up and down, tampering with my makeup, which I'd already worked on for hours. On my phone I had an app from the local taxi company that already had my address so I just needed to click on the 'Cab ASAP' button to get a vehicle to take me from the ball if I felt it was time to leave.

The cab turned into the narrow one-way road, which was lined with cars on both sides, so there were no parking spaces, and it wasn't broad enough for a second lane of traffic. I told the driver to let me out at the far end where it turned right on Paige's corner. I was usually quite chatty in taxis, but this time my mouth was anxiously dry. I gave a £5 note and told the driver to keep the change because I didn't want to mess with any fiddly coins. There was a warm orange glow coming from the living room window that fluctuated, giving the impression that the room was candlelit, perhaps by an open fire since it was such an old property. I traipsed up the granite slabs to the doorstep and found that the door was slightly ajar. A natural cordial scent welcomed me, while its musical equivalent caressed my hearing. I tapped on the glass of the door as I pushed it open and stepped in to the restricted hallway. I advanced toward the open wooden doorway from which hospitable sounds emanated and closed the door.

I stood framed in the doorway, looking into a stylishly retro decorated living space that had personality and character in spades. Original art that subtly blended ancient African images with Chagall prints bedecked the walls, producing a very impressive scene. The furniture was varied, with a Welsh dresser covering the majority of the wall opposite the tiled fireplace that emitted heat, light, a crackling sound and a homely atmosphere. Paige was perched on the far end of a small two-person sofa wearing an alluring Victorian-style smoking jacket above dark-patterned leggings and slip-on shoes. I could at last confirm that Paige was a woman due to the breasts bulging from inside the coat. Also, her hair was now down around her shoulders in a cascade of chocolate and chestnut hues – a gorgeous person in a very attractive house. She was engaged in an animated conversation with the only other person in the room; he was sitting in a high-backed wicker chair looking well-groomed in a smart pair of chinos and a quality blazer over a fine corduroy shirt with a silk paisley cravat around his neck.

"Yay! Good to see you, BJ. I'm glad you've come as I felt we've got something in common. Just occasionally I feel a link with someone the moment I meet them; you are one of them. This is my buddy Ian, who I've known for years. We had an interesting first encounter didn't we BJ." Paige greeted me enthusiastically.

Being a gentleman, Ian stood up and greeted me in a way similar to the French traditional style of 'la bise.' "Good evening. Can I get you a drink? What would you like? We do have a well-stocked drinks cabinet."

"Thanks. Here's a bottle of reasonable white, which would be better chilled, so I reckon you'd do well to fridge it and have it with a meal. Do you have any local beers? I try to check out local breweries when in an unfamiliar area." I spoke as I took up the other end of the sofa Paige sat on.

"Sure...You have a few bottles of something from Summerskills don't you Paige?" Ian put his glass of red wine on a shelf as he left the room to walk through the main corridor to the kitchen at the back of the house.

"He's a great guy, Ian. Very clever at psychology and also a bit sporty. Sailing and such, having been around on tall ships a few years ago. As you'll have seen from my website, I'm a freelance designer in creative learning. Last big job I had was with the People's Project here in Tamarmouth. I'm just kicking my heels these days waiting to hear about a few local vacancies and a possible ideal job. Did you know Tamarmouth is twinned with St-Malo in Brittany? I'm trying for a twinned artist-in-residence position, but I doubt I'll get that. What about you? Are you looking to move to a retirement place? When are you leaving?" Paige conversed with a lively manner and a look of interest on her face.

Now I had to really start lying as I couldn't let Paige know who I really was. I decided to stick to the truth as much as possible and just change details such as locations and names. I told her I was a bus driver but from Bristol rather than Tamarmouth. "Yes, been up in Bristol for years driving buses and used to come here on summer holidays with my parents. Now that I've got the chance, I think I could retire down by the sea like my dad wanted to."

We talked about Bristol and Tamarmouth till Ian returned with the only other guest already present, who was someone they both knew already. She came over and introduced herself to me.

"Hi! I'm Jackie. I work at a community interest company based in Cornwall. We do arts projects with people suffering from autism, learning difficulties and mental health issues. That's how I met Paige."

As I started to talk to Jackie, there was a knock at the door, and Paige went to answer it. I heard her talking to someone out in the corridor before she returned to the room and was followed by a tall, slender Mediterranean-looking woman. She had dark hair and well-tanned skin. Characteristic Cimmerian eyes looked out through a pair of John Lennon-style glasses. She wore a full-length dress bearing a floral design in fuchsia, vermilion and cream. Ankle boots could be seen under its hem, and a cape of faux fur was wrapped round her shoulders; she carried a bag that matched the boots. A pretty Alice band kept her hair back, which fell over her shoulders. It was clear that this was Paige's partner, and this was probably one of the foreigners she'd mentioned when we first met. I got up from the two-person sofa so that the couple could sit together. I was interested in talking to Ian, so I joined him when he headed to the kitchen to get some more drinks and some nibbles such as garlic stuffed olives, cubes of feta cheese and rolls of smoked salmon.

"I take it you are okay with dogs, yeah?" Ian called as we walked in single file to the galley-like kitchen.

I quickly told him that they weren't my animal of choice, but I didn't have a problem with them either. "I take it there's one around here somewhere."

"Too right there is. There's the mighty beast of Cattedown, the hell-hound Brutus." Ian's tone of voice implied a fearsome animal. Despite being familiar with Willow, I almost felt apprehensive. However, I was shocked when Brutus came striding in from the scullery. He was the most conceited, arrogant Chihuahua I had ever seen.

"He looks to be a real character, probably with canine personality disorder," I said, appalled at the vibes I was picking up from this concentrated attitude on legs.

"This is Lord Snooty." Ian talked while moving around the little kitchen confidently; he clearly knew where everything was. We soon had a decent tray of quality items loaded up ready to transfer to the front room.

"I've not studied it, but I'm interested in mental health, so I was wondering what you're into regarding psychology?" I opened the next part of our conversation with this and was a bit surprised by the honesty of Ian's response.

"I was abused as a child by close members of my family. After a traumatic childhood I ended up alone in the world with a lot of questions about human nature and morality. I travelled the world, exploring the mind and consciousness with drugs, meditation and prayers. I gained a lot of knowledge, one might even say wisdom if being generous. I learned a lot but had no qualifications. I found myself in Tamarmouth and persuaded a few people to meet me and convinced them I'd do a foundation course for a year and, provided that I succeeded, I could go on to a master's degree. By then I'd better know exactly what to focus on, philosophy, psychology or whatever." Ian seemed quite happy to talk about this kind of thing, and I found he had set up a group called Victim Aid Therapy, which provide help and support for people, especially students, who had been abused as children. We both returned to the living room, and I was glad I'd made the effort to come out to the party as I was enjoying myself and gaining useful information.

CHAPTER 28

D S Peter felt he was making progress with his family restoration activities, even if. he hadn't succeeded at much else. He wished he could do as well with the Blind Justice case. He saw that it was really messing up DI Tracy, especially with the poisoning of her cat, and so she had to stay away from her home. She was at least safe and secure at the police property. Some nights it was just her; occasionally officers came in quite late and woke her up because they been on a stakeout operation, and it would have taken them too long to drive home. These were often some of the more brawny than brainy members of the force.

Peter could see she wasn't sleeping well, and she had told that him her cat was better but was being taken care of by a friend. She'd often leave work, spend a few hours at the friend's with Arthur and then return to the shared house.

"Morning, ma'am. I was thinking about the guide-dog angle of things regarding that bit of footage and also the paw prints. A couple of things occurred to me last night. First, someone could dress up a dog so it looks like a guide dog when in fact it isn't a real, proper registered one. Obviously that dog wouldn't be on any list. We have a couple of guys working through the registered guide dogs in the area to see if they're connected to anyone with a criminal record and that sort of thing. The other thing is what happens when a guide dog dies. Is it checked out? What happens if, say, a guy says his dog passed away, but he's lying, so he still has the dog but it's not listed anymore?" These were the kind if ideas Peter had when having a good, quiet night watching TV at his own flat and wondering who to take as a partner to a family meal if it worked out. He was confident enough that his sister would wait till their mum had seen a sentimental film or something before asking if she'd be willing to meet their dad in the future. Kathy knew their mum well enough to get it right and not to rush it.

"Yes. Those are interesting but disconcerting points. We have used records from the nearest office and checked them against people with records No success, so you're probably right with that kind of thing. Dr Larsson's personality profile can't help much because we can't compare that information to the psychiatric outlines of anyone due to medical confidentiality." DI Hansard was clearly suffering from what is known as 'mid-case blues' and is a bit like the mid-novel writers block that some writers suffer. Something somewhere would happen soon. Either the criminal would get too confident and slip up or a witness would come forward; there would be a forensic result, or a link between the victims would be found. How an officer handles their own morale and that of their team is the difference between n average and a top-quality officer.

DS Anderson was digging farther into the dark pasts of the victims, sure that if he went back far enough, he would find a link between them or at least between the premeditated murders. It might be a place they had all been, hopefully at the same time, or somebody they all knew and who knew them.

He talked to himself when concentrating and alone. Just like how, when he was really focused on something, he stuck the tip of his tongue out without realising it.

"Right, Mr Collingwood…I want to know why you got divorced…Speaking to Alison, your ex-wife, it seems you were misbehaving. You had it all but threw it away for some reason. You weren't convicted but charged with child abuse…Odd, it was in the Channel Islands…Now Mr Westbrook is our local success story…Good education – up to Oxbridge to become a lawyer…Mostly working as a defence lawyer…That needs to be checked, any famous cases or names I'll recognise from this case…Now I think those two were pre-meditated, but then killing Murtlebury was a bit more opportunistic; he was available and vulnerable so, being more confident by then, you just did it. People don't usually take prisoners without at least a bit of planning, so Richards was targeted."

A knock came on the office door, and DS Peter looked up from the computer screen and piles of paperwork. "Yes, come in."

"Sorry to disturb you, Mr Anderson, but I thought you should see this. Ma'am isn't in at the moment." PC Watkins opened the door of Peter's broom cupboard office carrying a file of loose papers.

"Come on in, buddy. I could use a break, but I'll not have a fag break. However, I'll just have a nicotine mint to lull my craving for a cigarette. So remind me what you are doing this morning." DS Anderson stretched his arms up in the air and then got his mints from the jacket over his chair.

"I'm looking through the calls and emails from the public. You know what they're usually like. Lonely pensioners who just want a visit from a support PC, mad students living away from home for the first time, and young ladies who are asylum seekers." PC Watkins spoke while picking out a particular piece of paper. "But this email is different. See what you think."

From: frankie.franklinnewyorker@gmail.com
To: 101@devonandcornwall.pnn.police.uk
Subject: Blind Justice

Hi,

I'm a man in New York dating a drag queen named Michael Evans but who is known as Rocket Queen. Now I could be wrong, but I think he is friends with a lunatic in your city. They are going by the name Blind Justice and going around as a transvestite vigilante killing paedophiles. Having looked at the website for your local newspaper, I know you do have a psycho called Blind Justice messing things up for you guys. I don't know if I can keep my love life going and yet betray my lover's buddy from years ago with whom I still keep in touch on a regular basis. I'm going to do some serious thinking. I may be in touch again.

Best wishes,
Frankie

"Thanks for showing me this, mate, this just could be something. It is certainly worth having a good look at. I'm going to get in touch with Miss Hansard now." Peter had a feeling this just might be significant, and if he could also connect the past victims, they might be able to make some serious progress before the next weekend. He knew Tracy was out driving, so he sent her a copy of the email.

CHAPTER 29

I f there was one thing Tracy really hated it was wasting time, especially in traffic jams or queues of any sort. Therefore, as soon as she was caught in traffic, she started looking through the piles of paperwork she had on the passenger seat. It was also a chance to look things up on the internet using her phone. She couldn't remember or imagine what the world had been like before everyone was connected to the internet. She adored the 'information highway' despite all the cybercrime it permitted. She loved the shopping she could do without having to visit the supermarkets as previously she had become very frustrated waiting with her trolley behind families out doing their weekly shop. She was very tried by the young parents losing control of their rug-rats near the checkout where the sweets were stacked. She hadn't told anyone, but she was in favour of people having to pass a test of some sort before being allowed to reproduce.

She saw that an email had arrived from DS Anderson. He usually preferred to give her bad news face to face, so this might well be good stuff. She read the email from Frankie in New York and felt that this could well be a breakthrough. She also read what Peter had written about the links between the different victims. She had been thinking of taking a trip to a health spa to recharge her batteries, but she'd have to set that aside for now and go back to the station to talk to her IT specialist. She got a real adrenalin boost when an investigation progressed. The IT guy could probably find out if this really had been sent from New York. She didn't know anyone in the NYPD, but someone at the station probably did since there had been a link with America thanks to a career exchange a while ago. Officers had gone on a working trip to see how members of the world's most famous police department lived and worked.

Eventually she had the chance to get her car out of the gridlock and turned around to head back to work. She tried to imagine what the situation might be like for Frankie. He was in love with someone whom he'd met in New York, and while getting to know them better he'd discovered that they still had a close friend from years ago. This person they'd known for years seemed to be going crazy back in the UK. She couldn't tell, but she got the impression that Frankie was quite young, whereas Michael Evans was probably older and belonged to the same generation as Blind Justice. She guessed that they knew each other from childhood.

She realised she'd have to reply to Frankie's email, but she had to word it right, or they might lose everything. She needed to encourage him to communicate but couldn't pressure him because if this was Frankie's first love, the last thing he would want to do is betray the trust they had established by handing over his partner's lifelong friend to the law.

Tracy wished she was more familiar with the gay scene, but by chance, she had never really had to deal with it. She knew there were some officers who were involved with the LGBTQ crowd. She didn't think any of Peter's friends were in to it, but maybe his sister knew someone, especially since she was a hairdresser, and Tracy thought that a few of the guys in that trade were at least a bit camp if not gay. She thought she remembered hearing about a lecturer at the university who was quite popular with those guys. Ian was his name, but what was his surname, and what department did he belong to? Academia really was a mystery to her as she hadn't been a student anywhere except the College of Policing, and nobody there got drunk or took drugs like the students did at universities these days.

As she drove towards the police station she was annoyed by the vehicle in front of her. It was belching out huge black clouds of exhaust fumes. The driver couldn't be unaware of this as the smog was so thick and dark they'd see it in their mirror. She associated traffic cops with some of the boys who had been the first to get cars when they were teenagers, the ones Pete called 'petrol heads'. As he said, "They feel the need, the need for speed." Still, at least they were doing it legally because she was very displeased with people who committed driving offences, especially drunk drivers and mobile phone abusers. She was always very careful to make sure she wasn't driving when using her phone, even with her hands-free set. She didn't want to be a hypocrite. One of the worst things police officers ever have to do is break bad news to relatives; such as a person having been murdered or killed in a car crash. She often feels that the judges let them off a bit too lightly, and she has been sure in a few past cases that defendants had been paid to drive into other people, thus using a car as a murder weapon, but that was often very hard to prove.

She arrived at the station and went to the incident room, where she found Peter and a few PCs; as she had hoped, the station's IT expert, Nick, was on scene too. They were all clustered around a computer screen while Nick sat in the chair in front of it. She could feel the energy and enthusiasm emanating from them, so she guessed that they were making positive progress.

"Evening, ma'am. We have confirmed that it is from New York, but obviously that still leaves a lot to work on. God knows how many internet cafes there are in the city, never mind mobile phones, laptops and PC towers." She was greeted and updated by Peter who had a heavy five o'clock shadow on his face but also had a lively sparkle in his eyes.

"What do you think we know about Frankie? I want to send an email back to him to thank him for what he's given us so far. I need to talk to a psychologist or someone about how we can influence his decisions and make him feel responsible but not guilty. He is the only real connection we have to Blind Justice at the moment despite it being such a tenuous link." The other people in the room could hear the apprehension in her voice because she did not want to break this connection to BJ, so she'd handle it with kid gloves. It was a currently delicate silver chain, and she wanted to build it up to the sort of chain that the Torpoint Ferry uses to cross the Tamar.

CHAPTER 30

"I know LA is the City of Angels, including fallen ones, but why does New York have to be Psychoville?" Frankie asked himself aloud in the empty living room. He was back in the apartment he shared with a couple of moronic junkies who drove him mad. There was also a guy who had a room that he kept padlocked when he wasn't around, which was most of the time. He was a bit older than the other clowns, and Frankie reckoned that he probably was a lot more knowledgeable. He was called 'T', and he and Frankie had had a few excellent discussions about serious issues. The others just gossiped about the latest computer games, pop music or other such trivia.

Frankie was hoping that T would come back again soon so they could talk. He didn't have a phone number as T hadn't big on telecommunications ever since he'd spent a couple of years in the Himalayas, where digital watches were the peak of technology; there, he didn't use a mobile phone for months at a time, and those had been the best years of his life. Frankie found himself pacing up and down the room. He thought about how things could, should or would work out in the end. Ideally, he would still be close to Michael Evans. Maybe they could even live together – in Michael's place, he hoped, which was paradise compared to this dump. He was worried about

Blind Justice and felt he needed to be stopped. He didn't think he could 'grass' on him because if Mike found out, that would completely fuck things up. It would be the end of the only lifelong friendship he had, the one he had maintained for years across thousands of miles. Frankie didn't have any friends like that, but he could see what it meant to his lover, Michelle, known as Rocket Queen. Together they had helped each other through care homes, which had been the worst thing they ever experienced, and at such a young age.

Then there was the worst-case scenario, which could play out in a number of ways. Blind Justice could get scared and come over to the States. Maybe he'd panic and call Michael Evans to go and help him in England. Anything that risked the cops getting involved meant there was a chance of people getting shot or going to prison. Frankie was feeling trapped in an emotional maze, and he wasn't even sure there was a definite escape route. God, he hated it!

"I'm not even 21 yet, and I've got to work out how to deal with this. Half of me wants to just go and get high. That's just sticking my head in the sand, though. No help to or from anybody. I wish I had someone I could talk to about this. It's times like this I imagine parents or siblings would be good…" Being out of touch with his divorced parents and having no brothers or sisters meant that Frankie didn't agree with the idea that 'no man is an island'. He'd been living his life like he was Hawaii ever since he could remember.

Then, as he was about to go out for a run in Central Park (he kept very fit and worked part-time as a personal trainer), the flat door opened. T walked in looking and smelling like he'd been on the streets for a few days. He was carrying a clean white plastic box in his big dirty hands, and he was focused on it to such an extent that Frankie thought that if he didn't make a sound, T would go into his room without even knowing he was there. Talk or not? A problem shared is a problem halved.

"T! Can we have a chat, bud? I've got a moral dilemma, and I'd be interested to hear what you reckon." Frankie trusted T and felt he couldn't make things worse and maybe he could even make them better.

"Sure thing, dude. Can you give us 10 minutes to have a shower and put me washing on? Can you get a four pack of cold beers from the store, and I'll be ready when you get back?" This was a typical T thing. You do me a favour and I'll do you one.

"No worries." Frankie walked out to the stairs, wondering about the plastic box – he'd heard a scratching noise come from inside.

Frankie came back with a pack of chilled Budweiser's and found T on his knees wearing a bathrobe and flip-flops and looking under the sofa.

"Come on, out you get, you timorous little beastie." T spoke in a gentle voice and used his right hand to take some seeds from a bag in his left. "I told you about the hamsters I saw in the mountains, didn't I? Well, I've got a pet one now…A real Tibetan hamster called Dalai Lama. If I'd gotten a gerbil, a rat or a mouse I'd probably have called it Robbie, after the Scotland poet." T stood up with the cute little critter in his hands, stuffing its cheek pouches with seeds.

"Can we go in your room in case the others come back? This is a serious issue, and I'll show you some stuff on my iPad." Frankie picked up his drawstring bag and followed T into his room. A great odour of joss sticks filled the room despite the fact that none were smoking.

"Crack a couple of beers, and I'll put the rest in my mini fridge." T sat down on a prayer mat with crossed legs while the hamster ran from hand to hand. "What can I do for you?"

Frankie explained the situation he was in regarding his very close friend Mikey, the first love of his life and how he was connected to a psychopathic killer over in England. He knew T hadn't been involved in any gangs with the mafia, but he guessed he really wouldn't want to have to rat on anyone. It just wasn't a decent thing to do unless it was necessary to save a person's life. They both knew of people who had lost everything because they'd passed information on to the cops.

"I really don't like to have to lie to anybody. If I'm in a moral maze, I sometimes try to imagine what I think Jesus would do if he were in the position. I think he would go and tell the police, but I don't know if he'd do it anonymously or let them know where the information came from." This was T's fundamental position, and it made sense to Frankie.

"Thanks. I'll go away and have a think about it and the future. If I do split up with Mikey, I'm sure I'll find another lover soon or later, though I can't imagine it now." Frankie went out for his run in Central Park and wondered what, if anything, to say to Mikey next time they met up.

CHAPTER 31

When I woke up in the morning after the party at Paige's place, I wished I hadn't lost my nerve and panicked after a couple of glasses of beer followed by a vodka and Coke or two. They had all been friendly people with good accepting attitudes and been non-judgmental regarding sexuality and mental health. I had made contact with Ian so I could go to his support group now because it wasn't just for students. There was one meeting left before the Christmas holiday, and I had gotten the impression from Ian that it was going to a bit more informal than they usually were. People were invited to go along to the bar in the student union and meet up for a Christmas buffet, where mince pies and coffee would be provided.

They usually met in the evening, but this time it was a midmorning get-together as some of them were going to the local pantomime that evening. Ian would recognise me and anyone else who had been at the party, but I decided to go in a Father Christmas outfit so I could hide behind a fake beard. There was nothing yet, but I was worried an image of me might appear in the media soon. I'd also take Willow in an elf costume to improve my confidence. I had a little wooden barrel she could carry for me like the St Bernards do in the Alps so I'd have some brandy to put in my coffee if I felt like it.

"Morning, Willow, it's time for you to meet the local students of the LGBTQ crowd and those with psychological issues. I reckon it would have been good if Rocket Queen and I had known people like this who we could talk to. There was no such thing as Childline when we were kids. It had been the British stiff upper lip and all that rubbish for us; look what it made. A psychotic transvestite vigilante and a gay drag artist." I talked to Willow as I made a bowl of porridge for each of us; I found it was a good breakfast we both liked. I served mine with some soft brown sugar and mixed hers with a few meaty chunks from Simon Richards's muscles.

"How about I get a tin of Quality Street chocolates to show what a nice kind person I am? It will also be something I can use as an icebreaker if I see someone I want to start a conversation with, so I will. We can go to Lidl's on the way to the campus and buy a cheap bottle of booze to go in the barrel you'll be carrying."

We set off in plenty of time as I didn't know my way around the campus of the university, and it was quite sizable, as was the student population. Considering that one in four people is supposed to have a mental health issue at some point in their life, and it is often related to stress, I guessed there would be a fair number at the uni. Many students were living away from home for the first time, and obviously exam pressure would be an issue. Since it was a place with a ferry to the continent, a serious amount of drugs, alcohol and tobacco came through Tamarmouth. I wasn't surprised that Ian's support group was popular, and I hoped there would be a good-sized crowd at the union. I guessed they would mainly be kids in their late teens, but I was hoping to find more mature students, especially those who lived in the area rather than those who were there for the term from London or abroad.

Willow and I did our shopping and explored the university grounds, which we had ignored for years. I remembered when it was a small polytechnic institution. I hadn't really been back since then, when I occasionally went to events at the Main Hall. My generation had done O and A levels in fewer subjects than students these days. Now it seemed that students had to take courses like drama, which hadn't even been an option for me. Computers were the thing that got me these days. I remembered when rooms were filled with machines to do sums and calculate information. It seemed now that a smartphone could do everything the 1960s NASA computer banks had done. I imagined that soon, cars would drive themselves, so anyone could simply get in and tell the car where they want to go. However, I got the impression that there were two categories of people. Half loved technology and lived via social media, while the other half had serious doubts and sought a spiritual experience in life. Some of the modern churches were doing well, and Scientology seemed popular with celebrities.

"Let's sit down and have a cigarette by the reservoir; I like the view there. Swans and ducks with fountains in the background." We walked to the northern side of the campus and sat on the benches looking at the water, which would probably freeze in a few weeks' time. We still had a good few minutes till the union opened and we were expected to join Ian and his buddies. The whole area was pretty empty, but there was a couple intimately sharing a flask of coffee and enjoying themselves. Looking closely, I could see that it was two girls wrapped up in winter woollies – scarves, hats and gloves. They whispered to each other and giggled. They then came over to me and said hello to Willow first and then to me. It didn't take long to confirm that we were all waiting for the meeting in the union. We chatted to pass the time.

"Do you students pay much attention to the local news, or are you too busy?" I asked.

"Well, it's a personality thing, I reckon. Some people care about the local news, but others ignore it. Some guys I know hardly ever interact with the neighbours and just play

computer games against people in Shanghai via the internet. I
do also know people studying journalism and artistic subjects,
and they want to get involved with cultural activities in the
area. As do we – we're studying social work, so we have to
do placements." The girl who looked similar to Baby Spice
explained.

"Interesting. I was wondering about the Blind Justice story
in the press and what the people in the group make of it," I
said.

"It does have people's attention. We've been talking about
it the last few nights in our house." This was said by the
older looking student, who seemed to be the lesser half of the
partnership.

I looked at my watch and suggested that we walk towards
the union. We carried on talking as we went.

"People aren't scared – they can see that it is the criminals
who are the victims. Isn't there something about live by the
sword and die by the sword in the Bible?" said Baby Spice.
This was what I had hoped to hear, and I heard more and
more of it throughout the morning. The best was from a gay
guy who was one of the older members of the group. He said
he'd help Blind Justice if it came to it. I got the impression
from him that he only said that to stir things up in the group,
but when I talked to him one on one, he really seemed to
mean it. I persuaded him to give me his contact details, and I
gave him mine so that I'd have at least one possibility in case
of an emergency.

CHAPTER 32

T racy was not a gambler and never had been. She thrived on certainty; she didn't like to take chances. However, she had to bite the bullet on a couple of fronts. First she needed to go home and live with Arthur now that he was healthy enough because he clearly wanted to go home. She did too, but she knew the risks, unlike him. Blind Justice would not scare her out of her own home. After all, everyone knew where the Queen and the Prime Minister lived, but how often were they attacked in their homes? It was always when they were out doing things they were targeted, and the one that really stuck in Tracy's mind was the Brighton bombing by the IRA. If she couldn't go home and relax at her flat with her pussycat, life wasn't worth living. She also enjoyed walking in the local streets and parks and being recognised by the neighbourhood cats who each had their own personality and characteristics. There was a lovely couple of tabbies she often saw in the windows of a house past the corner shop. Sometimes seen individually, she was sure they were a male and female, but she didn't know if they were a couple or a pair of siblings. They had been there for years, and she felt like they were old friends, but they have never been in the front garden. Maybe they went out the back or perhaps stayed in permanently. Another one she liked she had first seen as a tiny black kitten with oversized eyes and ears. It was now a sort of teenager, behaving foolishly and overreacting to things.

The second issue to deal with was replying to Frankie. If she didn't acknowledge his email and express support and encouragement, it would be a waste of time. It may need to be done very slowly, word by word – even *War and Peace* had been written like that. As the Chinese proverb says, 'A journey of a thousand miles begins with a single step'.

She had discussed it with specialists, experts, professionals, authorities and felines and she now had to do it. She would also use her personal email address. Based on how Arthur responded, she felt that instinct was a significant factor. He just acted according to his nature, so she would do the same.

From: tracyhansard.di@gmail.com
To: frankie.franklinnewyorker@gmail.com

Dear Frankie,

I'm immeasurably grateful for your email. I understand how you must feel trapped between true love and honest moral decency. I think you need to be sure and confident that you have somewhere else to live because if you pass details regarding Blind Justice on to me and we successfully follow it up and take it to court, sooner or later, your friend Michael will become a problem. If you are going to provide evidence, a witness identity protection scheme will probably be required.

I have been in touch with the NYPD, so you can report to a precinct and mention the name Blind Justice to the officer at the reception desk, and he'll take you see the duty senior officer. They can then either take a statement from you or give you access to facilities to contact me. You can get in touch with me via phone or email.

The last thing I want to do is upset you because I think you could be a crucial person in this case, which is going to be significant for both of us and, obviously, other people too. Is there anything else I can do for you that would help?

Best wishes,

DI Hansard (Tracy)

She wrote it in pretty much one draft, and before sending it, she cleared it with her superintendent, who discussed it with a senior forensic psychologist. The plan was to give Frankie as much support as possible and an escape route if required. It was similar to situations where they had to negotiate with terrorists, kidnappers and hostage-takers to get as much as possible while giving away as little as possible, be it information, power or control.

The Metropolitan Police at New Scotland Yard were getting involved now too and sent a trained international counsellor familiar with American and British protocols who had worked for the United Nations Commission on Human Rights. However, as Tracy was familiar with Tamarmouth and its population, he wouldn't be leading the inquiry but would serve as an asset for Tracy to utilise as needed.

"So Pete, what can we do now but wait and see how Frankie reacts to this?" Tracy sat at her desk. Her DS sat across from her. He had just been on a conference call with the Devon and Cornwall Chief Constable and Mr Goldburg, the Met's UN man flying in from Switzerland.

"Well, ma'am. I think a few hours rest would do us all some good. The next few hours or days are going to be hard work. Are you going to go back to yours with Arthur, and do you have a surveillance team in the street? I doubt BJ will be trying anything like that again though! It was just his last move in this psychological battle of cat and mouse to try and upset you…getting under your skin and in your head." DS Anderson was right. It would do Tracy good to go and collect Arthur and for the two of them to go home. She also felt she should put out food for the other local cats as usual and maintain as ordinary a life as possible.

"Yeah, that's it. A good proper meal and a few hours' sleep in a decent bed after having my last quality bath for a while, I expect. I tell you, Peter, I'm getting too old for this type of work. I can see why a lot of the older, senior cops move to Headquarters and join committees, become school governors, work nine to five in offices. Having experience is very useful, but it has to be obtained by hard graft, which is paid for in the end. Did I tell you about my night in the police house with a guy who reminded me of my uncle from Princetown?" Tracy started recalling that night and childhood memories of time spent on the farm near Princetown. The locals were either farmers or guards at HMP Dartmoor back then.

The two of them walked to the secure car park. They knew it was possible that more civilians would die in this case, be they unconvicted criminals or innocent members of the public, and the death of Blind Justice was a high probability. Tracy said she'd go and shop at Sainsbury's before going to see her friend and cat-sitter, Julie, to pick up Arthur. Peter was not sure what to do. A drink didn't seem like a good idea, but it would be pretty inevitable if he stayed out or went to see any of his mates. This was just the kind of time that he felt he'd benefit from a significant other or lady friend. Pets didn't do it for him like they did for Tracy.

CHAPTER 33

Having had a surprisingly good Christmas meal, which was made even better by meeting Mary, I now needed a reason to get back in touch with her. I knew she was reluctant to stay up too late for New Year's Eve, and she usually met up with her family for that anyway. I didn't want to call her without offering an invitation to some kind of event as that was not very gentlemanly.

"What can I do, Willow?" We had agreed to wait till early January, but as the days slipped by, I felt like she'd be forgetting who I was and how much we had enjoyed each other's company. Also, she would likely be distracted by the mobile phone she planned on getting from her daughter as a Christmas present. I knew she was interested in making a family tree and discovering who she is and where she comes from.

"How about we go back to the church hall and see what other events they have on, hey Wills?" I didn't know if Mary had been there because she was told about it by her Christian friends or someone else. I knew she had appreciated the taxi home, so it was probably not her local church, but that didn't mean it wasn't her usual place of worship. I decided to go for a decent walk, so I put an extra layer of clothing on and planned to stop for a hot drink somewhere near the church hall. So many places were offering a ridiculous range of teas, coffees and hot chocolates. I still didn't know where I could go for a cup of Ovaltine or Horlicks. As I wrapped myself in my winter outfit, I thought I was sure Mary felt the same way I did regarding hot drinks and many other aspects of modern society. It was a Marmite issue: you love it or you hate it.

"Okay, Willow. Time to face the real world and see what we think of it. I don't know why your paws don't freeze, but I could do with pads on my feet like you've got. I've got two pairs of socks on under a decent pair of boots, but I'll have cold feet later. You'll be fine, though." I talked to Willow while I put on my scarf, woolly hat and gloves. I picked up my white cane from beside the front door, and we set off into the black and white world of frosted Tamarmouth. I generally enjoyed shades of grey and wearing dark glasses; it was what I knew.

We took a longer route than before to the parish church hall, and I recalled my conversation with Mary and wondered if she'd said anything useful about what she enjoyed doing. She wasn't a volunteer anymore but still used the charity shops to buy clothes and books. Most of her other shopping was for food, which was either done locally at the Co-op or with her daughter, with whom she took monthly trip that combined a meal out with whichever supermarket had shown the most alluring advert.

I remembered Mary saying that she knew about the Christmas lunch from a flyer she saw at a tea dance she had been to at another hall. I was reminded of this when I saw a poster for a concert in the city's Guildhall, which was where she'd seen the advert. I decided to go via the town centre and look for promotions and see if there were magazines or leaflets advertising events for the upcoming year. I'd then have a drink and proceed on to the hall. Afterwards, I'd take the short, direct route home so that I would arrive before dark, which comes quite early that time of year.

I tried to remember the last time I'd been to anything like a dance, and unfortunately it was in the previous century. Not many people with impaired vision danced, and it had never been my kind of thing even when I could see what I was doing. I preferred to sit and listen or watch. Going for a meal or a cream tea was a definite possibility as Mary and I had both enjoyed our lunch, so I'd invite her out for a meal, but I wanted a reason to contact her and break the ice. There were mainly classical music concerts performed by symphony orchestras in the Guildhall, and although I wasn't sure what Mary reckoned, I knew I wouldn't enjoy those.

I picked up the new season's schedule but hoped the church hall would be hosting an event geared more towards working men, their partners and their retired parents. I decided it was so cold that I'd use the next cafe I came across to get myself a cup of tea and sit in the warmth for a bit. It made me really angry seeing the pensioners being interviewed on the local news and asked what they would choose: food or heat? Considering the size of this country's economy and what its pensioners had done in the past, I was very disappointed with the government's social care provision and the treatment of the NHS. I usually admired the nurses and doctors; it was the politicians and the management I found infuriating.

Willow and I went around the next street corner and found a community cafe we were unaware of. Over the last year a lot of these community things had come and gone, so we'd lost track of them. This place had been shut down; the last time I'd been here, it was a shop that sold locally produced food and artwork. I didn't know it had become a cafe partnered with the charity Shelter, which helps the homeless.

"Come on, Wills, let's have a cuppa." This was the sort of place that filled its window with adverts for neighbourhood events and cards promoting little businesses. Its staff probably consisted of friendly locals working a couple of jobs to survive rather than accumulating debt. I opened the door, and we made our way to the counter. Most places didn't mind well-behaved dogs, and by law, they couldn't refuse a guide dog without a good reason. I was greeted with enthusiasm by a young man who gave me the impression that he was from the Middle East, maybe Syria, Iran or Iraq.

"Afternoon, sir. Would you like to take a seat near the gas fire or the window?"

"I'll sit by the window as I'd like to check out these posters and flyers, and this whole room is well heated by my standards." I pointed to the sofa in the bay of the window, and I started to unwrap myself and take off my coat. Years ago Michael Evans and I decided to always take coats off so that we'd appreciate putting them on again afterwards. I put what I could over a chair by the fire and got Willow to lie on the rug next to it. Meanwhile, my waiter had placed a menu on the table, along with a number, and went to serve the couple with a toddler at the table by the cake stand.

I hadn't intended to have a bite to eat, but the cakes were very alluring, and I try to support local businesses if I can.

"Can I have a mug of tea…and a piece of the chocolate flapjack, please." I told the young man with 'Ali' on his name badge.

"Sure thing, sir." He scribbled my order on a notepad and then tore the page off and passed it through the hatch to the backroom kitchen.

Looking at the posters in the window, I saw that most were out of date, advertising Christmas carol services, meals and New Year's parties. However, I did see one that mentioned an event held the last Friday of each month. It said that the Welcome Hall combined a tea party with a dance, at which a group of musicians played tunes my generation considers famous. People could bring partners or, if they wanted to attend alone but wanted to dance, would be paired up by the organisers. It sounded ideal; I could bring Mary, but she could have a proper dance with somebody who was more skilled than me.

I noted the details and enjoyed my tea with a flapjack, which was just the way I remembered it – not too crispy, but sticky due to plenty of golden syrup and tasty due to ground ginger. I also saw an advert for a film club that was being planned for the community cafe. It was going to be aimed at the more elderly members of society as a chance to get them out of their flats and do something together. They were getting a projector soon, and they'd use it on Sunday afternoons to show classic films such as *Citizen Kane, Ben-Hur* and *The Thirty-Nine Steps*. I now had a couple of events to invite Mary to, and I was sure she'd say yes to one of them if she really wanted to see me again. I decided to go home and have a warm evening watching TV. Then, when I'd boosted my confidence by 'Dutch courage', I'd give Mary a call and tell her about the tea party and the film club.

CHAPTER 34

E ver since he was a kid, Peter Anderson had liked to be a goodie. When he and his mates played 'Cowboys and Indians', he was the Lone Ranger or a similar character, and when they played 'Coppers and Robbers', he was always a constable on the beat. He was sure he would be a copper when he was in school because he grassed on bullies or inflicted a bit of retribution on them himself. When he was growing up he watched all the police TV shows and the documentaries about pathology, criminal psychology and case histories, such as *The Great Train Robbery*. *The Bill* had been a favourite till all the American shows came on. However, the one American show he had enjoyed was *Hill Street Blues*, and he'd been impressed by Captain Furillo and how he ran his precinct. It was fictional of course, but ever since then he had liked the idea of taking a break and visiting the New York Police Department, ideally arranging a chance for an exchange so he could swap roles with one of their officers.

This email from Frankie might just be a chance for him to have a weekend in the Big Apple, and that should be enough to at least put him in touch with people across the pond working for the US Department of Justice. He had always enjoyed the idea of Christmas in snowy, ice-cold Central Park but, having already gone to the trouble of organising his family, he felt he'd

159

have to settle for a few days in the US in mid-December and then return to Tamarmouth to try and get everyone together for a meal. His family had been at war to such an extent that in the past, he, his cousins and his sister had called his mum 'The Godmother'. As in the case of famous Mafia Dons, it was incredible what could be agreed upon if people could be persuaded to sit and eat together.

He didn't like eating by himself if he could help it. In the canteen he'd rather go and sit with strangers than eat alone. It was okay back at his flat as there was nobody else around. Unfortunately, when he couldn't take a fag break, he now regularly had a tea and biscuits to distract himself from thoughts of nicotine. Nicotine chewing gum or mints helped if he had to stay in the room, and he now chewed the end of his Biro relentlessly. However, he spoke to different people standing in the queue at the canteen; till then, he had talked to smokers in the corner in the car park. He found that over meals and drinks, people told him more intimate details than they did over a smoke. It was probably to do with appeasing an addiction rather than just satisfying the basic need of human motivation.

They told him about their family, friends and what they were doing. This gave him a rough idea of who had holidayed in the States and which members of the force had relatives living there.

"Evening, Peter, come and have a look at this!" A community support officer waved a postcard at him from their seat.

"Yeah. Just coming." He headed over to them once he'd picked up a cup of tea.

"It's a card from my cousin who is working in America. He doesn't live in New York City, but he is in that state. He works as an international corporate lawyer. Good pay, but it doesn't do much for his family life as he's always flying around the world. He goes to China and Japan a lot these days, Korea as well." The card showed a family scene and had been made from digital photo. It told the recipient he now had a nephew named Dwight to think of as well.

"Do you think I could contact him if I were to go to America in an official capacity?" Pete started to think about his potential visit. "Being a legal person, I expect he could put me in touch with senior officers there, either directly or via contacts with the legal practice."

"Yes, I can email him to say congratulations on his kid and combine it with a query about that. He works for a big company that also has criminal lawyers for defence and prosecution at trials," CSO Steve replied enthusiastically. "Shall I do it now, or do you want check things with the DI first?"

Pete took a swig of tea to wash down his digestive biscuit. "Yeah, can you write it ASAP and send it to me and I'll show Tracy? If she's happy with everything then you can forward it to your cousin. This could be really useful, mate, thanks."

DS Anderson knew that a number of people didn't appreciate the community support officers, but he certainly did. He often found that because they lived in the area where they worked and were known by the locals, they obtained information the constables couldn't. He remembered a case last year in which somebody kept committing arson. The officers were getting nowhere till the CSOs were allowed to talk to the local organisations, such as schools and colleges. From this information a short list of suspects was drawn up, and it didn't take long to arrest and charge the perpetrator.

DS Peter Anderson felt very pleased with the way the case now seemed to be developing, and he felt like having a drink to celebrate that he may well be heading towards achieving a major item on his bucket list: a visit to New York.

He'd fantasised about it for years ever since he'd been a teenager, and he wanted to tell someone who'd known him back then. He wasn't in touch with anyone he'd gone to school with, so that just left his family. He remembered that he'd gotten his dad's new mobile number when he and his sister had met him at the King's Head pub the other night. A drink with his dad would be a good chance for his father to sing his son's praises and also for the two of them to socialise and get know each other better, having been apart for years. He chose to call his dad rather than send him a text as his father, like most of his generation, wasn't too keen on digitally written things.

"Dad...How're things with you? I'm in a good mood, so do you fancy a drink and maybe even a meal if you haven't eaten yet?" Peter felt he was getting to know what his dad did and didn't like. For example, if they went out to eat, whereas Pete enjoyed trying new dishes and spicy things, he knew that Jack preferred traditional 'pub grub' – a roast on Sunday at a carvery or fish and chips, a mixed grill or maybe lasagne if he was feeling adventurous.

"Sure. I'll meet you at The Dolphin for a pint of ale. We can order a takeaway using an app on my phone while we have a drink, and I can get it delivered to my flat to arrive when I get in...Yes, modern technology is great. See you in 10 or 15 minutes."

Peter checked his emails and saw that Steve had already written the message to his cousin, so he forwarded it to Tracy, explaining what had happened and how he thought they could use it. The last few evenings when he'd gone to bed, he hadn't been very optimistic about the following day, but now, he was already looking forward to tomorrow, and he was about to enjoy a drink with his father.

CHAPTER 35

"Alright, Willow. It's now a new year, and I've got serious expectations for my health this year. I'm hoping I'll get my sight sorted out with help from my psychiatrist. Regardless of what happens we'll still be together, so you don't need to worry. I'll look after you no matter what." I spoke to Willow as I read the local paper, which reviews all the events from the previous year and describes what to look out for in the new year.

Willow looked up at me with her empathetic eyes. She had clearly put on some weight over the Christmas season by eating sweets, pork scratchings and mince pies. I knew why she had put on more than she had during previous Christmases – she'd been given extra portions of meat this year.

"Now that the students are coming back from their Christmas holidays there are going to be more people on the streets again, and there are the sales, so I think there will be enough cover for me to make another attack. This one is going to have to be very carefully planned as I'm in the news these days. Blind Justice is a real public enemy now despite the fact my goals are the detritus of society, and I know some people think I'm doing a better job than the cops." I talked as I sat doing research online, trying to find a way to identify a new target. It occurred to me that many of those who did get convicted in the courts these days were given too mild a treatment by the law, which was an ass. If I could find someone who was released on parole or put in a secure hospital rather than prison, I might be able to target them.

It occurred to me that the people in Ian's support group would have memories of the people who had abused them, and given how organised Ian had seemed, he probably got people to do at least basic paperwork when they joined the Victim Aid Therapy group (VAT). If I could get a hold of that information, it may well have statements about the victims' pasts, which would provide clues regarding the identities of the abusers. For example, a person might be asked to summarise what had happened to them in the past. If someone had written that they had been violated by their uncle, for example, I would target their uncle as my next victim.

The previous VAT meeting had been more of a social event than a therapeutic session, but it had informed me that in a couple of weeks, they would be meeting in Ian's waiting room outside his office. One of the socialites had shown me a picture and described its location and what it was like, so I knew there were a couple filing cabinets behind his secretary's desk.

"What do you think Willow? We can either break in or go and persuade everyone to leave; a fire alarm would do it." I decided breaking in was the better option. Ian's office was on the ground floor of one of the older buildings, which would be about as good as it could get for Blind Justice and the Heroic Hound, especially as they had both slowed down a bit due to their Christmas indulgences.

We had a plan now, so we had to wait for the right conditions in which to implement it. Sooner or later there would be what used to be called a pea-souper fog, which would create ideal conditions for a transvestite vigilante to embark on an intelligence-gathering mission. A good thing about my cat suit was that it was made of waterproof material and had no open seams, so it kept me warm and dry. Willow did pretty much the same with her fur and Kevlar coat.

It was mid-January when the weather turned from clear and ice-cold to grey, overcast and wet. Also, the wind died down, allowing the moisture to accumulate in the atmosphere. I watched the forecast, and it looked like the thickest fog would occur later that night. I hadn't been in touch with Rocket Queen much since before Christmas as I knew he was not happy that Frankie had gone to stay with fellow fitness workers at a sort of boot camp since they were all preparing to run a marathon and raise money for NYC Pride. However, I needed a morale boost before going out on my next mission, so I contacted Michael to see how he was and tell him what I was up to.

"Hey Rocket Queen! How are things going this year? Is Frankie back yet or is he still out running in the countryside like Forrest Gump?" I spoke to Michael via a video phone call. I could be wrong but I got the impression he was suffering from depression to at least a slight extent.

"He's coming back in about a week. He hasn't sent me much in the way of texts, cards or love letters. I know it isn't because of a lack of a signal because I know a guy named Tony who is at the same camp, and I've been in touch with him." Rocket Queen was talking to me from his apartment, and it was about midday in New York, but he didn't have any makeup on. This was a concern as when he was feeling good he put his face on as soon as he woke up and had a shower.

"Remember what you were like at that age? Something had to be right in front of you to get your attention. It was a case of 'out of sight, out of mind'. Yeah?" I tried to justify Frankie's behaviour, not knowing what he was thinking about or the moral dilemma he was in; he was using the time away to assess the situation. In fact, he was weighing future possibilities regarding himself and Michael, which would also have a major effect on me.

"So what are you and Willow up to these days? I expect you're glad the weather is getting better. I've decided not to get myself a doggy; commitment isn't my kind of thing." Michael talked to me from what appeared to be a dirty, untidy bedroom.

"Funny you should mention the weather. We are going to take advantage of a thick heavy fog to go out on a reconnaissance mission tonight. Remember the therapy group I told you about? I'm going to break into their office to check their records, which I believe will give me some clues about who abused the members of the support group. Then I can track them down, so I'll have some new targets. I don't know what it's like in America, but Christmas and New Years are just excuses to get drunk over here. It has helped people forget the recent past." I explained my idea to my lifelong friend while I put a bowl of Pedigree dog food down for Willow. "You can tell Frankie the next time you're in touch that if he runs that marathon, I'll donate to a charity."

"Sure thing. Thanks… I'm wondering what to do to welcome him back after his time away…He's on a specific diet for the running, so I can't really take him out for a meal or have a party yet." Michael was talking intermittently between putting his makeup on and getting dressed. He obviously had thought of something to do today. My getting in contact with him seemed to have cheered us both up and given us a bit more confidence.

"Okay…I bet you'll find something to do. Just do something spontaneous rather than planning anything. Ask him what he wants. You could buy him some clothes or go out to a show. Anyway, I need to start getting ready for tonight, so I'll leave you now." I finished the conversation feeling better about myself and happier about what Michael was up to, and he seemed to be a little less miserable being alone.

By the time Willow and I were ready to go out there was so much moisture in the air it was like a whiteout, and we could hardly see anything. However, we were used to moving around with no visibility, so it wasn't a problem for us. The weather would have put most people off from coming out, and it helped obscure Closed Circuit TV pictures. We'd had a nap after dinner and woke up a bit before midnight so as to have plenty of energy for what would be a very significant mission if it was successful because it would give us access to a lot of confidential information and thus open up numerous ways in which we could progress.

We navigated our way through the dark night and the white blanket of water vapour till we arrived at the cul-de-sac of old buildings, which had been converted to offices after having previously been private houses. We advanced up a couple of steps to the porch, which was so considerable it even had pillars on each side to improve its architecture. Until we reached the front door, we had been progressing in an overt manner, but now I crouched down as the operation took on a covert element.

"Willow, stand there and let me get my skeleton keys out of your pouch. This lock should be easy enough to pick, and we know we can break open the filing cabinet with a good bit of leverage." I bent down so that my line of sight was level with the lock mechanism. I was feeling excited as this was a new sort of crime for me. I soon had the main door open, and we slipped in and closed it behind us. Looking along the main hallway, I saw offices on both sides, each with a name on the door, a stairway at the far end and an unmarked door that probably led to either a toilet or a kitchenette. We went through the door marked *Ian Shore: Department of Psychology*. We were in the waiting room we had seen in the photos, which had a small receptionist's desk and a chair on wheels. Behind the desk were the cabinets, and the rest of the walls were lined with more comfortable chairs. Above the chairs were posters of quotations relating to mental health; the text had been hand-written in Gothic calligraphy. At the far end was a door surrounded by wooden panelling and frosted glass, which led to a small room where Ian could talk to people privately.

I bent down over Willow and removed the crowbar that was strapped along her spine for protection in case she was attacked; it was also a convenient place for her to carry our larger tools. I soon broke open the filing cabinets and found the Victims Aid Therapy paperwork in the bottom drawer. It was a sizable file, and I opted to take it all to give myself numerous possibilities for my next strike. I returned the crowbar and extracted the drawstring bag, into which I put the file of A4 sheets. Each form consisted of two sheets stapled together. I reckoned there must have been about twenty-five different sets of data.

"Alright, Wills. This will give us a bit to get our teeth into. Let's go back home now." I rubbed Willow on the top of her head, and we left the office. The break-in would probably be discovered later that morning as it was a weeknight. I didn't think there was anything to indicate that it was a Blind Justice crime.

CHAPTER 36

U pon receiving the email from DI Hansard in the UK
and getting a bit of advice from T, Frankie decided
to take some time to think on his own. Usually he
thought best when he was out walking or running, so training
for and then completing a marathon made a lot of sense.
Going away to a boot camp was an unexpected opportunity
to leave everything behind and clear his mind. T had talked
about going on retreats, having silent days, meditation and
things he'd done when in the Buddhist countries of the
Far East. He knew he'd have a physical trainer, but as sport
psychologists were more popular these days, he expected to at
least be able to contact one while away.

In a way, he liked the idea of taking on a new identity after
providing evidence for a trial, which would be very significant
and would change his life completely. To make a fresh start in
another country seemed appealing as he didn't have any family
he'd be losing. He could work as a fitness instructor in any
country where English was spoken, and he knew the sort of
places to go to make new friends. Plus, he could email friends
like T back in the States if he wanted.

Frankie decided to go get in touch with the UK police.
He emailed them, and within a day or two he was at the
local coach station waiting for a Greyhound bus to arrive

carrying DS Peter Anderson. A cover story had been set up that involved him posing as a journalist who represented the British LGBTQ community, so that was why he was visiting the camp. He had arranged to meet up with his parents and sister when he returned so he could tell them about his trip to America and show them his photos.

"Hi! I'm Frankie. You must be Pete." Frankie greeted him. He knew it was Peter because he'd been told to look for someone with their leg in a cast. This would explain why he wasn't out running all the time with the others.

"Yeah. Can you give us a hand with this rucksack? Are we getting a taxi now?" Pete was dressed in a tracksuit he'd bought the night before while sightseeing in New York.

They hailed a cab and Pete paid for the transport. He'd have his own room, while Frankie would share a dormitory with a few other runners. That gave Pete a chance to talk with Frankie one on one and work on his computer in private. The whole place was a converted ranch. The homestead was now the office, gym and housing for the staff. The cattle sheds served as a refectory and the sleeping quarters for those training.

A pack of runners came towards them, chanting a cadence, as it's called in the US military. The leader shouts a line, and the recruits either repeat it or respond to it.

"We are gay and we are proud!" The trainer called out.

"We are gay and we shout loud!" The runners answered.

They reached the parade ground and jogged on the spot as they waited for the last ones to arrive. They were then dismissed to take showers before their evening meal.

Frankie joined the others and went for a shower, while the senior trainer came over to greet Pete and carry Pete's bag up the steps onto the veranda. It really was an enormous sky, just like in all the classic Westerns.

The trainer was a retired US Marine drill instructor, and he looked like a human Hummer. "Come on in, buddy. We heard you broke your ankle, so you have a room on the ground floor by the kitchen. You can join us for dinner in about an hour."

"Cheers, that's fine. If you let everyone know who I am and why I'm here, they can volunteer to talk to me if they want to tell their stories about being LGBTQ runners and working to raise money for AIDS charities and gay pride. Tell them I can tell their story without mentioning their names if they want." Pete took the key from his room's door, went in and placed his bag on the bed. He'd seen a vending machine by the reception desk and went out to get a Coke.

He returned to his room after signing the guest book. Time to contact Tracy to say that he'd made contact with Frankie and describe his first impression to her. Later he'd get a hold of his file and details and send his picture back to the UK. He took out his Apple MacBook Air and pulled up the questionnaire he was going to use as part of his cover story when conversing to anyone who volunteered to talk to him.

Frankie had been told to have a good think about whether he wanted to stay in the States and if he'd like to move to the West coast or Texas or somewhere rather than leave the country of his birth. Obviously California, the Golden State, had appeal, especially if he could move to San Francisco. He decided to stay in America as he then still had the option to travel abroad in the future. Most of the other runners had come with friends or partners, so they socialised during the rest periods. Frankie just jogged around thinking about what to do and what the future might hold for him. He was quite happy to talk to Peter either in his room or as they wandered around the estate.

Rocket Queen talked to his friend Tony, who was at the camp with his bisexual partner, Jane, by phoning him, but he waited to see if Frankie would ring him.

"Hi. How are you and Janie doing? Have you seen Frankie? Talking to a journalist and by himself a lot?" It soon became clear to Mickey that his friend was not being 'the life and soul' as he often was. This struck Rocket Queen as unusual, and he was also confused by Frankie's behaviour as he normally planned everything in detail. If he was going somewhere, he'd buy the tickets weeks before because he enjoyed the anticipation and getting ready for it all. This trip to the marathon boot camp was totally different; he'd mentioned it less than a week before going on the trip. Rocket Queen didn't like it, but he couldn't help feeling a bit suspicious as Frankie had seemed a bit stressed, as if he were hiding a secret, the day or two before leaving.

Pete compiled a list of names of people who wanted to tell him their histories regarding charity work and running. He posted a timetable on the noticeboard so everyone knew when to visit his room. He had checked things with DI Tracy, so he added Frankie to the timetable when they would be able to Skype Tracy and get her talking with Frankie. After breakfast there was a gym session during which most people ran on treadmills, and it was a good chance for the trans-Atlantic link-up. Mr Goldberg had met with Tracy for a few hours by then, and they were going to try and get him talking with Frankie and working as a legal representative for him.

"I hope you're not feeling too jet-lagged, Pete. What have you managed to find out from Frankie's file?" The DI talked to her sergeant while she waited for Frankie to come in.

"I've got his surname and his social security number. We can give him a new one to help conceal his current identity if he provides evidence and then needs to take on a new identity. He told me that he was raised by a liberal Christian family, which seems to have given him the moral code he's working with. They were accepting of homosexuals, and although he didn't get too involved with the church, the idea of treating neighbours the way you want to be treated is his basis. Since being in New York he has broadened his horizons and learned about the world; he started off in a small Minnesota backwater town." Pete explained the information he had till Frankie knocked on his door and came in looking a bit nervous.

They soon set up a conference with Frankie and Peter on one end talking to Tracy and Mr Goldberg on the other side of the Atlantic. It seemed that Frankie had been horrified by what he had seen and heard regarding Blind Justice. He wasn't certain, but he had reason to believe that Blind Justice's mother had been murdered by a serial killer, which was why he wanted to do something about it.

CHAPTER 37

M ary and I agreed to meet up for the tea dance and then probably go to a film on Sunday afternoon. I still wasn't feeling very comfortable, so I took Willow with me for support and as evidence of why I couldn't dance. I knew the place, so I took a taxi to be among the first in and get one of the better tables between the dance floor and the counter where refreshments were served. That might've meant I'd have to sit by myself for a while as I waited for Mary to arrive, but it seemed like a worthwhile activity.

This was the first date I'd been out on for a long time, and I was feeling nervous. I'd already decided I wouldn't dancing, but I hoped this wouldn't be too negative in Mary's eyes. People were coming in and mulling around, often in pairs, or they headed straight for the cups of tea and tasty homemade cakes. It was just after four o'clock, and the band was scheduled to start playing at half past. In the meantime, there was music coming through the PA's loudspeakers to dispel the silence, specifically the music of Vera Lynn, Glen Miller and the Boston Pops Orchestra.

I was just starting to relax and feel a little more confident because I got the impression that the others were there not to dance but to socialise and just come out of their lonely homes. I then heard something on the sound system that I hadn't heard for years. However, it didn't take me back to 'the good old days'; rather, it was something I remembered hearing in Mr Blackheart's apartment, and it sent a chill to the core of my very being. It was a James Last track called 'The Last Waltz.' I began to feel very anxious and stressed. I had just sat down with a pot of tea and a spare cup, hoping Mary would be along soon. I began to have a feeling of dread, and my breathing accelerated, and I became sweaty, first on my palms and then up to my face.

I had talked to my CPN about being aware of things that trigger panic attacks and cause me to have episodes of blindness. This one was obviously caused the music, which brought up a memory from my traumatic past. I could feel my eyesight deteriorating, so I reached out and stroked Willow for reassurance. I could hear people around me but could see no more than dark shapes moving around in front of a pale blurry background. I was just about to get up and leave when I heard Mary's voice calling to me.

"Mark! Willow! How are you? Good to see you again." Her voice got louder as she wound her way through the chairs and tables to where we were sat. She put her hand on my shoulder, and, being a sensitive woman, she immediately saw that I was not right.

She sat down in the other chair at the table and slid it close to mine.

"Mary...Thank God you've arrived! Remember what I said about my episodes of blindness? One's just started now. I was about to get up and head home." I described how I felt and why I looked so pale. Apart from the medical workers, I hadn't really talked to anyone about this, certainly not when it was happening.

"Alright, Mark. Calm down, relax. First you need to slow down your breathing. I did a first aid course a while ago, so I think I can help you. You don't want me to see if there are any

St. John's Ambulance people here, do you?" She spoke quietly in a caring, reassuring voice.

However, I could still hear that music in the background, and I felt like a scared, vulnerable, lonely schoolboy. I couldn't see anything now, so with one hand I gripped Willow's harness, and with the other I squeezed Mary's hand in mine. I held on to both for dear life as if I were holding on to a rope over a bottomless chasm leading to the fires of hell.

"Ssshit…M-Mary, can you help me get out of here? I just need to get outside…Then I can start to get sorted out," I mumbled towards her. She agreed and put her arm around my shoulder. I instructed Willow to get up and head to the door. As we staggered through the flood of people progressing in the opposite direction, I felt weak and sick. So pathetic. Especially because I had meant to impress Mary that day, and maybe even persuade myself to dance with her if she wanted to.

We made our way out of the doors and into the car park. Mary said she'd call a taxi to take me home. She could either continue on to her home or join me for a while at my flat. That way she could ring her daughter from my landline and get a lift home when she felt like it.

I was grateful to Mary but also so upset and angry with the fact I still couldn't deal with things that had happened to me years and years ago. They still tormented me. I hugged Willow as we waited for a black cab to arrive. I didn't break down into floods of tears, but I did emit a soft, mild whimpering. I was what Mr Blackhurst would have called a 'snivelling wreck'. I hated everything to do with that disgusting, vile beast who had contaminated my life and messed up my future from my days in the children's home onwards.

"Mark, what's your address? Here's the cab," Mary spoke to me as she waved to the taxi driver.

"Home Sweet Home Terrace in Cattedown. It's a ridiculous name for a deprived street in a destitute area of a decaying city." I wanted Mary to have realistic expectations of my abode as I felt I might be about to have the first visitor for a long time who wasn't there because they were employed to be.

"You hear that, driver?" she asked the cabbie as she, Willow and I bundled in to the cavernous empty space in the back of a Hackney carriage.

"Yeah, I know it. That not take long," he called over his shoulder in an Eastern European accent as he set off towards the roundabout at the end of the road. I got my wallet out, and, despite not being able to see it, got out a few pound coins as I knew that would be enough. Mary said she would come in and join me for a cup of tea.

We were soon in my shared hallway with the door to my flat on the left and the door to the upstairs flat at its end. I imagined that Mary's flat was very clean and tidy, like those occupied by people with obsessive–compulsive disorder. Mine was the sort of place where a person would expect somebody with ablutophobia to live. That's a fear of cleaning and washing, and despite the time of year I didn't think my flat had been given a spring clean for years. However, having dealt with homeless people and other desperadoes, Mary was not put off going into my kitchen and making tea.

"Thank you for this, Mary. I'll make it up to you by taking you to the film club on Sunday, and I can take you to the proper cinema when there's a film we'd like to see." I apologised to Mary as I made my way across the room to my chair, the position of which I knew by memory. I sat down and took out my baccy tin. I was quite capable of rolling a fine cigarette without being able to see anything, so I made one and started to smoke it as I told Mary to put a splash of brandy in my tea and give herself one if she wanted.

Everything in my flat had its own place, so I got a hold of the remote control and turned on the radio. My sight was starting to come back now that I was feeling comfortable and relaxed. I could hear Mary entering the living room, and she sat down after putting my mug on the coaster. I was embarrassed by what had happened, but I felt that I needed to at least partially explain why I suffer these blindness episodes, so I told her a bit about what had happened to me in the past back in Jersey before she got a taxi back to her flat.

CHAPTER 38

I decided it was time to start meeting the public and promoting my cause, but I would do so on a one-on-one basis to start and under my own clandestine terms and conditions. Since I had gotten the contact details from Christian at the mince pies get-together in the student union, and he'd said he would help Blind Justice, it was time to put him to the test with an unexpected visit.

I'd gotten the impression that Christina had always lived on the edge of society and that that suited him. I had noticed that he had smoke-stained fingers, and from his tattoos I saw that he liked cannabis. I used his home-made business card to find his address, and Willow and I got in the camper van and drove to a dark back street around the corner from his street. We waited till dark and used the space in the back of the vehicle to dress in our vigilante outfits. It was time to see if we truly had any allies out in the real world. It was an unpleasant night in what wasn't the greatest part of town, so we didn't have to worry about company. We eventually got ourselves organised and, feeling secure, crept out of the van and down the pavement to Christian's house. I decided to try the back door, which only provided access to his place; the front door led to a shared hallway, where we might bump into someone else. I tapped on a window next to the door with my white cane a couple of times, and sooner than I expected, he was standing in the door frame looking out into the murky night. As soon as I saw his silhouette I strode forward into the light bathing his yard.

"I am Blind Justice, but fear not. As you know, you are morally strong and don't commit crimes against mankind, so you aren't about to receive retribution." As I spoke I proffered my épée to show him that I was serious, and we quickly entered his living room, where we sat on opposite sides of his coffee table. It wasn't decorated with fashionable books displaying voluptuously decorated homes but was littered with tobacco and cannabis paraphernalia. It also bore a variety of paperwork that reflected that he was a student of psychology who was as politically active as possible. He seemed surprisingly unworried considering that a psychotic killer had entered his home and was obviously carrying his weapon of choice.

"Can I get you or your hound some refreshments?" He pointed towards the kitchen, and as I gave him a negative reply he asked for permission to get himself something – a can of beer or at least a cup of tea. I granted him permission, wishing to show him my humanity despite the negative publicity in the media.

By the time he returned I'd rolled a couple of cigarettes and lit mine, leaving him one in the ashtray as a gift. He sat down, appearing comfortable, which was one reason I'd chosen to call on him at home rather than meet somewhere else.

"What can I do for you, my vigilante friend? I admire what you are doing, but I think you already know why you are here. Yes?" He seemed shockingly enthusiastic and friendly, and when we met before, I'd gotten the feeling he was sincere. I also felt that he was eager to do something that would make a difference and be noticed. Ideally he wanted a way to get himself in the history books.

"I need to get the support of the members of the Victim Aid Therapy group as they seemed to understand what I said about being abused as young and why I now want revenge. I'm sure I'll be caught soon or later, and then I'll need backup from everywhere available. I reckon we could record some interviews or chats about things and then post them on YouTube. We'd need to do it soon as I'm sure I'll be remanded when I'm caught, and there's always a long time till trial." I explained my idea to Christian, and he was happy with it.

"That seems a pretty good plan. The big question is do we conduct a spontaneous interview, or do we have a script to work with? I could let you know the questions beforehand so that you can at least have an idea of what you'll be talking about," Chris proposed while he rolled himself a spliff with some skunk.

I was more than familiar with alcohol but had never encountered cannabis on any of my adventures. I had found that sharing a drink with Mary had improved our relationship, and as weed is supposed to be a social drug, I asked if I could have one too. That was fine with Chris; having a smoke helped us get to know each other. I didn't tell him it was something new to me because I didn't want to appear naïve. The only thing he talked about that caused me uncertainty was the fact that he wanted to get a friend of his involved who could help record the videos and post them on the internet. It made sense to have another person operate the video camera while he and I were in front of the lens. He had a mate whom he trusted and had known for years, and he said he'd contact them in a day or two after we had sorted out a few details.

I was not familiar with 'the munchies', but it was certainly something I experienced there and then, so to bring the subject up I got some biscuits out for Willow, who was well behaved as always.

"Have you got something we can eat? Not a full meal, just some biscuits or something for us? I'll have that cup of tea now if that's alright." Looking around the living room, I got the impression that my host was a hoarder as there was hardly any wall visible. He had shelves of books, CDs and DVDs, and all over the walls were posters, postcards and old tickets with flyers.

With my cup of tea he obligingly provided some Garibaldi's, which seemed unbelievably chewy but quite tasty, which I attributed to the fact that I was a bit stoned.

"Okay. Now that we have made contact with each other and agreed on something, I think I'd better be heading off. I'll wait for you to get in touch with your mate; you can email me when you are ready with some questions. I'll think about what message I'm trying to get to people and how best to say it." I stood up with Willow and was glad that she could lead me back to the van as I was unfamiliar with the sensations of being stoned. It was a very educational experience, and I could see why it was so popular in modern culture. However, there were additional effects I became familiar with as I went out into the real world and had to deal with it by myself. The plan had been to change back to Mr Wilson in the van and then drive home, but this was before I had smoked cannabis. I didn't want to drive in the dark under the clouds of a stoned brain. We could have slept there in the van, but a clearing night sky lured us into walking home after abandoning Blind Justice in the van.

CHAPTER 39

Tracy was glad to have moved back home with Arthur as she was only really able to relax one hundred percent in her own place with him for company. He still didn't feel brilliant, but he was clearly well on his way to recovery. She had decided to buy him a treat, which wasn't the sort of thing she usually did. Catnip – some cats go absolutely mental for it, but some simply don't react at all. She knew from previous experience that it ticked the box for him, so she left the police station and bought a catnip toy at the supermarket, where she also bought herself a quality piece of fish and a bunch of flowers to give to her friend who had looked after her cat for a day or two. As she drove through the tiresome traffic she wondered about DS Peter and the automobiles in America. He was not a petrol-head, but he was a quite capable driver, and he had successfully taken part in chases in the past. Everything about America seemed to be bigger to her, and she wondered how he would handle the size of the drinks if he came across any. He may be alright and avoid them as she knew he was staying in a healthy fitness place.

She had agreed to call him later that day and would do so from home, but she was going to make sure she had Arthur on her lap first as it might be a long phone call.

"Julie, I bought you these flowers as a little 'thank you' for taking care of my beloved pussycat. I can't thank you enough." Tracy handed the bunch of blooms to her old school friend.

"You know I love cats, but because of all the traveling I do these days I can't have my own anymore," said Julie, who invited her long-time buddy in to see Arthur curled up sleeping on the windowsill.

They had a good long natter about a wide range of subjects over a cup of tea and some homemade cake – baking was one of Julie's talents. Their conversation ranged from American politics to the joys of living a rural life on the edge of moorlands. This was something that they could both relate to because when they first met they were both living in remote farmhouses.

"Okay, Arthur. It's time to get in your box, and we can go home," said Tracy as she picked him up and cuddled him while he hung in her hands like a rag doll. He seemed to know he was going home rather to the vet or some such place as he didn't resist.

It was past twilight when they pulled up outside Tracy's flat. They had seen a police car patrolling the area, not that they thought that Blind Justice would return, but it helped keep people's morale up. She first went in and let Arthur out of the box to explore his territory and get settled in again; then she got the shopping bag out of the car, locked the car and took the bag up to the kitchen. It was still early enough to put the pasta bake on and wrap the salmon steak in foil after drizzling it with flavoured olive oil and adding a little sea salt and freshly ground black pepper. Once these were in the oven she sat in her chair with a Tribute beer and called Peter. They would have over half an hour to talk before her supper was ready. She could then talk while stroking Arthur on her lap and rubbing under his chin.

"Hi, Pete. How are things going with you and Frankie?" She went straight to business as she was feeling more positive and energised by being at home with her favourite companion.

"Ma'am. He seems keen to stay in the States but wants to cross the continent and live on the West Coast. I'm sure we can get him to make a statement soon, in which he'll give us all we need to get a hold of his friend Michael Evans in New York. Through him we can then determine Blind Justice's identity and track him down in Tamarmouth. Has he been doing anything you're aware of, or is it still nice and quiet with you for now?" the DS asked, remembering how stressed she had seemed before he left. Just from her voice he got the impression she was feeling better, and he understood why when she explained she was at home with a good tasty beer, cooking a quality meal and tickling her critter's belly as he lay on his back with his paws up in the air.

"That sounds good, ma'am. Hopefully we can make a move on him before he does anything else and get him where he should be: behind bars in our custody. Then we can search his premises – this seems the kind of case where there won't be any trouble with evidence or the Crown Prosecution Service. Once we have this one I think he'll be going down for a fair stretch and quite possibly to Broadmoor with the other psychos. I'm enjoying it here in the US, and I'll definitely be coming back on holiday. Everything is just so big over here, it's like I'm looking through a magnifying glass." Peter talked with enthusiasm, and it made Tracy feel even better and more confident about what they were doing.

"Cheers, Peter. I've got to put together a handful of salad to go with my supper. Also put out something to satisfy my furry monster or he'll be after my salmon steak. Get the written statement as soon as you can, and we can also use a recorded video version. It should be alright to get the New York police to move in under 24 hours, and then the day after that we can make our move over here, and you should be able to get back and join us for it. It has been good work, and I'm happy with the way the team is these days." Tracy spoke as she gently pushed Arthur over her knees down to the floor. She then stood up and led the tiny tiger to the cupboard where his culinary delights were kept. Unlike most of the senior officers she didn't have any children and grandchildren to buy things for, so she spoiled him. She chose a can of terrine with salmon for him, and he could play with his catnip toy after they had eaten.

PART 4

CHAPTER 40

Willow and I left the van parked near Christian's flat and set off for a night-time walk, starting in less familiar streets than usual. I enjoyed looking at the constellations of the stars on a clear night if my vision was good, and Willow was always glad to have a walk, especially somewhere we were unfamiliar with. I used to take great pleasure in watching Sir Patrick Moore present 'The Sky at Night', and Professor Brian Cox on Horizon had a Northern charisma that was growing on me. I often read the horoscopes in the paper or a TV magazine because they amused me – I didn't think it meant anything. I'd enjoyed the total eclipse at Tamarmouth years ago when I was still driving local buses. Comets and shooting stars were good too, and I was disappointed I'd never seen the Northern Lights and probably never would now.

"This is good isn't it, Wills?" I encouraged her as we headed to the park between Christian's house and the town centre, which was probably the best way home. It felt safer in the dark now that the lights were upgraded to LEDs, and the CCTV was operative.

I felt physically abnormal; my senses were especially sensitive, so the stars were particularly twinkly, and the Milky Way seemed brighter than usual. After smoking the joint, all my senses were heightened, as was my emotional consciousness. As we wound our way along the footpath I became very aware of a couple of other people in the park and the nocturnal sounds of other life forms. I recognised the sounds of insects and an owl but wasn't sure if the barking noise was that of an urban fox as it didn't sound like any breed of dog I knew. We walked up the slope and arrived at the crest of the hill. One way was an avenue of lime trees, or we could take the route past the pond towards the cafe. Obviously that was closed at this time, but beyond it was a twenty-four-hour garage. I liked being able to buy a hot drink at any time, but the garage also sold alcohol all day, which I didn't approve of. I didn't think petrol stations should sell booze at all, really.

I got Willow to head towards the pond, and I wondered what, if anything, would be active there tonight. Also, a nearly full moon was rising, which I wanted to see reflected in the black-looking water. I remembered being a boy in the children's home, collecting frog spawn in a bucket to watch it develop and become tadpoles, then froglets. It was a pastime I'd engaged in with Rocket Queen in the limited free time we had. We had to stay on the grounds of the estate as we could only go out when escorted by an adult. Some people handle being restricted a lot better than others, it occurred to me. I knew I was better than Rocket Queen had been at coping with detention, but he was the one who could handle physical pain. It was why he'd let Mr Blackheart spank him rather than me on a number of occasions. We had been so close back then, and I don't think I've ever been so close to anybody else since.

I ambled with my dog to the stream, and we followed it to the pond. I decided to sit on a bench and have a cigarette while observing any wildlife at the pond for a drink. I knew the biggest visible crater on the moon was called Tycho. It was named after a Danish nobleman from the late 1500s. We enjoyed the tranquillity of the scene, and I didn't know it at the time, but it was the last period of real peace and quiet I'd have for a quite a while. I saw a few things swimming in the water, heard an amphibian croaking and saw a bat fly dipping down for a sip of water, causing ripples to spread out to the rushes at the far side.

Suddenly voices entered my consciousness, and I was aware of a couple strolling up the way I'd go down towards the twenty-four-hour shop at the filling station. They progressed at a snail's pace, holding hands and mumbling to each other. As they approached it became clear that they were teenagers. He wore jeans, a t-shirt and a smart leather hooded jacket, while she was in jeggings with a blouse or suchlike under a scruffy denim coat with loose threads at the cuffs. They didn't notice Willow and myself as they were only interested in each other. Soon they were pretty close, and by then he'd put his arm round her shoulders, and they lent their heads together to kiss passionately.

When I'd walked with my CPN, Jane, I'd mentioned the number of used condoms I saw lying in the streets these days. They were disgusting like the needles, but at least they were not as dangerous. We didn't think either were involved in my blindness episodes since they were so common that, if they did trigger a response, I'd lose my vision all the time. I began to feel embarrassed as the two moved closer to the bench while only looking at each other. They were embracing intimately while exploring each other's bodies through their clothing, so I coughed to alert them to my presence on the other side of a weeping willow tree across the pond. I pretended I was unaware of them as I stood up and spoke to Willow.

"Come on, buddy, time to go and get a hot chocolate for me and something for you. I think I need some fag papers too," I said as we returned to the pathway that cyclists could use. As we went around one side of the tree the youngsters moved round the other side and took up the bench. By the time I'd gotten halfway through my rollie I looked back and could see that they were lying together on the bench.

Intimacy. I'd never properly known since I'd been abused by a paedophile. He had corrupted my personality and made part of it into a psychotic cross-dressing vigilante. The rest of my personality was unaffected by it, but I had to deal with anxiety-induced blindness. I had so many problems, and I felt so lonely that I thought of travelling to visit Michelle in America to boost my morale. The other appealing option, which I considered again and again over the years, was suicide. However, I'd gotten through the Christmas season, and everyone was cheered up as spring approached, and there was more light in the daytime. Also, I now had Mary, and she was a light at the end of the tunnel getting brighter and brighter. I'd call her tomorrow and try and organise a trip to see a film or go to a museum or art gallery together and absorb some of her positive energy. I hoped she felt about me as I did about her.

I left the park and crossed one of the main roads to Tamarmouth's city centre, which was peaceful at this time on a weekday morning, and an odd delivery truck and a rare taxi were the only vehicles around. Willow and I went to the attendant's hatch and got a Costa hot chocolate and a packet of green papers for me and a bag of Frazzles for her because those are the closest thing to pork scratchings. We headed back to my flat along more familiar streets to have a bite to eat before going to bed. I recalled when Mary escorted us back there. I hoped she hadn't been too freaked out by my blindness and what I told her about my history in the children's home. God, I hated Mr Blackheart for what he done to me and my life. I felt gratitude to Rocket Queen just as strongly, and I wanted to find a way to express it. I didn't think there was a method to release my anger at the bastard who had screwed up my life and probably done the same to many other unfortunate kids. We were victims, unseen by society.

CHAPTER 41

The Skype session had gone well, and Pete got the impression that Frankie would trust his boss, and they could use Mr Goldberg's knowledge of international law, the CIA and other useful information to their advantage. What Peter had to do now was get Frankie to write and sign a statement. He would then read it aloud so they would have a recorded version on video. Once they had that, the CIA could progress with assigning him his new identity and moving him to the West Coast.

The details about Michael Evans could be given to the NYPD, as it would include his description and address, so they could raid his apartment and investigate his laptop for details regarding Blind Justice. That may not include his actual address but with the help of a computer technician, they could determine it using the email account. Once they did that, the data would be passed on to DI Hansard so she could set up surveillance and determine his identity. During that period Pete would fly back to England, and they'd be ready to arrest Public Enemy Number One in Devon.

When Pete had seen Frankie earlier that day they had set up a meeting for later in the day. Pete was now in his room with everything he needed for the interview. He'd type everything on his laptop and then read it back to Frankie. If he was happy with it the interview would be printed in the office, and the two of them would sign and date it. Either then or later, if Frankie wanted a break, he'd read through it aloud so they'd have it on file.

Pete wondered why he was still alone as Frankie had seemed keen to get on with it now, and the meeting should have started a few minutes ago. He remembered seeing Frankie talking to a male and female couple at lunch, and they had passed him a mobile phone. He had used it to talk to someone. This made him suspicious as Frankie usually hung out with single men. Did they know him? Who had been on the other end of the line?

Pete waited for another five minutes, but there was still no sign of Frankie, so he decided to find out who the people he had been talking to were. The first thing to do was to use the information he could get from the retired Marine who had organised the boot camp. He went to the office and asked the person on duty where Mr MacBride was. At this time, it was early evening.

"He went in to town to pick up some kit. Have you got his mobile number?" The woman at the desk, like most people at the establishment, had a good figure due to regular exercising but had a fuller figure than most UK residents.

"No, I haven't. Can you either give it to me or call him yourself?" Pete asked as he took his mobile out of tracksuit jacket pocket.

"I'll ring him." She picked up the handset from the cordless phone and made the connection by pressing just two buttons.

"Thanks, love." Pete realised that there was still no sign of Frankie; if he had knocked on the door of Pete's room, Pete would have seen him.

"Okay, Scott? Mr Anderson wants a word with you…Here he is." She passed the handset over the counter to Peter.

"Hi…No, nothing wrong, but I could use a chat with you when you get back in…I'll see you then…I'll be in my room." Pete arranged a meeting for about seven o'clock.

"Thanks." He gave the phone back to the woman and hobbled back to his room, thinking that the broken ankle was a convincing cover story, but he was glad he wasn't in pain, just the discomfort of wearing the plaster cast.

He realised that it was quite later in the UK, but he wanted to talk to one of his family members to tell them he was alright and looking forward to seeing them again. It was Friday night in England, so he guessed his sister would still be up. She'd be watching a film or enjoying a romantic meal with Gary or Phil. She might be in bed by now, depending on which boyfriend she was with. He realised he'd not spoken to his mum much recently, so he chose to call her.

"Mum…Yeah, I'm having a good time. How are you guys?…Cold? Yeah, I know." She told him about the latest events in Tamarmouth, especially those relating to family and friends. They talked for a bit, and then he said that he hoped to be flying back in a couple of days. "Good night. Sleep well, Mum."

A knock on the door told him that Scott MacBride was ready to talk to him. The knock, like the man himself, was a thing not to be messed with. As he opened the door, he said that he thought they should go to the office for a few reasons. One was that there was a wall with a board with passport-type photos of staff and clients, as the others were called. Pete's plan was to use this to identify the people whom he'd seen with Frankie. Then he could find out who they were and what Scott knew about them.

He pointed out Antonio Romano and Jane Knox from the rogues gallery, and immediately Scott said that they were a couple and had come from New York City, but so had most people there. The thing that struck Peter was they were both a considerable number of years older than Frankie, so between them they probably knew a number of people in the LGBTQ community. Thus, it was feasible that they knew Frankie partner, and they might well be of the same generation as him. Pete considered the situation and elected to leave the couple alone for now so as not to raise suspicion and instead find Frankie. They knew he was still on site somewhere, they just needed to find and talk to him. Another reason Pete had wanted to meet in the office was because the CCTV was run from there. He asked Scott to activate the feed to the screen to see if they could find their target. Just as Peter was beginning to get a little nervous a camera in the Quiet Room picked up Frankie in the room by himself. It was a room most clients rarely used. It was only big enough for a few people to sit comfortably and was typically used for meditation or private prayer by visitors who were spiritual or religious. Close up it appeared that Frankie had been crying. Pete considered whether he should wait to see what the man would do next or visit him in the room; he chose the latter. There were beverage facilities in that space, so the two of them could have cups of tea and a relaxed chat. Peter explained to Mr MacBride what he was going to do and asked him to somehow ensure that Antonio and Jane didn't interrupt them.

As he limped across the courtyard to the block with the Quiet Room, Pete tried to imagine what the couple might have said to Frankie and wondered how he would feel if he had to 'grass' on one of the first people he'd really cared about who wasn't a family member. It was all very alien to him as he'd always had a lot of family support, unlike Frankie. He approached the room's door and saw that it was ajar, with ambient music easing out from within.

"Aaah…There you are, Frankie…" Pete greeted him in a calm, non-accusing way and shuffled in, heading towards the coffee table. "Fancy a cup of something? I'm a tea-lover, being British, so that's what I'm having."

He had turned his back towards Peter when he came in, but he now recognised the voice and accent and faced him, wiping the smears from his cheeks. "Why does life have to be so bloody difficult? I wish it were like a computer game so you could choose a difficulty level and play easy till you were familiar with everything. Maybe even go back and try other ways of doing things, put it all on pause to give yourself time to think and check the instruction manual. Ya get me?"

"I see what you are saying, yeah." Pete had felt similar things but wouldn't express it like that. "I wasn't spying on you, but I saw that couple from the city talking to you earlier. Does this have anything to do with them?"

"Yes. They know Rocket Queen, and they talked on the phone with him and myself. They've known him pretty well for quite a while, and they've seen him at his best and at his worst. Reckon if he loses me he'll get depressed and hit the drink again. Almost killed him last time."

Peter sat down with his cuppa, leaving the tea bag in since he couldn't see a bin anywhere. "Obviously this is about you and him, but you've got to remember what is happening in England. There have been four brutal murders, at least...It won't stop till he gets caught."

"I know. That's why I need to bite the bullet. We've got to go and make this statement...I'm pretty tired now. Can we leave it till tomorrow morning? How about if I get up early and tell people I'm going on my first run of the day? I'll come to your room, and we can do it over a good coffee and a Danish or muesli."

"Okay." Pete looked at his watch, knowing the seconds and minutes would drag like a nasty root canal in ultra-slow motion. "I'll be ready at six in mine."

CHAPTER 42

After talking with Christian in such a cool environment as his flat, I felt that things were taking an encouraging step forward, especially if we could conduct a decent interview and have his pal record it. It would be pretty easy for us to get it to go viral, we reckoned. I got out the files I'd stolen from the Victim Aid Therapy office at the university. Each member of the group had their own file. Each file had the individual's information sheet, containing contact details and a summary of their history. Looking at the handwriting, it seemed each individual had filled out their sheet themselves. However, what I found really interesting was that the pages also all had writing in the same hand, which I assumed was Ian's. They were basically blank pages that were dated and consisted of post-interview notes. Thus, they had details specific to each history. To be fair to Christian, I put his aside to destroy later. To keep as much information as possible Ian had scribbled down almost everything that was said and then seemed to have gone back and annotated it with a red Biro to show what he deemed significant.

I did something similar but used a highlighter pen to emphasise personal connections. For example, "my uncle abused me" and "raped by St John's choir master." These gave me things to look into and try to track down. Many of the events had happened a long time ago and all across the country, but by filtering, I identified a few local incidents. Most had occurred enough years ago that the victims could now talk about it. Moreover, the offenders were probably elderly now and might offer little resistance if I could find them.

I really liked my smartphone and the internet access it supplied. I preferred Samsung rather than Apple. "We like underdogs don't we, Willow?" I talked to her to keep her happy as she was the only friend I had in this country. I wondered what was going on in America with Frankie and Rocket Queen. As I was thinking about past and present events I was reminded of how old Willow was. Man's best friend doesn't have man's life span. Police and guide dogs retire after a few years of active service. She had done so much for me; I had to make arrangements for her future. I didn't know, but I imagined I'd be caught eventually, after which she'd probably be sent to a local dogs' home. I wanted to make better plans. I couldn't help remembering the death of Hitler. He shot his hounds and then himself when the Russians closed in on the bunker. If I could steady my resolve I'd be able to go out with a bang, set things up for a media circus with police marksmen, my victim, myself and her. I just had to find somebody in the files and create pre-recorded statements and explanations with Christian and his associate.

I was glad to see how quickly I got the email saying the three of us could record using a portable video camera that had a quality microphone built in. I could get Christian and his friend to join me in the flat. That was probably the best option as I could be in my full Blind Justice outfit with my companion who was seeming a bit worn out these days. I could reveal and share my world, say who I was, what had happened to me and why I did what I did. Then I could embark on my final mission and catch whomever I'd been able to find via the files. I reckoned that at least two abusers described were still residents in Tamarmouth: one in a nursing home and the other living alone. I had to work out how to get into each of their homes. I didn't want to upset those who supported me by unnecessarily stressing out uninvolved people such as care workers. That would make a black mark against my name, which was clearly respected for radical morality. I was just doing the job the police and justice system should be doing but weren't able to. It had become increasingly obvious that the public wanted to get rid of child abusers, and many thought that life sentences were too good for most of them. Even a life in Broadmoor was better than they deserved. Prison life was too easy for them, so instead of the taxpayers wasting their money as they lived out their pension years in warm comfortable cells, I'd execute them.

To be honest I expected to be shot by the police in a final stand, but I couldn't help wondering what would happen if I were caught and taken to trial – 'Blind Justice goes to the Old Bailey to meet Lady Justice'. 'Mr and Mrs Justice in London'. All sorts of possible headlines in the newspapers; the situation had immense potential to spark human rights activism, justice reform and a re-evaluation of social values.

Still, now I had to think about the interviews and my next victim. I told Christian I needed to meet our technician, Kevin, as soon as I could to break the ice and make sure he was suitable to work with. By following histories, comparing dates and employing a process of elimination, it seemed a member of the VAT support group was living by himself had been molested by his football coach when he was in a local youth club. They were connected to the Tamarmouth Pilgrims Football Club and had been to court in the past. The charges were dropped, but clearly everyone was convinced that the man was guilty. It led to his early retirement and a decline into a lonely isolated life in a council flat. He probably never went out these days because he could shop via the internet and have everything delivered to his door. He'd pass the time watching dirty videos, remembering playing football with appealing innocent boys and wondering about repentance and karma.

I arranged for Kevin to call in at my place for a chat on his way back from work. It was then that he explained aspects of recording and the use of the social media to get the interviews out into the world. He worked at the local theatre in the technical department and had completed a degree in a related field. Therefore, he was qualified and had experience conducting live recordings. I must admit I was a bit anxious because I considered him the weakest link in the chain. Christian knew him from their school days; that's where they had met. They weren't best friends, but they had done a number of things together, like camping trips and protest marches, so they knew each other well. Trust was a definite issue in my life and always had been ever since I met Mr Blackhurst. The only serious trust I had these days was in a drag queen who lived hundreds of miles away and a decrepit old Labrador. I was sitting looking at my Samsung phone, wondering what the police were up to and if they had any real leads, when I heard the doorbell ring. I had a sticker in the window saying I didn't want any cold callers, but considering the time, I guessed that Kevin must have finished work early. It was Friday, so he might well be going out to see a band or maybe doing some extra work as a roadie technician. It flashed into my mind that with the economy being what it was, I might be able to pay Kevin and thus feel more secure about his services and security.

I used the automated door release after I'd confirmed it was him so that I didn't have to answer the door in my full outfit. He was dressed as I imagined he'd be based on what Christian had said about him: well-worn black leather boots and jacket, old blue jeans and an Iron Maiden t-shirt. He was carrying a webbing rucksack, which held his electricity tool box, a light meter, a notebook and a pen. He seemed more stressed than Christian had been when I'd visited him, but I could understand that.

It didn't take him long to work out what lighting apparatus he wanted and where we would all be positioned in the living room, including Willow. He told me about a couple of networks he was involved with that focused on spreading subservient news. They did a lot to try to disrupt the North Korean government, the Chinese communist state and white supremacy movements. He would use them to get our films around the world in a very short period of time. After he'd chosen the lighting, determined our positions and told me about the previous projects he'd been involved with I was much happier, and he was pleased to know he could earn a few hundred pounds. He had a partner he lived with and two kids who lived with his ex, which meant he lived life on a tight budget.

CHAPTER 43

Tracy was very pleased with the information Peter had gotten Frankie to include in the statement as she was sure the NYPD would soon make a move, considering the seriousness of the case. They had a good description of Michael Evans, known as Rocket Queen, and his address. Now they just had to seize his computer, which would give them all they needed to identify Blind Justice. In the meantime, her sergeant could fly back to England and join her and the authorised firearms officers to make a move on their target. She needed to contact the lieutenant in charge of the operation in America and familiarise herself with who he was and let him know the situation. In fact, after thinking about it, she decided it would probably be best if Peter could do it as it wasn't too far away, and he'd be glad to get the cast off his foot even though it had worked well as a cover story.

She checked the time and felt it was a reasonable hour to try to talk to Peter about the next steps in the investigation. She still didn't feel comfortable using Skype, so she called him on her mobile.

"Peter, thanks for what you have done. I've been thinking, and I reckon you should leave the boot camp soon and get back to New York City so you can be with the cops when they move in on Rocket Queen." She was feeling excited. She was sure it was just a matter of time now. They had all the pieces; they simply had to fit them all together. Thinking about the famous speech by Churchill, she was sure they had passed the end of the beginning and had now reached the beginning of the end. She felt that the result was inevitable now.

"Okay, ma'am. Do you want me to stay in touch with Frankie or shall I leave that all to the CIA? They are sending an agent over today to talk to us, so once they are in touch with Frankie we can leave it to them to sort out his new identity and so on." Pete felt a bit sorry for Frankie and his position, but he could see that he'd be able to make a clean break and then follow it with a fresh start in LA, so all wasn't lost.

"See if Frankie and his CIA contact hit it off. Remember we have Mr Goldberg here, and he can fly to the States and work on our behalf. He hasn't met Frankie as such, but they were fine talking to each other via Skype." Tracy was keen to do all she could to support Frankie as she considered him a victim of the crimes, but in a different way to the others.

"Sure thing. I found out a bit more about Rocket Queen from a couple who are also at the boot camp. They have known him for years and reckon he might commit suicide if he loses Frankie, which he obviously will. Maybe drink himself to death, they were saying, knowing what he has done in the past." Peter explained what he'd gotten from Antonio and Jane, which Tracy found rather depressing because it meant another victim made to suffer due to the crimes committed by Blind Justice. She finished the conversation with Peter and wondered about contacting the New York Lieutenant based at the 10th Precinct at 230 West 20th Street. She decided she might as well break the ice, and then if she found out anything useful, she could pass it on to Peter later. She had wrongly assumed it was going to be a male officer, so she was a bit surprised when a woman's voice answered the call after it was put through by the switchboard.

"Hi! Lt O'Neil here; is that Detective Inspector Tracy Hansard in England?" The voice was strong and had a distinct New York accent.

"Yeah, that's right. Have you seen the statement my sergeant got from the informant, Frankie, at the boot camp? He will be leaving there soon to join you and your officers when you arrest the suspect, Michael Evans, also known as Rocket Queen." She got straight down to business as she felt there wasn't any time to waste.

"That's fine. Sergeant Peter Anderson, isn't it? It's best if he just watches since he won't be armed unless we sort out a short-term permit." Lt O'Neil seemed to be pretty well informed about what was happening.

"Yes, he's not an authorised firearms officer anyway. What can you tell me about the housing at the address you've been given? Is it likely to be big apartments in a skyscraper or are we talking a brownstone terraced house with people sharing each place?" Tracy had no idea but guessed that the address would say a lot about its resident.

"Yeah, I'll check. It is probably a terraced house with about four floors and reasonable-sized apartments, which are shared. Maybe they have been split into smaller apartments so they'll be alright for an individual. To be honest that's what I think we'll find. I imagine we are dealing with a bit of a loner, but not as bad as yours." Lt O'Neil made it clear that she knew why the information was being collected and what was happening in England.

"Thanks. If you let my sergeant stay with the computer while it is accessed, he can get the information on Blind Justice as soon as possible. I don't suppose we will make an arrest till Peter is back, but we can start surveillance at least." Tracy explained and was glad she'd chosen to contact Lt O'Neil as she felt the two of them were similar.

"I've got to go and attend a briefing now. I guess I'll meet your sergeant tonight, and we can move in early the next morning. Okay?" Lt O'Neil spoke while checking her sidearm in her handbag and brushing down her uniform. Once she heard Tracy hang up, she applied a fresh touch of lippy.

Despite the fact that it was early evening Tracy thought it would be worth getting a few hours' sleep if she could since she'd need to be ready for action the next day in the UK as that was when Peter and Julie would go to Rocket Queen's apartment in the wee small hours. She'd at least be able to relax even if she couldn't sleep because she'd learnt some techniques about 'power-napping' and meditating. She wished she could catnap like Arthur; she was jealous of him in a couple of ways.

CHAPTER 44

I hadn't been apart from Frankie for so long – since we decided to begin a relationship – and I was feeling very lonely. I wanted the two of us to go out and get drunk, but I knew that was out of the question till after he'd run his marathon, so I opted for a retail therapy session ASAP once he returned. Till then I'd had to settle for a talk with my oldest friend for an ego boost and hear him tell me about the tadpoles he'd seen when out in the park the other day. This time I used the phone as I had plans to use my computer while we talked.

"How are you doing regarding your video diary or whatever you are doing to record your activities for posterity?" I asked him.

"I've found people who will work with me, and I've got an idea of what to say. We just need to do it now. That's always the hard bit, you know what I mean?" he replied, explaining the situation to me. "I had an interesting evening the other day – I got a bit stoned with Christian, the guy who's going to operate the camera for me. I'd rather go for a bit of Dutch courage for the filming, though."

"Yes, I get what you're saying. I'd go for a line or two of coke or speed to get my confidence up or a blue or two to help me chill out and overcome my nerves." These things were easy to get down at the LGBTQ clubs here, but not in

Tamarmouth. I knew he wouldn't be interested anyway. It was one of the reasons I lived in the America and he was still in England. "No news from your nemesis, DI Tracy Hansard, yet? Poisoning her cat has probably got her too scared to move these days." I cajoled him with a bit of banter as we had done since we were kids.

I couldn't admit it, but it was at times like these that I was jealous of him and his loyal canine companion. A dog can have a significant effect on one's morale when one lives alone in a flat in a big lonely city. Even if it were just a pygmy Chihuahua, it would be there to talk to and play with. I knew many people took their dogs out for walks; it was a way to break the ice when meeting new people, and that was one reason he had a dog. Obviously, he had Willow for his blindness episodes too, but responsibility was far more his thing than mine.

"How are you doing with your trick cyclist and sorting out your vision?" I asked him because I wanted him to join me and Frankie in America for our wedding, but I hadn't mentioned it to anyone yet. My goal was to propose to Frankie and have Mark Wilson come over with Willow to be my best man at the wedding ceremony. "Can you stay online while I call Frankie using my laptop? I want to talk to the two of you together while you are both hundreds of miles away." It seemed a good idea at the time, but by then I'd had a few drinks because I'd been lonely and felt that if I proposed to Frankie while he knew we were being listened to he was would be more likely to agree.

"Don't take too long. I'm tired, and I've a lot to do tomorrow with Christian and Kevin." Blind Justice sounded drained, and I wondered if he ever drank energy drinks loaded with caffeine and glucose. I knew Frankie did, especially now that he was in the last week or two of marathon training, and would use them on the day of the race.

"Here we go – I'm just calling him up on Skype with my laptop. He's expecting a call, so he should be waiting now." I told him what I was up to, but didn't mention my plan to propose.

"Hi, Frankie. I'm having a chat with BJ on my mobile as I've got something I want you both to hear." I couldn't be sure where Frankie was or if he had any company at the time, but assumed he was alone somewhere at the boot camp.

"Greetings to you both. How are you feeling these days?" Frankie replied casually, but I sensed he might not be alone.

"I'm talking to you both because I want to put forth an idea to you, the two most important people in my life… Frankie, you said you'd marry me, so can we set a date for a month or two's time so we can make arrangements, including having Mark come over with Willow and be my best man." I came straight out with it. My inhibitions had been washed away with glasses of Jack Daniels and Coke. I saw Frankie frown quickly, but then he hid his face behind a paper cup, which had a familiar logo on it. I focussed my attention on the handset and heard a voice asking Willow what she thought about going to America.

"Willow, at last we might be going away to enjoy the land of the free. I think that would be good for us. I think I'll need a new passport, and maybe it's time to sell a few things to raise some money." There was definite enthusiasm to be heard, but Frankie seemed speechless, and he looked partially upset.

"There's nothing wrong is there? Are you okay, Frankie?" I wondered what was on Frankie's mind; he wasn't reacting as I'd expected.

"Sorry, buddy. I've been too involved with my training, and I've heard a lot of HIV horror stories from people here at this camp. A few hate crimes from guys and girls who used to live in the homophobic deep South; I didn't realize how bad people could be. Only now am I understanding how lucky we are to live where we do." Frank's explanation made sense, but

I wanted to talk to Antonio and Jane about what he had been up to.

However, I was glad to see that there was enthusiasm on the other side of the pond. I hadn't thought about it till then, but I don't suppose my friend had left England since he returned from the Channel Islands. As I considered his life it, seemed pretty pitiful that he had never managed to leave the past behind and go out and explore the world.

CHAPTER 45

D S Peter Anderson was very glad to leave the boot camp as he was sick of the participants. He was also very relieved when he was able to get rid of the plaster cast on his foot. To be honest, he'd be glad to leave behind the US and return to his family, friends and work companions. He did like the American dream, but at times it was a bit overwhelming for a small-town boy from Devon. It seemed funny, but he'd be glad to have a paper cup of watery tea in his office, and he was looking forward to talking to DI Tracy face to face.

One thing still had to be taken care of, though, and in a way it was the riskiest and most dodgy part of the whole operation in New York. He had to meet up with Lt Julie O'Neil, and they had to make a move on Michael Evans, Rocket Queen. He was one weak link in a chain that led to the killer, Blind Justice. As far as Peter could tell, it was the part that was most likely to go wrong. He knew he'd feel responsible if things went wrong in America even if it wasn't his fault. He had seen all the TV series where they storm in, guns blazing, and before anyone knows what happened the suspects are lying dead, with cops standing around, wondering just what had started the shootout. There certainly was a very different attitude towards guns in America than in Great

Britain. Firearms are part of the American way, but that's not the case in England, and Pete was very glad of that. He knew guns didn't kill people; other people did that. However, the acceptance of guns was part of the culture in the States. It wasn't good; he knew what his sister and mum thought about it. He considered getting in touch with them but decided to leave it till after he'd finished the last part of the job. They would just worry, and then he'd get stressed about that.

He took a train to Grand Central Station just so he could brag about it to his dad and other masculine companions such as Phil or Gary (depending on whom Kathy was seeing). He was met at the station by a member of the NYPD who escorted him to a car. They then drove to the precinct headquarters and found that a briefing about to start. He had spoken to Lt O'Neil before and was quickly introduced to her first. He knew he was just there to watch and be a witness. Looking at the sizes of the officers, with their weapons and body armour, he felt a bit intimidated; he couldn't imagine what it would be like for a perpetrator.

He thought about what they knew regarding this Rocket Queen character. He'd been at a children's home in Jersey and had made friends with a lad called Blind Justice in those days. Something about their friendship seemed to convey that they had total trust in each other. They had probably helped each other survive in one way or another. With no other family members to turn to, they would have just had each other. Peter remembered what Frankie had said regarding Rocket Queen talking about those days. Abuse seemed the most likely thing. Not that long ago there had been cases in the news regarding Sir Jimmy Saville and other famous celebrities who had thought they were above the law but had since come crashing down.

"Sergeant Peter Anderson? Do you think you are ready? Do you have anything you'd like to say to the men before we set off for the apartment?" Lt O'Neil asked from behind her desk in the office that consisted of a glass box, which enabled her to see and be seen if she wanted, but the blinds were closed now.

"I suppose I'm just concerned that our target will be killed or seriously injured, so we won't get to talk to him. Guns and killing are much more accepted here than in England," Pete explained, but he also knew that the required information would be on the computer in the residence.

"We know that this person isn't responsible for the murders, just a lifelong friend of the killer. In fact, we know from our records that he doesn't have a gun license, so it shouldn't be a problem." Lt O'Neil did what she could to reassure DS Anderson.

Peter couldn't believe how similar it was to the episodes of Hill Street Blues he had been inspired by as a kid. He almost expected to see Captain Furillo come around the corner talking to Sergeant Esterhauser. The uniforms with the 'To serve and protect' logo and the New York accent made it all feel a bit unreal, like he was on a film set.

Three cars were dispatched on the job, two with standard pairs of officers and one with an officer who was considerably more experienced than his 'rookie' partner. An additional vehicle had Peter and the lieutenant in, and they led the way through the streets of this famous city towards the darker corners, which the tourists were glad not to see. It was the same in every city, really. But one didn't have to look too far to find the real people with the real problems.

The cruisers, without any sirens or lights, headed down the long well-lit roads of central New York towards a waterfront area. Using the radio, they organised one car to go to the back of the block to block any escape attempt, but since it was so early in the morning, that was pretty unlikely. As they approached the building, Peter remembered what Frankie had told him about the good times he'd had with Michael Evans when they had first met and fallen in love.

"Okay. Here we are. We can get in the block, and we'll go up to the third floor, where his apartment is. We will smash the door in, and these guys know what they are doing. Some of New York's finest and most experienced guys. I doubt we will even need to fire a shot as he will probably be in bed, out cold," the lieutenant explained to Peter, and they made their way up the stairs. "You just stand in the background until we have gone in and secured everything. We will at least get the computer, and I don't think it will take long for our tech guys to get the required info."

Peter recognised what the cops in England called an enforcer: a manual battering ram that would be used to break open the apartment door by one officer to allow the others to go streaming in and overpower any resistance. Remembering his conversations with Frankie, he imagined what it had been like when the two of them had first come here together and how different the situation was now. Just as Peter was reflecting on the situation, the officer carrying the enforcer got the nod from his sergeant and smashed the door off its hinges, allowing the others to move in.

As Peter had expected the apartment was not particularly anything, just average. Indeed, Michael Evans would have seemed just as average if it hadn't been for all the women's clothes in his wardrobes and drawers. There was also a sizeable collection of makeup items in front of the mirror at the dressing table, which was where he was sitting when the police burst in.

"Everybody freeze!...Don't move – this is New York police," the leading officer shouted as he waited for his colleagues to secure the other rooms.

"Aaah...Oh my God...What the fuck is going on?" Michael Evans was clearly flustered and in a panic.

The police could now arrest and charge Michael Evans, aka Rocket Queen, and confiscate his computer. However, if he gave them the information they wanted immediately, arrest wouldn't be necessary. He had no real reason to try and protect Blind Justice, and when he found out what had happened regarding Frankie he didn't think there was even much reason for living.

CHAPTER 46

Tracy was thinking about what she would do for a holiday after she'd completed this case. She knew that these days some people took their pets with them on holiday. Would Arthur like a trip to the countryside? He could discover all the wildlife. Maybe she could even take a sailing trip on the Norfolk Broads or hire a longboat on the canal as that kind of thing always seemed to be so slow and relaxed. She felt that they'd deserve a very relaxed time, and depending on how things went with the court case and the Crown Prosecution Service, she might start thinking about eventually retiring.

She was just fantasising about sunbathing on the deck of a Bermudian sloop with Arthur and a cocktail when the phone rang. This was it. She'd told them not to put any other calls through to her office. She was in a secure environment, but she felt nervous, which was uncharacteristic, especially when she was alone, as she had been most of her life. As she said to Arthur, she talked to herself when she was alone so that she could ensure an intelligent conversation.

"Hello...Yes, put the American call through." She was going to talk to Peter about how things had gone.

"Okay, boss. We've got him. Yes, he has told us what we wanted to know, and we are just confirming the details by comparing them with the information on his computer. I don't think it will take very long – he was feeling lonely and was blown away by us turning up on his doorstep." Peter explained the situation and sounded very relieved that it was time to head back to England.

"Right then, Pete. You just get yourself back home ASAP... I'll set up a surveillance team on Blind Justice once we have his address confirmed...You say his real name is Mark Wilson? Do you have a date of birth?" Tracy was talking a lot faster than usual, and it was obvious that she wanted to get this criminal under observation at least. She'd be feeling a lot more comfortable now that she had him in her sights.

"Ma'am, I'll be back in Tamarmouth and ready for action in under twenty-four hours. That gives you time to set up surveillance and get the gun squad briefed and prepared. Also, I think you'll want to read the information the police here will be sending you." Peter imagined her back in her office with a picture of Arthur on the desk and her mug of hot sweet tea steaming away.

She just had to get through the next night while her sergeant returned to London; then he would fly to Exeter and take a train from there to Tamarmouth. She called up the detectives on duty that day and told them the address for Mark Wilson, showed them the portrait photo, which had been confiscated from Michael Evans's apartment in New York and was the best picture they had of him. However, it was a picture of Blind Justice wearing a party outfit, an extensive supply of makeup and an extravagant hair piece; it was surprising how different the two looked. One ordinary-looking gentleman and one flamboyant psychotic transvestite. Two very different sides of the same coin.

Using the data she had received from Detective Anderson she found out all she could about Mark Wilson by checking his criminal record and National Insurance history. He had been in Tamarmouth most of his life, ever since he had arrived from the children's home in Jersey. That was where he had met Michael Evans, who had gone on to become Rocket Queen and then successfully emigrated to the United States. He seemed to have pretty much just lived his life by himself, working for years as a bus driver, until he retired for medical reasons. He had then been on the sick payment for a number of years, and spent a lot of time with his guide dog. He had probably had psychiatric issues ever since he lost both parents in a car crash. Back in the 60s bereavement therapy was unheard-of. It was a time of British stiff upper lips; boys and men didn't cry or show emotional weakness. Child abuse was largely institutionalised by the Catholic Church and the Department of Education. Nasty, unpleasant things were done to children because they were thought to build character, despite actually being rather soul destroying.

DI Tracy Hansard was beginning to get an idea of who this person she was chasing was. Or at least who the two characters who made up the physical entity were. She could understand the letter she had received from him a little better now. She decided to contact Pete's buddy, Professor Larsson, as these sort of mental conditions were his speciality, so he might be able to help, and she guessed he would certainly be interested in conducting a case study. Fortunately, he wasn't too busy at that moment, so he came over to her office almost immediately and said he'd be very keen to help the investigation and also give the individual an in-depth psychological examination.

"Welcome, Professor, come in and sit down. Yes, we haven't actually got him in custody yet, but we have an address and an identity. We're just waiting for Peter to return home, and then we'll make an arrest. Is there anything you think I should know regarding split personalities? All my information so far comes from Wikipedia." Inspector Tracy was confused about how two or more identities could exist together in a single body and yet be totally oblivious of one another.

"Okay, Inspector. Well it is certainly a complicated subject, and there has only been a limited amount of research done so far. This is why I'm keen to meet your subject, Blind Justice, and his other identities; he could be very helpful in this field of psychological research, which is also related to psychiatry. The trauma of losing the two parents in the violent way he did is characteristic of such cases. The shock is too much for the child's personality to handle, so the identity breaks into separate parts. It's hard to explain...I do have a book here that I can lend you that explains it well. *A Fractured Mind: My Life with Multiple Personality Disorder*, by Robert Oxnam. He explains it from the inside as he had the condition himself." The professor took the worn, dogeared paperback from his Tamarmouth University bag and gave it to Tracy. "Fortunately, none of his personalities become very aggressive or violent. He has written it for lay people rather than scientists, so he hasn't used jargon or complicated medical phraseology." The professor was definitely an asset, and she imagined he could be a professional witness for the prosecution when the case went to trial.

CHAPTER 47

I woke up and realized it was a lot later than I usually got up. I remembered that I'd walked home late with Willow; I'd overslept. I recalled walking in the park, seeing the teenagers and deciding to contact Mary. I'd have to get up and have breakfast before phoning Mary to invite her for a coffee or something.

"Good morning, Willow. How are you today?" I spoke, and I could hear a lively note in my voice that wasn't usually there. I looked out and saw the blue sky with some picturesque fluffy white clouds flying past in a strong wind. The seagulls were screeching; I didn't usually like them – in fact I often hated them – but not today. I had an instant coffee after getting dressed, and just because I could, I decided to walk to town with Willow to have a cooked breakfast. A change is as good as a rest, so I'd do things differently today.

We set off with an inexplicable vigour, and despite having my cane, we made rapid progress to the city centre. We took an uncommon route in, walking beside the sea for quite a ways. Mary and I had both enjoyed watching the sea on Christmas day, and it occurred to me that perhaps we could catch the ferry to France for a weekend. I hadn't done anything more adventurous than take the ferry to Torpoint recently, so felt it time to do something radical. I could show Mary that I still had a passion for life, which she was boosting. I saw the large floating hotel that was arriving from Spain and had all sorts of wild dreams and images in my head about what we could do together.

We arrived at Captain Jasper's for brunch and enjoyed the world of renowned food, which I washed down with a hot sweet tea. Like many of the best restaurants these days it had a water bowl for dogs, so Willow wasn't thirsty either after eating my crispy bacon rind.

I was still a person of the older generation who managed to get by without a mobile phone, but after seeing the prices in the January sales and thinking about Mary with hers and remembering what my CPN had said, I thought I'd have to get one. It occurred to me that Mary could help me figure out how to use it as she had been given a phone by her daughter over Christmas. So, it was time to call her via a phone box.

"Hi! Good morning, Mary, it's Mark...Yes, I'm feeling much better today. Thanks. It's a beautiful sunny day, and I'm out having a walk with Willow; I feel I owe you something after that incident at the tea dance when you got me home." I felt guilty for messing up the event and was wondering what she'd appreciate as compensation.

"Mark? Oh, yes...I didn't recognise the phone number, but I know it's a Tamarmouth one...A box, not your landline as I have that in my phone's memory. Yes, the weather is looking better than I expected today. How about we check out the new retail park at Endsleigh for some gardening things because that fits in with my New Year's resolution? There's supposed to be a good teashop there too." Mary had plenty of energy, which I could feel through the phone, and I liked the idea of visiting the garden centre. Usually the only green things I grew in my flat was mould.

"Okay, yeah Mary. Shall we meet there, or do you want to join me and Willow here in town first? You'll get a lift from your daughter and then take a bus back probably..." We organised our rendezvous, and I hung up feeling pleased with things so far. I'd have time to get there first and find us a comfortable table at the tearoom.

Mary was already at her daughter's house when she received the phone call from Mark Wilson. She regularly went to see Alison, her one child who lived in town, on Saturday mornings; it was a chance for them to chat about what had happened at Alison's workplace. They would then indulge in some retail therapy either online or at Trago Mills if the weather permitted. Mary had talked about Mr Wilson quite a bit since meeting him at Christmas, so Alison was glad that she'd get a chance to meet him for a chat and a cuppa. She had worked with a wide range of people over the years in a number of jobs. She had started as a holiday rep for a couple of years in Spain, dealing with drunk tourists and pissed off local residents. She got the impression that things had been sleazy when she was there, but now it was worse due to the prevalence of cocaine. She now managed the franchise of a major beauty products store in Drake Circus, which was the South West's biggest retail site other than Bristol's Cabot Circus.

She didn't have any particular suspicions about Mark Wilson, but the world these days had too many wolves in sheep's clothing, and her mum had changed recently. Also, when Mary had told Alison about the episode at the tea dance she was a bit curious at least. The two of them often quoted *Alice in Wonderland* to each other, saying, 'curiouser and curiouser' about a person or thing that needed a bit more investigating.

The bus ride to Endsleigh wasn't too bad as I lost myself in the local and national newspapers' reviews of the past year and their expectations for the new year. I saw that Blind Justice was in the national press was expected to be caught now that the Devon and Cornwall police were being helped by top forensics and psychology scientists in the area.

"So what would you like as a late Christmas present, Willow?" I asked my faithful friend. I knew cats got high on catnip, but I wasn't aware of an equivalent product for dogs. I knew a lot of dogs chased squirrels in the local parks, but that's not really what guide dogs do. Then, walking up and down the aisles, I saw I could buy Willow a quality waterproof jacket and matching boots. It could be personalised by having her name embroidered on it, but then it would have to be ordered and sent back to the leisure activities centre or on to my address. Since I wanted something right then, I settled for an unembroidered green barber-style jacket as well as some of the Christmas doggie treats on sale.

I was heading towards the car park to have a cigarette and look for Mary and her daughter even though I didn't know what model car they were in or whether Alison was just dropping Mary off or planned to join us.

"Hi, Mark! We're over here!" I was hailed by Mary, who was waving at Willow and me. She was walking towards us in the company of a smartly dressed lady who was clearly a relative judging by their similar facial features. Two attractive ladies were in my company; I was optimistic about what this new year might provide.

"Afternoon, Mary. Nice to meet you, Alison. This is my companion, Willow, yes, a faithful friend. Would you like to look around first and then have a cream tea?" I knew Willow was an asset when it came to meeting people for the first time, and she made for a great icebreaker. Alison crouched down and stroked Willow on her head then rubbed her under the muzzle.

We set off towards the hanging baskets – that was one thing Mary wanted to invest in this year. As I talked with Alison about Christmas and the family's plans for the next year I was reminded of when young adults start dating and take their new partners to meet each other's parents, trying to give them a good idea of who they are but not wanting to seem too overpowering as first impressions are difficult to forget.

I wanted Alison to know about my health condition and financial situation so that she didn't discover it later and think I'd been hiding it, but I wasn't trying to garner sympathy or seem a weaker, lesser person than I was. Things seemed to go fine, and I expected I'd been given a good review by Mary, who was the one I was really trying to show off to. I was happy by the time we left as Alison had meant to simply leave her mum once she had seen me and could put a face to my name. However, she liked Willow and seeing her mum enjoying herself, so she stayed and joined us for Earl Grey tea, scones, jam and clotted cream. Afterwards, she gave us a lift back into town, dropping Willow and I back at Cattedown roundabout before taking her mum home. As we had talked about the extensive availability of beauty products and the vanity of society these days, I had an idea that wouldn't have occurred to me had I not talked with those women: I decided to take Willow for a grooming session.

CHAPTER 48

"Come on, Willow. I'll brush you down and put your coat on. You're looking smart after having been shampooed and trimmed. Then, I'll put my outfit on and do my makeup and hairpiece. By the time I've done that Christian and Kevin should be here. We can have a chat, probably a beer and a spliff or two, and then record the first interview. I'm looking forward to it, feeling excited rather than nervous." I was pleased with how things had gone recently, but now that the new year was underway, it meant that the police would resume their usual work having after having endured the 'silly season', as I knew a lot of organizations called it.

I was dolled up in a good outfit and wearing a face of expensive makeup with my wig properly attached when I went to get a beer from the fridge. I opened the can and poured it into a tankard, then sat at my computer desk.

"Wills, why do you think I haven't heard from Rocket Queen in the last day or so? I think it might be that Frankie is back from boot camp, and they are having a bit of a party, but I know that really has to wait till after the run." I was talking to Willow to try and help myself relax. I didn't have a clue about the situation regarding Michael Evans. He was in custody in New York and had used his one phone call to ring Frankie, who was the reason he was arrested in the first place.

Christian and Kevin had met up beforehand so that they could arrive together. They each had a rucksack of work items: a video camera, a light meter for Christian and a wireless microphone and laptop for Kevin. They also had some provisions for us to share and snacks for Willow. I let them in the upstairs flat and gave them an enthusiastic greeting as they came out of the stairwell and into my living room.

"Come on in. I'm having a beer and a smoke, and as I said to you before you are each welcome to have something of mine unless you have brought you own." Knowing the things I did, I was guessing that they had already had a line or two of coke each to boost their energy, and depending on how things went, more pharmaceuticals or other drugs could be taken as required.

It didn't take long for the two technicians to get everything set up and ready to go. We had decided that I'd perform the first pieces as more of a monologue rather than an interview. We could record interviews and questions later and maybe even have questions sent in to us via email or Twitter.

"Greetings to you all! My name is Blind Justice, and I have been made by the despicable society we live in these days. As in the past, weak despondent societies have formed those who will correct and repair them, such as has been happening these days. In the past the Russian revolutionaries and many others were formed by the dictatorship of the country's rulers. On a more personal level it is often said that people who are abusers are formed by having been abused themselves.

Having been the victim of serious abuse myself I now feel I am in a position to go after paedophiles. After I'd been an orphan in a children's home, my personality coped by splitting in to the transvestite vigilante you see here and my original ordinary self. Here with me is Willow, my guide dog, who helps me when I suffer episodes of psycho-somatic blindness."

We decided to carry on recording and edit the piece at the end. Just as I was getting Willow into the shot my phone rang, and I could see it was a call from an American landline. Since I had seen what Rocket Queen and Frankie were up to, I answered it. I was surprised to find it was from Jane and Antonio, Rocket Queen's long-term LGBTQ friends who had had been at the marathon training camp.

"Hi guys! How are you?" I greeted their video call, expecting to get a congratulations regarding Frankie's and my engagement. However, I quickly saw that they were not in a party mood.

"Have you heard from Queenie? It's about Frankie." I could hear the emotion in Jane's voice and saw that she was upset.

She explained that the NYPD had arrested Michael Evans following a raid based on evidence from Frankie that he provided while at the camp in upstate New York. It seems there had been an undercover English police officer there to get a statement from Frankie about his friend, Rocket Queen, and, more specifically, what he knew about a UK associate known as Blind Justice.

From this it became clear that I was the target of the operation, and Queenie had just been used to get information about me. The cop in America was obviously working for DI Hansard. I became paranoid and realised I needed to move out and go incognito. I grabbed Willow and started breathing slowly to make sure I didn't have a panic attack or a blindness episode.

"Forget the recording, guys. I need to move out and set up a new HQ. Once I've done that I can contact you, and we can carry on. Use what you've got so far to set up a Facebook account and anything else you can do to promote this. I'll give you some more later when I know what's going on, but here is a couple hundred pounds for each of you now. I hope that's enough to buy your silence and pay for the work." I gave them each a wad of £20 notes as I stuffed things into my wheeled suitcase and a rucksack. "Off you go now, lads. I'll be in touch."

I was in part talking to myself, Willow and my other personality as the two guys left in a state of confusion. I was also imagining what I'd say to Rocket Queen or Frankie if I could, which I might never be able to do again.

My two conspirators had left, and once I was ready to head to my van looking like an ordinary pensioner with a few health issues, I had an idea. Should I set the place on fire? Being charged with arson was no worse than murder, which would be the case if I were ever caught. Yes. I set things up so that a candle would burn down and eventually reach and burn through a thread. That would allow a pot of white spirit to tip and be ignited by the candle, thus setting the papers alight.

Since I was a smoker I didn't have a smoke alarm in the flat, and if the curtains were shut, I reckoned that the fire could become well established before anyone knew anything about it. By the time it would be extinguished it could destroy a lot of evidence, so there would be a confusing mess for the detectives and fire service officers to examine. I unfortunately felt that doing so would end the relationship I had with Mary, which would be a real shame. Maybe she felt strongly enough towards me that if I got in touch somehow she'd reply in a positive way.

CHAPTER 49

I t was the last day of the marathon boot camp, and Frankie was keen to get back to the big city. He had organised to get a lift back with Antonio and Jane; he would have had a lift out there if he'd known they were going too. None of them knew it, but their last night on the ranch was the morning before the raid on Rocket Queen; as they returned home he was taken in to custody by the New York police.

"How soon are you going to call on Queenie when you get back? I don't suppose you guys have been apart for more than a couple of days since you got together." Jane was chatting with Frankie while Antonio loaded up their station wagon.

"Well, I've not heard from him in the last day or two, but I think he had a couple of jobs on. Also, there were a few gigs he was going to check out. Especially if he could find some of his old mates to go with him as it is music from that generation; a bit before my time." Frankie wasn't one hundred percent certain but he was pretty sure Michael Evans had been busted by then. He expected he'd be in custody, and if not, it was likely because he had been released and would be getting drunk due to the shock of the situation he found himself in.

The weather took a turn for the worse as they drove along the freeway, and a heavy blanket of snow started to enshroud the entire locality. A grey sheet hid the blue sky from view, and the white snow that smothered the ground quickly darkened thanks to the pollution in the air.

"Can you take me back to my place? I want to leave my stuff there, have a shower and put on a different outfit. Thanks, pet. How are you feeling about doing the race in a couple weeks? Shall we meet up for a run round the park in a few days – you've got my number haven't you?" Frankie was trying, pretty unsuccessfully, to make chitchat.

"We're just running it to complete it and raise money. We're not looking at it as a race as such. Instead, we're just going to get together and finish it. That will be enough this time. Maybe try and run a better time if we do it again next year." Antonio and Jane explained their situation, smiling at each other in the front seats and exchanging caresses while we waited in gridlocked traffic. Meanwhile, Frankie was restlessly twitching in the back seat like a young boy in need of a washroom.

"One thing I like about having a few days away like that is that I can forget about all the gossip, rumours and fake news. I wonder what has been going on." Jane spoke as she connected her iPhone to the in-car charger to check texts and emails. She could see the news both locally, nationally and globally, too, if she wanted. She and Antonio didn't know it but they were about to get a very shocking and appalling piece of news, which Frankie already knew about. He'd have to use all his acting and bullshitting skills to convince them that he didn't already know that Rocket Queen had been picked up by the local police officers following a raid.

The couple knew a lot of people and were very active socialites. Frankie felt like he didn't know many people in the local community, and he had no family to worry about. It was one of the reasons he was not bothered by the idea of relocating to the other coast. It was clearly going to be a long slow drive back home, so he told the couple he'd listen to some music on his headphones. It meant he could go to sleep or at least pretend to be unconscious. Their conversation might be different if they thought he wasn't listening, both with each other and if they spoke on the phone to anyone.

He started with Apple Music, playing some alternative tunes from the 80s. He enjoyed bands like Jane's Addiction, Sisters of Mercy and The Cult. Lyrics such as 'Love is always over in the morning' seemed particularly poignant presently. He meant to stay awake listening to the music quietly in the background but he accidentally fell asleep. He was clearly more tired than he realised, both physically and emotionally.

He had talked to his friend T back in the apartment in the city about a number of things, using his wide range of experiences to help him align his moral compass. He knew that T had been influenced by his family, but his parents had passed away, and his siblings occasionally wrote him letters.

Frankie had numerous uncertainties regarding his folks. One involved a recurring dream he had again while in the station wagon heading home. In the dream, a young Frankie just old enough for elementary school is picked up by a yellow school bus and dropped off with his mom after a day of classes. His pa would be home later with his elder sister, whom he picked up from the local high school. A lot of the year it was cold, dark and remote in the Minnesota backwoods. However, back then there was no internet, and weeks could pass before one saw another soul if one lived in a lonely cabin. Physically active people dreaded the cold; spiritual, emotional people feared the isolating cabin fever.

It is hard to measure time in a dream, but it feels like many hours have passed, yet there is still no sign of the Dodge returning with Eleanor and the family hound in the front seat next to his father. His mom is getting a little nervous as the climate doesn't suit her like those who'd grown up there. She is from Saint Paul, which was the state capital originally.

Then, it is hard to tell memory from previous dreams, speculation and images from film and TV. What he sees in his mind's eye is this. He and his mom go to bed after waiting up for a few hours. They don't panic, but aren't happy, either. In the morning, if her family hasn't been in touch, she calls the sheriff.

In the middle of the night the cabin is open, and an alcoholic hunter who has gone stir crazy while living in a cave in the depths of the woods enters the house. Frankie and his mother don't know it yet, but he has already ambushed and shot Frankie's father and sister. He had then come to their homestead, not realising who lives there. He wakes them both, but Frankie's mom has his attention, so he doesn't realise Frankie was present. This allows him to hide under the bed in the secondary sleeping and storage area. He hears terrible animal-like noises from across the room for an hour or so. Eventually his mom is killed, and the lunatic has breakfast and then leaves. He isn't certain but thinks that the local law enforcement workers rescue him and kill the perpetrator after tracking him back to his fortress deep in the lonesome pines.

He awoke with a start and made sounds that surprised Jane and Antonio.

"Alright! Were you dreaming, Frankie?" Jane leaned over and stroked his arm and shoulder. "You're okay now."

He regained his bearings and was glad to see they were back in the urban jungle. They didn't have far to go until he'd be back in his apartment.

PART 5

CHAPTER 50

Tracy was going to see the superintendent to explain the situation and get clearance for the firearm officers, which she required for Operation Barber, which was going to be at its peak in a few hours. She knew Sergeant Pete Anderson was on the train back from Exeter, so they'd be ready to move in during the small hours of the morning as they liked to do.

Or at least that would have been the case if they hadn't recognised the address when a fire was reported in Cattedown. The detective working with the fire investigation officer saw that the address was that of the house under surveillance.

"Pete! You won't believe this but Blind Justice's property has just gone up in smoke. Probably arson, but we're not sure yet. There should still be DNA that we can use, both human and canine. I just hope he hasn't got a bolthole we are totally unaware of. Tracy ranted into her desk handset to her sergeant. She knew his location on the railway, so she knew he'd be passing through a few tunnels and losing signal intermittently.

She had a few minutes of definite conversation left, so she said she feared that Frankie might've had a change of heart and told his partner's friend out of guilt and remorse. However, it was just as likely, if not more, the couple who had known Frankie at the runners' boot camp. They probably knew about

Rocket Queen from Frankie and had contacted Blind Justice not knowing who or what he was.

This made sense to everyone, so the next thing to do was move into the razed remains of Home Sweet Home Terrace. Fortunately, not too much damage had been caused to the neighbouring houses. The first thing Tracy decided to do was house to house inquiries, and while she was doing that DS Pete arrived at the station. He was happy to be back home in the grey relentless streets of Tamarmouth, an old English city so different from places in the States. He drove out to Cattedown, which had streets with older histories than the entirety of America as a modern country.

"Good to see you again, Peter." Despite being British police officers, they went so far as to give each other a bit of a hug. "This is Alan Jackson of Devon and Somerset Fire Service. He is leading the investigation into the arson of the house. It looks like there was an accelerant downstairs in the living room, but we can't say much more presently." Tracy and Pete stood at the front of the house's remains with the fire officer and waited to hear details.

It was established that the resident of the house in Home Sweet Home Terrace had an old camping van of some sort and had left in it shortly before the fire broke out. Unfortunately, since this was an older part of the city, there was no CCTV until the nearest main road, and that seemed to have been avoided but was being scanned by the officers.

Based on the size the vehicle the officers guessed that Blind Justice was now operating from it. It was a mobile HQ, which would not be very easy to hide, so unless he could find another property he would be under a lot of pressure. Obviously, this had good and bad aspects. People under pressure make mistakes, so it doesn't take long to catch them. However, they also act in a more desperate manner, are more violent and take greater risks.

The next source of information regarding Blind Justice was a video Tracy and Pete saw on YouTube that showed him introducing himself and Willow. It was soon clear that the film had been made in the house before it was burnt down. He apparently had a couple of allies as somebody had clearly filmed and posted the video for him. The cops asked the locals if they had ever seen anyone else on the property, but people had only ever seen a gentleman slightly older than middle-aged with his guide dog and a curiously dressed transvestite who visited occasionally. Using the address, the police accessed Mr Wilson's medical records, so they contacted the CPN to determine the house's resident.

Jane Vickery was called in for a conversation with the DI, rather than an interview, and Dr Larrson was also taking part given his knowledge about MPD.

"Do you know anyone who Mr Mark Wilson, your patient, would consider a trustworthy friend? We know he isn't in touch with any of his family," DI Hansard asked the nurse as they talked in an interview room off the record.

"Not really, ma'am, no...I think, however, that he has a new friend he met over Christmas who he's been seeing more of these last weeks. She's named Mary, but I can't remember her surname, I'm sorry to say." Jane gave an apologetic statement to the frustrated policewoman who she could see was not very happy with the situation.

"Do you know anything about her or her family or anything we might use to get a hold of her?" Tracy wondered if there were any receipts linked to debit cards that could be traced, but doubted it. She and Pete felt that they needed Blind Justice to show up and maybe make a mistake due to a lack of resources, and they were about to talk to the media about a release in the local rag and TV news program.

There was one other line of enquiry to check out first that related to Mary. Nurse Jane remembered calling on Mark Wilson, and she was surprised to find a few items in a House of Fraser bag as she knew he didn't shop there. She asked and was told that Mary's daughter worked there. If they could check staff records at the local shop, it could lead to Mary's daughter and then maybe to Mary to Mark Wilson. This might enable them to successfully complete the operation, but it was not something they could count on.

CHAPTER 51

Willow and I managed to get to my van while it was still dark that night. I knew I was basically on the run now, and I was Public Enemy Number One in Tamarmouth. Because I had seen this on the horizon, I had thought about CCTV watching the city. I was parked in an old backstreet that looked like it was still in the 1970s – old council houses in terraced rows, no serious gardens, occasional dilapidated caravans and small fishing boats landed due to quotas.

I had previously looked at the local roads to see where the CCTV cameras were, so I had mapped out a route that avoided most if not all of them. Once I left the city and entered the moors I would be free of them. However, the local force did have a helicopter, which I knew they could use to get a good aerial view. So I decided that I needed to determine the residence of the man who'd molested the kids on the Pilgrims Football Team youth squad. I had his address and, as I discerned using Google Maps, he had a garage in which I could put my van. I knew I might have to empty it out first because he might have a car that he didn't used much, if ever. I just had to use the remaining dark hours to drive to his house and put the camper in his garage after emptying it if needed.

"Willow, if he's got any pets you aren't to misbehave, okay?" I gave my furry friend instructions, knowing that she would be alright. She might respond to other dogs, but she wouldn't make the first move. Cats were more likely to be an issue, especially if they were particularly cheeky. They'd go for her with their little retractable razor blades and then jump somewhere Willow couldn't reach. Also, since she was on a lead, her response was obviously very restricted. We drove a very circuitous route via county lanes and suburban housing estates to avoid being seen, and we passed many personal cars and bikes, which I looked at. To distract myself and help pass the time I looked at the registration plates and made words using the letters in the order I saw them. For example, when I saw the number plate R847SDL I was inclined to think 'ReSiDuaL'. It had occurred to me that if I recorded the words and looked at them later, it might be similar to checking results from Freudian word association. I expect that a clever psychologist could read some meaning in to it all. I didn't know it then, but Dr Larsson would do so soon. The newer style number plates were harder if I used all the letters or easier if I just used the last three and ignored the area code. Here in the West Country, the local plates all began with 'W' followed by letters A–J.

The estate we sought was made up of longer roads called drives with numerous short cul-de-sacs coming off them called closes. I was keen to reach my target soon and resolve the situation regarding the van and garage. I wasn't a fan of F Scott Fitzgerald, but if I'd known of his famous line, 'In a real dark night of the soul, it is always three o'clock in the morning, day after day', I would've agreed. We entered Pennon Close and edged along looking for number 21. It was a semidetached house with a ramshackle garden in front that extended along the side to the garage. I parked the van, the curtains of which were already closed, and then clambered into the back and changed my outfit. Since the future was unknown, and there was a wide range of possible outcomes, I had to be dressed in a good-looking costume. It also had to be durable and a bit resistant, so I selected the catsuit from New York.

I remembered a conversation I'd had with Christian and dug around in my shoulder bag. I found that he had left an AVI Petcam to attach to Willow's collar, I put that on Willow along with her latest jacket from Endsleigh so I could record evidence. I was assuming I'd be able to use a computer belonging to the house's owner. Time to break in and find out.

"Don't move, buddy! Silence!" I'd picked the lock on the back door easily. Pensioners in rundown bungalows and houses were often lax about security, but it might still be an issue on his PC.

I woke him in his grotty bedroom by putting one leather-clad hand over his nose and mouth and using the other to wave a carving knife in his peripheral vision.

His eyes expanded as wide as possible for a few nanoseconds, and I was reminded of the figure in *The Scream* by Edvard Munch as the men were both bald figures in nightmarish worlds. He nodded his head while it was still on the pillow, so I leaned back and gestured at Willow.

I had been in the news a lot recently, so I guessed he knew who I was. But because I enjoyed it as much as anything and since it was a chance for me to get revenge, I gave him the full introduction.

"You are going to be judged by Blind Justice! I'm going to judge you and pass a sentence. You may have been able to hide from society and everyone previously, but now I'll reveal your crimes to the world. You shall be named and shamed." As I spoke I strutted my stuff around his bedroom. Like a cross between a French rooster, a performer at Rio de Janeiro Gay Pride Parade and a top QC in a big trial. "Get yourself dressed. Then we will go to the kitchen and have a refreshment. After that we will examine the evidence on your computer. You will cooperate and provide passwords etcetera, unless you're a very foolish masochistic lover of pain."

I backed away from him and stood in the bedroom doorway, watching him as he got up in a state of shock. His striped pyjamas and thin skeletal frame reminded me of Holocaust victims in concentration camps. However, they deserved sympathy and pity, while he did not.

"Your name is Robert Fielding, isn't it? You used to be a football coach with the Tamarmouth Pilgrims Youth Team." In a court when on trial the accused must begin by confirming their identities and residential addresses, which was what we did, but in a slightly different manner.

"Yes. I can't deny that…However, I went to court but none of the charges against me were proved." He seemed surprisingly confident considering the position he was in. I was shocked.

"True. But if you are innocent, then why have people in Victim Aid Therapy mentioned you by name and talked about what you used to do to them at the training ground?" This was the convicting evidence he couldn't argue with, and he seemed astonished by it. "Now that you are dressed we can look on your computer while we have a coffee."

CHAPTER 52

P ete was feeling physically exhausted due to jet-lag; he was also emotionally drained. This was because he thought they would have Blind Justice in custody by now, and he was missing his family – he hadn't seen them over New Year's. He and Tracy agreed on a statement to release to the local newspaper and current affairs TV program. While that was passing through the required channels, he would be available by phone if required but would be basically be resting and relaxing.

Due to all his flying and other traveling over the last week or so, Pete found that he had lost track of the days of the week. Lying in bed in the morning, he turned on the TV and was a bit surprised to find that it was Friday, already half past ten. It might be time to contact Kathy as she often went for a meal on Fridays and Saturdays. He could find out if she had spoken to their mum about having a meal together and also inviting their dad, Jack, back in the family as well. He knew they liked photos of holidays, so he could have his pictures from his trip to America printed.

"Hello! Can I talk to Kathy Anderson, please?" He called the salon where she worked and decided she could do his hair for him, and they could chat there and then.

"Hi Pete! How are you?...Yes, come and see me, and we can book a table for a family get together." She was very enthusiastic about seeing her brother again and also reuniting their mum and dad.

Pete went into town. He was enjoying being back home. He walked the streets he knew well and had pounded on a beat when he was still a uniformed officer. He walked through the local park past the bandstand and the café, which was good for a Sunday carvery but didn't offer evening meals, so was no good for them tonight. He was sorry he had missed the Plymport Park Community Choir Christmas carol gig as he enjoyed seeing and listening to his friends singing with the Salvation Army. He felt sorry for all the homeless people who they supported, especially over Christmas. He had been too busy with work to be aware of whether there were people on the streets in America, but he knew there were ones in Tamarmouth.

As always there was a lull in business for the salons just after New Year's, so Kathy was glad to see a friendly face to work and chat with when Pete arrived to have his short back and sides re-cut.

"Pete, would you like an Americano to drink while I cut your hair? Still with milk and sugar?" Kathy greeted her brother from the refreshments counter at the back of the room.

"No thanks. I'd rather have a cup of proper tea, please. It's something I've really missed since I last saw you. How are you doing regarding Mum and Dad? What's the score with Gary and Phil these days?" Pete sat down in the hairdressing chair and laid back for a shampoo before the cut.

Kathy gave Pete an update on the family situation, and he was reminded of why he didn't watch soap operas. There was quite enough drama surrounding his own friends and family.

"I tell you what, bro. I think we can get Mum and Dad together because they have both been talking about the anniversary they would be celebrating at the start of February if they were still together. It would be their fortieth, which is ruby. I'm not suggesting we buy them any rubies, but we can get semi-precious garnets, which look good but are a fraction of the price. Also, I know there is ruby port, which is something I think they might enjoy." Kathy could dye her mum's hair a shade of red if she wanted, but she knew that most older people prefer a blue rinse.

"So how was America? Are you going to show me the photos now on the tablet, or will you get them printed so we can pass them around? I know which the folks would prefer. We should share a meal and then pass them around while we chill out over a shot of ruby and a cup of expresso or hot chocolate. Maybe a cigar or two for you and Dad." It was clear to Pete that she was imagining a euphoric scene.

"Who would you have for company: Phil or Gary? How have they been over the holiday season?" Pete had his suspicions about which would get on better in the family.

"Gary enjoyed a really romantic, traditional kind of family Christmas, where he is really sweet and has a good time kissing under mistletoe, which we did. We went to a midnight mass carol service lit by candles together, which I enjoyed, and so did he since he was the one who organised it." Kathy was sounding more and more enthusiastic as she mused about Gary. Pete was interested to see how things would pan out over St. Valentine's day in a number of weeks.

"I think we should try and get our folks together for a meal soon, and I've got my eye on a possible speed dating event on the Barbican, so I'll be busy then. You call Mum and tell her I'll be joining you so I can tell you about America and show you the snaps. I'll come with Dad from his place, or if he seems a bit nervous I'll pick him up from his local pub" Pete talked while his sister cut his wet hair; he was looking pretty smart by the time she finished.

"If you go to that dating thing would you like me to tint your eyelashes and thread your brows? I expect I could organise a few other things, too. Your skin tone is looking pretty good, and if you can keep that it'll help. It's probably from being outside in America." She finished him off with a quick spray and held a mirror up so he could see how he looked from behind.

"I can help you hide the grey hairs that are starting to show next time, or are you going for the George Clooney silver fox look?" She mocked him as he left, feeling confident and invigorated.

CHAPTER 53

"Time to check out House of Fraser to see if we can find Mary's daughter and find out who she is," Tracy said to her Americanised sergeant. He was looking like a lead detective in the latest US police series. His smart haircut was combined with smarter clothes than he used to wear. He had gotten used to wearing Chinos and a shirt and jacket to fit in with the other officers in the States. He'd fit in better in Hose of Fraser now than in Primark.

"Her department manager has been contacted, and we're meeting her at the store office. Then if we are sure we want to talk to her, Alison, Mary's daughter, will be called from the shop floor as she's at work today." Peter was feeling happier about going to what his family considered posh shops these days. He felt classier with his smart haircut and quality aftershave. He was looking forward to the family get-together that night, and he was confident that his mum and dad would be talking again by the end of it.

Meanwhile, Alison was feeling anxious about her mum, who seemed to have lost contact with Mark Wilson. Her mum had seen that his house had burnt down, and that had freaked her out. She had gone home in a state of shock and hadn't been able to contact the emergency services. It had taken her hours to even be able to call her daughter, who had to go to work rather than visit her upset parent. Alison had told her mum to call the local church minister or at least a friend of hers in the congregation. She went to the church more as a social activity rather than because she was seeking salvation. Initially she'd felt guilty about that but soon found that it was common, especially for people in her age group. The majority of the congregation were pensioners and had only started attending church in their sixties. Younger people went to the 'happy-clappy' Evangelical services or became Jehovah's Witnesses.

Alison had reassured her mum as much as she could till she had to hang up to drive to work, but she wasn't comfortable with the situation. She tried to remember if she had the contact details for anyone, such as a churchwarden.

It was an icy morning, so she had to forget her mum's problems and focus on driving in the foggy rush-hour traffic. She made it in to the private car park and sat for a minute or two, doing her makeup using the rear-view mirror. She was focused on work rather than family issues now, and she guessed that today she would be trying to impress the deputy manager, Mr Scott, with her customer service skills since she knew he already liked her selling ability after having seen her sales statistics.

"Morning, Mrs Neil…How are you finding the weather? A problem?" Alison was gregarious by nature, but since she wanted the promotion she'd be going out of her way to seem like the friendliest person in the store for the next few days.

"No, Alison. I don't have far to walk, and now that the worst of the frost has gone it's not a worry anymore." Mrs Neil was checking the cash register before the store doors opened in a few minutes. She didn't have OCD, but she checked things numerous times, over and over again, because she got nervous till business began.

Alison was surprised to see Mr Scott unlocking the customer doors and letting in a couple of people. However, he locked the doors behind them. The security staff normally unlocked the doors, but they just stood back chatting. She saw the two people follow Mr Scott towards the 'staff only' door, but before entering it they all turned towards her, and he nodded in her direction. Were they recruitment consultants or staff from another store up-line? She knew that mystery shoppers were employed sometimes. There was a two-sided policy with House of Fraser; it involved, on the one hand, being an average shopper who doesn't stand out from the herd and, on the other hand, being a difficult customer who needed to be handled with kid gloves and given a lot of care and attention.

"Is the new Calvin Klein display ready for action, Miss Green?" Mrs Neil had already checked the taster bottle, but Alison knew what to do to keep her happy so she did it.

"Thanks for your cooperation, Mr Scott. We want to have a word with Miss Alison Green because we think her mother can help our ongoing investigations. She's just a potential link in a chain to gain access to someone; she hasn't done anything wrong. Well, not that we know about or want to deal with at the moment," Tracy explained face-to-face after having spoken to Mr Scott on the phone to arrange things. She had dealt with him previously in shoplifting inquiries when a family had committed multiple thefts to pay for drugs and alcohol.

Just as Mrs Neil was making nanometric adjustments to the positions of the perfume bottles and her hair, she took a brief call from Mr Scott on the in-house phone line.

"Alison, Mr Scott wants you to go to his office before things get busy. As soon as you can. Okay?" Mrs Neil requested from the next counter.

"Yes. That's fine, Mrs Neil." Alison was glad to leave the shop floor as it didn't look to be very busy that day, especially so early on a frosty morning. She knew that Mr Scott would give her a cup of quality filter coffee, and she could use it since she'd missed hers that morning due to the call from her mum.

She briefly walked past the full-length mirrors and brushed her outfit down using her hands. A gentle tug on her suit jacket, a tweak on the silk neck scarf, and she was satisfied and confident. She knocked rapidly on the door and was invited into the deputy manager's office.

"Morning, Mr Scott."

"Good morning, Miss Green. Do come in and sit down a minute; this shouldn't take long." She was surprised and disappointed by the invitation. She looked round the room and saw that the visiting pair were holding coffee cups sporting the brand logo. They both had steaming coffee, which had left the machine's jug empty; it was just beginning to refill, drip by drip. They were both sitting on the two-seated sofa under the window and sharing an iPad, wearing not exactly smart clothes that clearly hadn't come from House of Fraser.

"These are two police officers, Miss Green. Detective Inspector Tracy Hansard and Sergeant Peter Anderson. They need to ask you a few questions." Mr Scott introduced them, and they each nodded when named and flashed their warrant cards.

"Miss Green, we understand that your mother has been in touch with a Mr Mark Wilson over the last month or two and that you have met him. Is that right?" DI Tracy recognised the type of girl Alison was, working in the better part of retail. No point faffing around – it was best to just get straight to it.

"Yes, miss. However, I was phoned by my mum this morning. She said she'd seen that his house has burned down, but she didn't think anything had happened to him… She hadn't heard from him for a few days, and she was very upset about it when I talked to her. She's probably going to get some support from a friend this morning and then contact the hospitals to try to find him. She likes him a lot, so I'm sure she'll go and visit if possible. Do you know if he's in a ward somewhere, miss?" Alison guessed that the housefire was an accident. She couldn't imagine the truth. It was inconceivable.

This didn't really help Tracy, but she thought she'd still better talk to Mary about Mr Wilson and what he was like. He might yet try to get in touch with her, and obviously that had potential.

"Thanks for that, Miss Green. We'd better have a word with your mum so can you give her a call, and we'll all go and talk to her at home. Is it okay, Mr Scott, if Miss Green comes with us for the rest of the morning?" Tracy knew it would be as he'd said he was willing to do anything he could to help the local constabulary.

CHAPTER 54

'Robbie' Fielding had taken advantage of being born with a natural football talent in a couple of ways throughout his life. Since he wasn't gifted intellectually, while in school, he focussed on being a sportsman so he could impress the local school girls. He played for the local team as a job till he was forced into retirement at a young age following an accident. That was when he went off the rails and started going downhill. I had discovered this from the notes in his Vulnerable Adults Therapy file I had stolen from the University office.

"Sit at your desk and turn on your computer, so I can see what files you have. I also might want to see your emails," I instructed him as I stood in the doorframe between the living room and the kitchen, looking similar to the Statue of Liberty dolled up in a pink outfit. "Watch him, Willow."

My épée was visible, so it acted as a deterrent to misbehaviour. I went to the counter and made myself a cup of instant coffee slowly and carefully; I wore thin coral kid leather gloves to look chic and avoid leaving fingerprints.

"I suppose you'd like some coffee as you probably need a dose of caffeine to get charged and woken up?" I talked to Mr Fielding as he typed. It was a very slow, old Windows system, which I found infuriating. He didn't know any better, so I couldn't really complain.

"Yes, with milk and sugar if you don't mind," was his reply.

"How about a bite to eat?" I was reminded of how prisoners in a cell on death row are allowed to choose their last meal. This would probably be his last meal; I wasn't sure and didn't care if he realised that yet.

I came over and put the two mugs of coffee on the desk, which supported the computer tower, grimy keyboard, mouse and decrepit printer. Eventually I was able to look at the files on the desktop screen. The icons were mainly arranged in alphabetic order. However, in the lower right corner, where people often put their trash, he had a folder labelled 'Personal'. I stood behind him with a cup of hot coffee, which I'd gladly pour over him if he didn't cooperate, and demanded that he open it.

"Look, you've caught me; you know enough of what I've done. Do you really need to do this?" He spoke in a subdued tone of voice, and I got the impression he was feeling guilty for once.

"It's just to see if I can find any other dirty old men who need to be exposed." I wasn't sure what my future was, but I could send pictures to Christian to put on the web. I had seen a documentary about people pretending to be kids to lure and trap paedophiles. They were on the same side as I was, and I knew it. They were also criticising the police; they succeeded using their own skills and abilities to get the job done. Many of the had children had been abused or had suffered themselves. They focussed their bitterness and rage on getting revenge. Many members of the public supported them, and according to the senior officer's statement the police didn't approve of it. I bet some of them did, though. Anything to clean up the streets these days, especially with budget cuts to emergency services.

Robbie seemed to be slowing down as he went through the files and showed me the horrible photos he'd either taken himself or imported. I guessed that his slowness was due to the few drops of ketamine that I had put in his coffee. I hadn't expected it to affect him so much; I thought it would just reduce his resistance. I had considered a possible overdose for myself and Willow, but I didn't have the willpower to kill my best friend when she'd be able to live a few years in retirement after all this. I felt she deserved that. Also, if I were taken alive, I would need to make statements and be seen in court. I knew that some people would hate me, while others wouldn't love me, but they would understand. It was a very divisive issue. He seemed to have guessed that I had spiked his drink, and it was knocking him out rather than stimulating his consciousness.

"Right. It's time for you to get back into the bedroom, you perverted bastard. Leave the computer as it is. You won't have to worry about being exposed to anyone else now, anyway. Your only concerns now are what I'm going to do to your body and then where your eternal soul will go." I called Willow over and took out a pair of handcuffs from a pouch on her utility coat. They were just toy ones, but they were enough to restrain the remains of what had once been a fit and healthy football player. Now, he was just a weak body with even weaker conscience and sense of morality.

Unfortunately for me and the sake of revenge, he was fortunate, and the stress and strain of what we had done so far caused him to pass out while lying on the bed. I must admit that I was feeling tired too since I'd been up all night after burning down the flat. I sat down and wondered with Willow about our futures and decided to garrotte Mr Fielding with a piece of washing line. I took a piece from Willow's utility jacket, which I kept for use in emergencies. It had loops tied at each end, so I just needed to put it around his neck, insert an object and then twist it tight. After I did that, I took a wooden spoon from the kitchen and placed the loops around it. Then I slowly rotated it so he had time to regain consciousness have a minute or two to realise what was happening to him and why. By then, was lying dead on the bed. I decided to have a nap to recharge my batteries before killing my last victim.

First I went into the kitchen and found a can of Spam, which I fed to Willow. I also gave her a bowl of tap water to drink. While she ate and took a snooze I went and lay on the sofa under a couple of moth-eaten blankets. I managed to get a few hours' sleep before cutting *Blind Justice* in to his chest. I then took a teaspoon from the cutlery drawer and scooped out his eyes. I put them in the dish and fed them to Willow, who seemed to quite enjoy them. Then I took a couple of photos of the corpse and sent them to Christian. I also sent him the personal file from Robbie's computer and the footage from the Petcam Willow had worn. He said he'd edit it and upload onto an appropriate platform. He showed me what he had done so far with the recording we'd already made.

"I need to think about what I'm going to do next. I can call DI Tracy Hansard and let her know about Robbie. I can wait for her here so that I get arrested or set it up so that she comes with the firearms officers. I could try to escape, but non-stop running and hiding doesn't seem appealing, especially with Willow and my health condition, so I doubt I'll do that. Thanks for what you've done, but I think it's over now." That was my email to Christian.

CHAPTER 55

Alison was escorted by the two police officers to their marked car in the staff car park. She sat in the back with Tracy while Peter got in the front and started driving. Alison had called her mum and asked her to wait for her to come back to have a talk. So as not to raise suspicion, she said she wasn't feeling well, knowing that her mum had no other commitments that day and would stay in for her, wanting to nurse her daughter.

"Did you ever meet Mr Wilson?" Tracy asked Alison. "If so, what was he like?"

"Well, obviously there's the fact that he has a guide dog. He explained that she wasn't required all the time, but he has episodes occasionally. A bit like panic attacks, but they cause him to lose his sight. I expect that my mum can tell you more about that." Alison had liked Willow, and Mr Wilson seemed okay. Since they had met at a church Christmas event, she guessed that he was safe.

Alison wondered what all the local curtain twitchers would make of her coming back so early in the morning in a Panda car. One thing she liked about her mum's road was that it was quiet and serene. Mostly retired inhabitants in bungalows potter about in their gardens, volunteering the charity shops, especially local ones such as St Luke's hospice and Devon Air Ambulance.

Peter parked the car on the drive as it was empty as usual; now, Mary only used buses for transport because she gave up driving years ago. He backed in as he liked to be free to drive away quickly if required.

The three of them went up to the front door, and Alison opened up the unlocked door. She ushered in her escorts and called to her mum, who was in the kitchen, as she expected.

"Mum! I've got some people with me who want to talk to you. Can we all sit down and have a chat over a cuppa? It's nothing to worry about; they are just concerned about your friend Mr Wilson," Alison called to her mum while herding the officers in to the living room to sit on the suite.

Mary entered the room. She sat down in her chair, and Alison took requests for beverages and made them while the police explained the situation.

"Here are the drinks. You can all add your own sugar and milk as I've done mine and Mum's." Alison put a tray down on the table, sat down near her mum on the sofa and picked up a ginger nut to dunk in her coffee.

"...No, we don't think Mr Wilson was hurt in the fire. We've checked the hospital and reports from the local paramedics who man the ambulances. Also, there is no sign that his guide dog, Willow, was injured, so we think that they weren't in the house at the time of the fire. He hasn't tried to call you, has he?" Tracy was establishing the situation before asking if Mary had the mobile number. She'd probably ask her to call him. The question was how much she needed to tell Mary to persuade her to cooperate without giving away too much about Mr Wilson.

"No...I haven't heard a word from him, and I'm worried about them. I was going to ring the hospitals today to try to find him. I presume you have checked them already," Mary explained, seeming a bit flustered by the whole situation.

"Mary, do you have a phone number for Mr Wilson? Obviously it needs to be a mobile number. Also, I'm assuming he has your phone number." Tracy was wondering if perhaps her nemesis had upgraded his phone but kept the SIM card.

"Yes, I tried his number, and it said he was unavailable. I didn't leave a voicemail message as we both don't like them, but I could if you like." Mary was being as cooperative as she could but still didn't know the significance of it all.

"Thank you, Mrs Green. Can I talk with my colleague, and then we'll decide how to proceed? If you and your daughter can give us a few minutes alone we'll know what to do next." Tracy could see that Mary was just worried about a friend, not concerned about any possible criminality. She still thought the house had burned down by accident, not intentionally to hide evidence.

Mary and Alison retired to the kitchen and closed the frosted glass door behind them to give the police officers some privacy.

"Peter…What do you think? Do we get her to call him and leave a voicemail message even though that's not what they usually do? Still, having a house burn down and a man with a dog disappearing isn't a usual situation is it?" Tracy wanted to be proactive and do something rather than wait for a call that might never come.

"I think we can ask Mary to try ringing the number, and if he doesn't answer, I think she should send him a text. I know they haven't done much texting yet, but she can explain why she did it. I think he must know how to read and write texts even if he'd rather talk. It makes sense for her to leave him a message following the fire." This was Peter's take on the situation, and it made sense. They could tell Mary what to do, but she couldn't say, "The police want to talk to you." It had to seem like a personal message, and she must arrange a meeting. They decided to tell Mary that they thought he'd accidentally burnt the house and then panicked. They wanted to talk to him about that, but they wanted to confirm his and Willow's health and get them rehoused. It was not an issue of blame, but Tracy understood why he didn't want to talk to the police, especially since, due to his health, he'd be worried about being sectioned under the Mental Health Act.

They two officers called Mary and Alison back in and described what they wanted to do: try a phone call and, if Mr Wilson answered talk to him and arrange a meeting, somewhere where a few police officers could be waiting, not necessarily in uniform but probably with easy access to armed officers and hopefully a limited number, if any, of members of the public. If he didn't answer the phone, she was to send a text saying that she was worried about her friend, propose a meeting and recommend a time and place. To close the text, she could ask him to call her ASAP to let her know they were alright.

CHAPTER 56

I found that when I woke up on a sofa I was with Willow, but there was a dead person lying on the bed in the next room, and we were in a house I didn't recognise. My phone's ringtone had woken me up, and looking at the screen I could see that my friend Mary was calling. I was very confused, but I knew she cared about me, and she seemed to have at least a vague understanding of who I was and my problems. Therefore, I answered the phone but really didn't know what I was going to say about where I was and the situation I was in.

"Hello Mary…How are you?" I said, feeling very glad this was not a video call.

"Oh…Mark, I think the question is how and where are you? I tried to visit you but found the house gone up in smoke. Razed to the ground. I contacted the hospitals but, there was no sign of you, and the police were examining the remains of the house." Mary was clearly glad to be in touch with me again, but she was obviously not happy.

"Umm. Well, yes. I'm a bit confused about what has been going on. My life is a right mess at the moment. I just don't know what's happened…I think I need to talk to my psychiatric community nurse. I'm not even sure where I am." I spoke clearly to Mary, but I'm sure my voice must have sounded emotional. "God! What the hell's going on," I said to myself and Willow and partly to her.

"What do you want to do? Can we get together for a chat somewhere? What can I do to help you? I'm sure we can sort things out." Mary talked in a stilted way, almost like she was reading what she was saying. I thought I could hear something in the background but guessed it was the radio.

"I think I need to call Jane Vickery. You know, my CPN. Perhaps she can give me advice. I'd like to see you too. I think maybe I need to call an ambulance, but I'm all right myself. I can't explain now." I wondered what to do since I was in an unknown place with a dead body on the bed next to me with *Blind Justice* cut in the torso. I'd had suspicions about my other personality, which this seemed to confirm, but in a way, I was still responsible. It reminded me of a murder case in the press a while ago when someone said they were sleepwalking when they murdered their partner. Something like that in the news would certainly raise awareness regarding abuse, mental health and psychiatry in the NHS.

"Mary, I think I need to leave where I am now, and obviously I don't have anywhere to go to now that my flat has gone. Can I come to you? At least for a talk, and maybe I can call my nurse from there. I can get a taxi, so it shouldn't take too long." I needed to get out of the house as soon as possible, and I was glad I still had Willow with me.

"Let me check my diary as I think I've got an appointment that I've had planned for a few months. Mark, you can call me back in a few minutes, okay?" Mary was very supportive, and I wished I knew her better and longer.

"Sure...I'll get myself and Willow ready to get a cab to you, yeah?" It occurred to me that I didn't even know the address of the house I was in, but a little look near the front door should sort that out. "I'll ring back in about five minutes." I hung up and stated to look around for any possessions I might have left in the room. Since I didn't know

how I'd gotten there I had no idea what, if anything, I'd
brought with me. Suffering for MPD really isn't very good for
one's blood pressure, especially if half of one's personality is a
psychotic killer.

"Willow, let's get ready for a walk," I called to her,
knowing that she often went to my stick or put her muzzle
against my baccy tin before a walk since I always took those
with me. She got up and wagged her tail, then padded to the
doorway where my stick was propped. I found my smoking
paraphernalia in my pockets and rolled myself a fag. I lit it up
and looked out the window from behind the closed curtain.
I wasn't sure but got the impression that I was in one of the
housing estates built on the outskirts of Tamarmouth to house
the boomer generation. Many were owned privately following
Mrs Thatcher's 'right to buy' campaign.

I was feeling better, having appeased my need for nicotine,
so we went to the hallway to look for post and find an address
to give the taxi company. I found piles of junk mail, free
newspapers and the yellow pages. This was 21 Hardy Close, in
a quiet cul-de-sac in a corner of an estate with streets named
after successful naval officers. I finished my rollie and dropped
it in the toilet to flush it away with my urine, which was my
usual final act before leaving a place, be it my home, someone
else's or a public house. I went into the kitchen to see if I'd
left any evidence there and then leant on the table to phone
back Mary.

"Mary…I'm ready to get a taxi, but I'll be a while as I'm
out near the hospital, and I think I'd better call in to a garage
to use their cash machine, get some fags and stuff, okay?" I
blurted out to Mary what I wanted to do.

"Umm…Yeah, you know my address is 37 Lamorna Street.
The taxi should come round the back as the road has been
pedestrianised. Then I can let you and Wills in to the garden,"
Mary explained so I could call the cab. I knew we used the
same company, so they'd know her address anyway.

"I'll be so pleased to see your place and the garden I've heard about. We should be there in time for elevenses. Nothing you want me to pick up, like milk or newspapers, is there?" I wanted to do all I could to keep Mary happy.

"No, you just come here, and then we can discuss the situation, see what has happened and what to do about it." Mary seemed surprisingly relaxed, which I was glad about.

I finished the call and then typed in the cab company number. If I were into technology I'd have it saved in the phone, but I'm not. I booked the cab and was told to expect a 10-minute wait or so.

CHAPTER 57

T racy was not happy that the meeting had been arranged at a residential establishment, but obviously it was time to get the case progressing and to catch Blind Justice. The officers had limited time to prepare; the police helicopter was scrambled, and the armed officers were given details of their target. A couple of them hid in an unmarked van down the road, and a couple were in Mary's house and the unmarked cars around the local corners. Tracy didn't expect Mark Wilson to be equipped with a firearm, but she wanted to take him, preferably alive. She couldn't risk not getting Blind Justice off the streets now.

As she found out from Mary, who had selected the taxi company, they were able to tune in to the short frequency radio call and monitor the vehicle's progress without the driver knowing.

Tracy decided that the safest thing to do was to get Alison out of the house but keep her ready to support her mum when the arrest was made. They would be required to go to the police station and give statements. Mary would answer the door to Mr Wilson, and once the front door was shut behind him they'd ambush him, bursting in to the hallway from all points of access. This would allow them to have three guns covering their target: one from the living room, one from the downstairs water closet and one hidden around the house corner outside. A fourth would be from the front door – an enforcer would knock it open, allowing the SO19 officer to enter. They didn't expect much resistance, knowing what they did about who Blind Justice really was, his history and what Mary had told them.

However, Tracy had to admit to herself that what she disliked the most about modern policing was the increasing firearm activity. Even as a little girl, despite being a tomboy at a very young age, she had never liked cap guns. The smell of cordite that lingers after rounds are discharged made her feel sick. She couldn't imagine how it had been for Peter in America. However, some people thrive on petrol fumes, others on the scent of gunpowder and, she guessed, others on the smells of agriculture.

She got Pete to do the liaising with the SO19 officers as she was responsible for keeping an eye on the taxi and working out when it would arrive. She could hardly believe that she was about to meet the person who had occupied so much of her time and energy for months; he'd be in custody within the hour. He'd soon be a problem for the Prison Service and Crown Prosecution Service, and she would be able to relax fully for the first time since the name Blind Justice had appeared in her world. There would be a long and complex trial with a considerable media attention due to the many psychiatric issues that were obviously involved. She'd have to give interviews to the reporters and evidence to the jury when cross-examined, so there was still a lot of work involved. However, she felt it was like climbing a mountain, and once the arrest had been, made she'll have reached the peak and would then be on the way back down.

Peter kept looking at his watch every other minute. She understood that it was a sign of nervousness. He seemed even more anxious than she expected, so she wondered if there was something else on his mind.

"Peter, how are you feeling about this operation?" She asked.

"I'm alright regarding this, but I'm supposed to be meeting up with the family tonight. A bit of a one-off thing that I've organised, so I don't want to be late. Kathy and I are getting our mum and dad back together to meet up for the first time in a while. These days they both live alone, and they don't want to admit it, but loneliness is creeping into their lives. It's not too bad for Mum since Kathy is there most of the time, but she's getting ready to move in with the new boyfriend. I'm not sure about Dad these days, but he seems to be drinking too much. If anyone could put him back on the straight and narrow, it's Mum." Peter said a lot, and it was clear to Tracy that this evening was significant.

"Are you going out for a meal or getting together at home?" Tracy hoped that Peter had applied his tactical brain to his family manoeuvres as he had to their current action. She was pretty sure he would after considering the worst-case scenario and all possible outcomes.

"The plan is that I tell Mum that I want to show her my America photos, so she and Kathy go to a booked restaurant. Then I'll move in with Dad for the culmination of another long-term operation." He smiled as he could see the similarities between the actions.

She knew the importance of locations in these sorts of thing, so she asked, "Which eating house are you going for?"

"I have some good memories of past events at Tamarside, so I've booked a place there. It's just a Wetherspoons, but that will be a fine place for us to get together and talk." Pete smiled as he explained remembering previous parties at the establishment.

There was a tone from the radio that drew their attention, and they were suddenly back in the heart of an armed police operation. It was a call from an officer a few streets away saying that the cab was approaching on the expected route and would be arriving soon with a very significant passenger.

Pete, Tracy and the SO19 sergeant checked that they had gotten radio contact, and once he had spoken to each of his officers, they all took up their positions.

CHAPTER 58

I've never been comfortable in taxis by myself because I don't enjoy small talk strangers, especially if I know it had no future since we wouldn't talk again. However, sitting in silence while being driven around is not a way I like to spend my time either. This time I decided to talk to Willow, giving her a pretty inane load of drivel regarding what I knew about Mary's house and garden. Since she was so well trained, Willow wasn't the sort of dog that liked to go running about playing games and chewing up sticks. Comparing Willow to most dogs was like comparing people attending Royal Ascot in their tops and tails with drunk football fans.

Tamarmouth is a large city, so despite having lived there for such a long period of time there, were still parts I hardly knew at all. The names of the different districts brought up several mental images. Some conjured up historic dire housing estates, while others endless streets of post-70s plain cardboard boxes, neither of which appealed to me. To reach Kings Point, where Mary lived, we drove away from the waterfront towards houses with larger gardens and access lanes around the back. This involved more traffic nowadays as the original road had been pedestrianised to make it greener and safer for families. The taxi driver had driven Mary in the past, so knew where to park to let Willow and I out.

"That's going to be £8.60," the driver said as he pressed the buttons on his meter and looked at me over his shoulder.

"Keep the change," I replied as I handed a £10 note through the plastic screen dividing the cab.

Willow got out of the cab first as I held her lead, and I carried my cane in my other hand. My vision was average at the time, and it was a bright, sunny day, which meant there was a colourful flower-filled garden in front of us with a crazy paved path to the front door that divided the trim lawn. It was not the kind of street I had ever imagined myself living on, but it was fine for a visit, and at the moment I was more than short of alternative places to go.

Willow seemed quite comfortable, and I expected that she could smell Mary as well as all the flowers and other aromas, so we made our way to the front door. I pressed the doorbell while looking at the panels of frosted glass, which comprised the upper part of the door and enabled shapes and colours to be vaguely seen. I saw Mary approach the door; she opened it and invited us to join her.

"Come on in! It's good to see you both," she said as she stepped back. She used one hand to point towards the open door that led to the lounge and used the other to rub Willow on her furry forehead in greeting and encouragement.

We felt welcome and relaxed as we made our way down the hallway. The place was clearly decorated with a woman's touch, and there were numerous feminine characteristics. Mary was asking if I wanted to have a tea or coffee, and if so, how, when everything suddenly changed at lightning speed, and I felt like I was in Hiroshima on 6th August at 08:15:44. FLASH. BANG. WALLOP.

I was instantaneously met by two police officers carrying sub-machine guns in the door frames next to me. They were a most imposing sight, dressed in their heavy-duty black outfits and body armour. I heard a shocked sound from Mary as I saw her disappear around the corner and into the lounge. Willow gave an upset growl, while I called out in distressed alarm.

"Armed police! Don't move! Hands up!" Instructions were shouted at me from all directions, including behind me, as I could hear I was now being approached from my entry point as well.

Due to the high-stress situation, my sight started to decline almost straight away. I raised my arms while dropping the cane and Willow's lead. I could feel my heart rate and breathing accelerating as I panicked. I soon found that I couldn't see anything, and I was handcuffed, and my rights were read to me. I was then introduced to a senior police officer named Detective Inspector Tracy Hansard. She told me that I had the right to keep my guide dog for now at least. We would be taken to the station, where we would both be strip searched. Then I'd be placed in a cell, while Willow would be put in a holding pen. I would have a chance to make a phone call and choose what to do regarding legal representation. Since I am partially sighted, I'd be given braille versions of all the usual documents involved if I wished.

Things progressed automatically as expected, and before I really knew what had occurred I was in a police cell at Charles Cross Police Station wearing a forensic outfit since my clothes had been taken away for DNA testing. Since I was a psychiatric patient with the NHS I was now waiting to see a doctor, and I expected to see a mental health worker of some sort too. I'd been given a cup of tea by now and was told to just sit and wait. My vision had slowly returned to a degree, not that there is much to look at in a cell.

"Mr Wilson, you can make your phone call now if you want," a voice shouted at me through the grille in the door. I recognised the custody sergeant I'd been introduced to before.

"Thank you Sergeant. I'd like to call my friend, Mary Green, please." I got up from the mattress on the floor and stood back while the door was opened.

I was then escorted through a corridor of cells to the reception desk. The cells were being washed out while they were empty. They were getting ready for the upcoming weekend.

The cells were primitive, but there was a hi-tech kit at the desk. I'd had my prints taken earlier using an e-scanner rather than ink, and I'd had a swab of DNA. taken for a sample. I stood at the desk and was handed a handset for my call.

"Hello, Mary...Yes, it's me." I tried to talk to Mary, but I didn't really know what to say. My prime concern was getting legal and medical assistance, so I asked Mary to contact my PCN. I didn't have a lawyer, so I used the one allocated by the police to start. I'd look into finding someone who specialised in medical or psychiatric legal issues later.

The first issue was going to be bail, but I knew I wouldn't get it, so I didn't even apply. I was going to be remanded in custody by the magistrates without a doubt. As a result, I'd be going to the hospital wing of HMP Exeter. Willow was to be held at Police HQ, Middlemoor, Exeter. This was where the Devon and Cornwall Canine Development School was, and they had accommodations for dogs.

CHAPTER 59

D etective Peter Anderson couldn't believe how easy it had
been to arrest Blind Justice and put him in custody, so
he was feeling celebratory by the time he'd finished his
shift and done all the requisite paperwork. He knew that he
and Tracy would have a tsunami of documents to overcome,
but his confidence was now restored. Still, it was now time
focus on the other big operation, so he called his father.

"Hi, Dad…Do you fancy a bite to eat and a drink at the
Tamarside, and I'll show you my pictures from the States?" He
proffered the carrot to his father, knowing he'd take it up as
his Dad loved a pint of Tribute along with a sirloin steak and
a peppercorn sauce. "I can give you some good news resulting
from my America trip too…I'll see you there at about seven."

Peter left the station and saw a couple of the constables
having a quick smoke. He decided to join them and thank
them for their effort in this case. He took out the last cigarette
from his packet and sparked it as he walked towards the bus
shelter-like structure.

"I bet you're glad we've caught him, Peter." He was hailed
by PC Watkins, with whom he had become familiar after they
helped each other out with smokes for months.

"Too true, John. This case has been a real endurance test,
especially for Tracy." Peter thought about the emotional effect

of the cat poisoning and having to stay at the police house for a night or two. "I think that if the government had done more for mental health issues and abused kids, we wouldn't have had this case in the first place, you know."

"When this goes to trial it'll raise that to people's attention. With a bit of luck it'll also take place alongside an election, so we can get some more money for social issues and fight the cutbacks we and the nurses are suffering." Watkins was very clear regarding his political beliefs.

"Sure, but I think DI Tracy is going to have to retire after this or take a holiday and then a desk job, anyway." Peter hadn't mentioned it to anyone else, but he felt this had taken its toll on her over the weeks.

"Yeah, you reckon? You fancy being DI? I think it's open for you or someone new to the station." PC John Watkins stubbed out his roll-up and headed back in to confront the abundance of Blind Justice-related files and documents.

Peter decided to go and get cleaned up and put on a fresh shirt. He'd gone to a lot of trouble to sort out the family get-together so that it'd be worth it. He knew his mum and Kathy always did. If his dad was looking a bit rough that might encourage a sympathy vote from them, which would help get them back together.

Kathy and her mum felt that a short walk would be good to stimulate their appetite, so they walked to the pub. Peter took a bus near to the Tamarside, expecting to get a taxi back home following his first night of serious drinking for quite a while. As planned, he was the next to arrive, and he was recognised by the deputy manager since he used to be a regular when things were going well and his finances were comfortable. They sat at their usual table around the corner from the main entrance and out of the draught. It was also near the open fireplace, but that was not a concern tonight.

"Evening, Mr Anderson. How are you tonight, sir? Not seen you for a bit," the wife of the deputy manager greeted him while restocking the bar.

"Yeah, I've been away to the States for work, so I've come back for a family reunion and a decent beer," he said, feeling relaxed in his environment. "I'll set up a tab for tonight as my sister and both my parents should be along later, if they're not here already, and I'm covering the bill," he said while selecting a pint of Jail Ale to refresh himself.

He stood at the bar and saw the TV in the far corner giving the local weather at the end of the BBC early evening news. He tried to imagine what the media coverage would be like when the news about Blind Justice came out. Press officers, authorized statements and dealing with the senior officers were about to become the order of the day.

"Okay, Peter," his sister called from the table where they had already been seated. He waved at them and went over, knowing the beer would be brought to his table, and saw that they were already sharing a bottle of sauvignon blanc.

"Mum…Kathy. How are you?" He was glad he'd had a shave and shower as they were both looking good, wearing things they had been given as Christmas presents or bought with gift vouchers. His mum had a slightly different hairstyle, which he guessed had been done by Kath, partly at the salon and partly finished at home.

"We're fine. We want to see your photos and hear all about the trip to America. You're looking like you've lost a bit of weight. I would have thought you'd be heavier, if anything, after a trip to the States. It's not due to the stress you're under at work, is it?" said his mum; she hadn't seen him for a bit. He didn't pay much attention to his weight, but he imagined he might look tired.

He pulled a chair up to the table next to his mum, but he could also see the door to the bar, so he would see when his dad arrived. He knew his mum liked printed photos for albums, so he'd had a couple of sets printed out at Truprint. He took them out of his inside pocket and passed them over.

"You won't believe the size of everything over there. Look at these pics, and you'll see what I mean. Cars, steaks, people. It was overwhelming. The only things that weren't big were subtlety and quality beer." He gratefully acknowledged the delivery of his pint by the barmaid as his mum took the pictures and held them as she sat between her children. The first was a selfie taken at the airport. They progressed through the collection, seeing where he had been and who he had worked with. There were a lot more tourist-type pictures in the second half taken in New York that featured the Statue of Liberty, Central Park and the Empire State Building.

They were just reaching the last few pictures when he saw his dad out of the corner of his eye. He left the snaps with them, got up, slipped over to the bar and greeted his father.

"Dad! Yes, as you can see we are all getting together for a family reunion to see my pics and have a chat over a good meal. Kathy and I have got some things to talk to both of you about, so this seemed the good way to do it. Alright?" He knew his father would not object but might feel a bit indignant about being manipulated. In fact, all he did was tut.

"You'd better have some good stories about the American cops' lifestyles, and I've got a hunger for a three-course meal followed by a cigar and brandy, son." His dad was very predictable, which was a gift.

They stood at the bar while Jack chose a beer. He could see his daughter and her mother talking animatedly; the two were obviously aware that he had arrived. Kathy was probably explaining what had happened.

"Go on over, I'll bring your beer with the menus, okay Dad?" Pete encouraged his dad to join the family group. He sheepishly made his way over to his family and sat down across from Sue.

"You're both looking good. Feeling it too, I hope," he said as he picked up a set of the photos and started to peruse them. "How have you been over Christmas? I've had a bit of a cold, but I'm better now." Jack was clearly happy to be back with his family.

Peter put his father's Guinness on the beermat and gave them each a menu. "Don't forget the specials on the blackboard." He pointed to the board next to the bar as he sat down, wondering about the future of his family.

They enjoyed a decent three-course meal together for the first time in years. As a result, Jack and Sue would see more of each other, and Kathy broke the news she was pregnant and engaged to Gary, so they needed to start thinking about a family wedding. If they were clever they could combine it with a ruby anniversary party. They talked a lot about distant nieces and nephews of various generations and who had which children. Thinking of Kathy having children and all the other ones mentioned made Peter think about morals and ethics. He could understand why Blind Justice had done what he had to the paedophiles. Who's to say what's right and wrong? A freedom fighter to some is a terrorist to others, so one man's vigilante might be another's guerrilla. That was that. It always had been, it was now, and it always would be in the future. Life is subjective, and that is a fact.

Printed and bound by CPI Group (UK) Ltd, Croydon, CR0 4YY